Anthony Gilbert and The Murder Room

››› This title is part of The Murder Room, our series dedicated to making available out-of-print or hard-to-find titles by classic crime writers.

Crime fiction has always held up a mirror to society. The Victorians were fascinated by sensational murder and the emerging science of detection; now we are obsessed with the forensic detail of violent death. And no other genre has so captivated and enthralled readers.

Vast troves of classic crime writing have for a long time been unavailable to all but the most dedicated frequenters of second-hand bookshops. The advent of digital publishing means that we are now able to bring you the backlists of a huge range of titles by classic and contemporary crime writers, some of which have been out of print for decades.

From the genteel amateur private eyes of the Golden Age and the femmes fatales of pulp fiction, to the morally ambiguous hard-boiled detectives of mid twentieth-century America and their descendants who walk our twenty-first century streets, The Murder Room has it all. ›››

The Murder Room
Where Criminal Minds Meet

themurderroom.com

AF888343

Anthony Gilbert (1899–1973)

Anthony Gilbert was the pen name of Lucy Beatrice Malleson. Born in London, she spent all her life there, and her affection for the city is clear from the strong sense of character and place in evidence in her work. She published 69 crime novels, 51 of which featured her best known character, Arthur Crook, a vulgar London lawyer totally (and deliberately) unlike the aristocratic detectives, such as Lord Peter Wimsey, who dominated the mystery field at the time. She also wrote more than 25 radio plays, which were broadcast in Great Britain and overseas. Her thriller *The Woman in Red* (1941) was broadcast in the United States by CBS and made into a film in 1945 under the title *My Name is Julia Ross*. She was an early member of the British Detection Club, which, along with Dorothy L. Sayers, she prevented from disintegrating during World War II. Malleson published her autobiography, *Three-a-Penny*, in 1940, and wrote numerous short stories, which were published in several anthologies and in such periodicals as *Ellery Queen's Mystery Magazine* and *The Saint*. The short story 'You Can't Hang Twice' received a Queens award in 1946. She never married, and evidence of her feminism is elegantly expressed in much of her work.

By Anthony Gilbert

Scott Egerton series
Tragedy at Freyne (1927)
The Murder of Mrs Davenport (1928)
Death at Four Corners (1929)
The Mystery of the Open Window (1929)
The Night of the Fog (1930)
The Body on the Beam (1932)
The Long Shadow (1932)
The Musical Comedy Crime (1933)
An Old Lady Dies (1934)
The Man Who Was Too Clever (1935)

Mr Crook Murder Mystery series
Murder by Experts (1936)
The Man Who Wasn't There (1937)
Murder Has No Tongue (1937)
Treason in My Breast (1938)
The Bell of Death (1939)
Dear Dead Woman (1940)
aka *Death Takes a Redhead*
The Vanishing Corpse (1941)
aka *She Vanished in the Dawn*
The Woman in Red (1941)
aka *The Mystery of the Woman in Red*
Death in the Blackout (1942)
aka *The Case of the Tea-Cosy's Aunt*
Something Nasty in the Woodshed (1942)
aka *Mystery in the Woodshed*
The Mouse Who Wouldn't Play Ball (1943)
aka *30 Days to Live*
He Came by Night (1944)
aka *Death at the Door*
The Scarlet Button (1944)
aka *Murder Is Cheap*
A Spy for Mr Crook (1944)
The Black Stage (1945)
aka *Murder Cheats the Bride*
Don't Open the Door (1945)
aka *Death Lifts the Latch*
Lift Up the Lid (1945)
aka *The Innocent Bottle*
The Spinster's Secret (1946)
aka *By Hook or by Crook*
Death in the Wrong Room (1947)
Die in the Dark (1947)
aka *The Missing Widow*
Death Knocks Three Times (1949)
Murder Comes Home (1950)
A Nice Cup of Tea (1950)
aka *The Wrong Body*

Lady-Killer (1951)
Miss Pinnegar Disappears (1952)
aka *A Case for Mr Crook*
Footsteps Behind Me (1953)
aka *Black Death*
Snake in the Grass (1954)
aka *Death Won't Wait*
Is She Dead Too? (1955)
aka *A Question of Murder*
And Death Came Too (1956)
Riddle of a Lady (1956)
Give Death a Name (1957)
Death Against the Clock (1958)
Death Takes a Wife (1959)
aka *Death Casts a Long Shadow*
Third Crime Lucky (1959)
aka *Prelude to Murder*
Out for the Kill (1960)
She Shall Die (1961)
aka *After the Verdict*
Uncertain Death (1961)
No Dust in the Attic (1962)
Ring for a Noose (1963)
The Fingerprint (1964)
The Voice (1964)
aka *Knock, Knock! Who's There?*
Passenger to Nowhere (1965)
The Looking Glass Murder (1966)
The Visitor (1967)
Night Encounter (1968)
aka *Murder Anonymous*
Missing from Her Home (1969)
Death Wears a Mask (1970)
aka *Mr Crook Lifts the Mask*
Murder is a Waiting Game (1972)
Tenant for the Tomb (1971)
A Nice Little Killing (1974)

Standalone Novels

The Case Against Andrew Fane (1931)
Death in Fancy Dress (1933)
The Man in Button Boots (1934)
Courtier to Death (1936)
aka *The Dover Train Mystery*
The Clock in the Hatbox (1939)

A Nice Cup of Tea

Anthony Gilbert

An Orion book

Copyright © Lucy Beatrice Malleson 1950

The right of Lucy Beatrice Malleson to be identified as the author of this work has been asserted in accordance with the Copyright, Designs and Patents Act 1988.

This edition published by
The Orion Publishing Group Ltd
Orion House
5 Upper St Martin's Lane
London WC2H 9EA

An Hachette UK company
A CIP catalogue record for this book is available from the British Library

ISBN 978 1 4719 0994 8

All characters and events in this publication are fictitious and any resemblance to real people, living or dead, is purely coincidental.

No part of this publication may be reproduced, stored in a retrieval system or transmitted in any form or by any means without the prior permission in writing of the publisher, nor be otherwise circulated in any form of binding or cover other than that in which it is published without a similar condition, including this condition, being imposed on the subsequent purchaser.

www.orionbooks.co.uk

For Gwennie with my love

CHAPTER ONE

AT HIS OFFICE at 123 Bloomsbury Street, Mr. Arthur Crook was discussing with his A.D.C., Bill Parsons, the mystery of the unidentified victim. A recent case had set society by the ears, when it became known that a man had, over a period of two years, disposed of some eight victims whose disappearance had never been noticed by anyone.

"That's what gets me," said Bill. "If you or I were to vanish someone would start asking questions pretty soon."

"You and me are public characters," Crook pointed out modestly. "But you examine the case histories of these people. All born murderees, all murdered for the same reason, what they possessed."

"But they possessed so little," Bill objected.

"That's the point. That's where Guthrie was so clever. If a rich man or woman disappears, sooner or later someone's going to notice it, most probably sooner. Rich people always have friends, and most of 'em have relatives. That's one of the laws of nature. But if your sole capital is, say, a hundred pounds—and two of the girls Guthrie put underground had less—who's going to bother with you? There are two kinds of people who can disappear without leaving a ripple behind. Take the case of Bessie Archer. Brought up in an orphanage, put into service when she was fifteen, drifts from one job to another, pretty soon from one man to another. At the time of her disappearance she had been working in some third-class hotel, had a row with the manager on account of visiting guests in their rooms, sauced him and was given her cards. In wartime he'd have reported that to the Exchange. Now she can walk out without anyone asking questions. The other girls with whom she worked don't know anything—why should they ? She was only there six weeks and she'd only been at her last job six weeks, too. She's known to have had men-friends but no steadies. She leaves A and goes to B. A don't care. He can get another girl any day of the week. Nobody reports her, police ain't notified, no family, nothing. Why should anyone get suspicious ? Not until a body's found, that is, or someone happens to notice, as they did in Guthrie's case, that his lady friends change their identity suspiciously often. It wasn't Bessie Archer who got Guthrie sent to the little covered shed. It was Guthrie getting careless as sooner or later they always do.

" That's the explanation of the Alice Hunter mystery. She's the other kind nobody bothers about. Elderly woman, only child, parents been dead these twenty years. No employer because she's too old and anyway she ain't trained, lives in one cheap boarding-house, or in this case one cheap furnished room, after another —y'see, there's no one likely to keep tabs on her. She's not one of these old dears who make friends, gossip in the butcher's queue, are always looking round for someone to go to the pictures with. She don't go to the pictures or if she does she goes alone. Of course, there are the tradespeople but they wouldn't notice. There are so many of them and she does nothing to make herself noticeable. What's that bird that can sink into the ground when anyone comes near so it's practically invisible ? "

" Partridge," said Bill mechanically.

" That's right. Well, landladies may remember her, but once she's gone they don't give her another thought. Never sends a post-card or leaves anything behind and has to write back for it, it's simply a case of nobody having a clue."

"Local vicar?" asked Bill.

"Even if she's one of the church-going lot he's not likely to pick her out from the others. She don't take the bag round or become secretary to a missionary association. She don't run accounts at the shops—she's more or less anonymous. If she ever had any school friends she hasn't kept up with them, she don't play bridge—she's simply a body with a label. Body disappears, someone else as like her as one sixpence is like another comes in her place, and even if someone does wonder why they don't see her any more the answer's easy. She's moved on, gone to the seaside, gone to another part of London, died maybe. The only hope of tracking her down would be if she had her money from a lawyer and her quarterly cheques were returned. But in this case—Miss Hunter—the dividends are paid into the bank and she draws cheques."

"Bank might notice she hadn't drawn one for a long time," Bill suggested.

"With all the clients a bank has it's going to be a precious long time before they start thinking about her. And even if they do, well, she might have got a job, companion to an invalid, lady housekeeper living on perks. No, it could be months before anyone started askin' awkward questions. I reckon the cat that walked alone may have saved itself a heap of trouble but it was laying itself wide-open to anyone out for a free skin." Here the telephone began to ring and he picked up the receiver. "Same like Miss Hunter," he wound up, and added casually, "Poor old girl!"

Miss Hunter was sixty-four at the time she started to make history, on a minor scale admittedly, but history just the same. She had been a good daughter to an invalid mother, whom she had contrived to keep alive until the old lady was eighty-eight, by which time Alice was nearly sixty. For the first year after the happy release Miss Hunter went about in a daze, alternating between great gratitude at being free from what had been civilised slavery—the old lady had had a tongue like vitriol—and a sense of appalling loneliness. After the doctor told her the old woman couldn't last much longer, her imagination, disciplined for so many years, began to peep out of its hole and picture a life that would be perfect freedom. " Think," it murmured to her, " of nights of unbroken rest." For the old lady was a poor sleeper and liked to be entertained in the small hours. " Think of only having to cook for yourself. Think of all the queues you need never stand in again. Think of never being afraid any more." Such knowledge was too wonderful for her. She couldn't accept it.

After the funeral, which was attended by herself and one neighbour who hoped she might perhaps attract the lonely mourner to come and share her house—half-expenses, half-work—Miss Hunter recklessly sold all the furniture of the gloomy flat and went down to Westbourne for a change. She had had visions of herself making friends easily, learning to play bridge, making up cinema and theatre parties with her contemporaries ; but at the hotel nobody else seemed alone. She was given a small room for an enormous weekly charge and she became unpopular because she didn't understand about tipping.

" A pernicious system ! " old Mrs. Hunter had called it. " They're paid, aren't they ? Then why should they be paid twice ? "

If anyone performed a special service then you might perhaps add a small tip, but only if it was something over and above the duties for which they were remunerated, and very few services were crowded out of this category. Mrs. Hunter had been a spoilt beauty in her youth, and she never forgot it. When she looked in the glass she didn't see the sunken yellow face of old age, she saw a laughing girl with a ribbon in her hair and a love-letter in her hand. " A smile's as good as a shilling any day," she used to tell Alice. But smiles had lost their value by the nineteen-forties, and poor Alice's timid smile could never have been worth more than threepence in its palmiest days.

Well, the holiday at Westbourne was a mistake, and a very expensive one at that, but it had taught her one thing, which common sense should have told her long before. If you're elderly and plain and uninteresting and your clothes look as if they'd been picked up at a jumble sale, don't expect people to pay you any attention—unless, of course, you're a millionaire in disguise. So, at the month's end, back to London Alice came. She would settle in a little flat, she thought, join one of the Church associations at St. Joachim's, and go to the Missionary Sewing Party, where she would begin the exciting process of making friends. But that didn't work out either. To begin with she couldn't get a flat and had to go into rooms. And her social efforts were a worse failure than her search for a flat. The truth was she had been so long her Mother's sole companion and, even more important, Mother had so long been hers, that she couldn't separate their identities. When she met a stranger she was tongue-tied ; she simply didn't know what people talked about. So she talked about Mother. Later in desperation she began to go to movies, or occasionally one of the cheaper seats of a theatre, but that didn't really help.

One day when she was waiting in rather a long bus queue she heard someone in front whisper, " Don't look round. That Hunter woman's behind us and if she sees us she'll want to join up; and if I have to hear any more about what Mother liked or what Mother said I shall scream."

Alice Hunter flushed scarlet, then went white, and dived hurriedly into the nearest shop. So that was what they thought of her. Poor Mother! They weren't a bit interested, which was ridiculous of them, she told herself valiantly. Mother had known so many great men, had lived in a more gracious age; Mother had been full of little anecdotes of what the great men had said to her—oddly enough there were never any great women—and surely these were interesting still, just as interesting as what the housekeeper or the woman at the chemists had said. But no, Mother had had her day. And if she stopped talking about Mother what on earth was poor Alice Hunter to talk about?

She didn't give up hope at once. She went to a parish party and she wrote—on Mother's paper—and asked the vicar to tea. But he was too busy to come. She went round to decorate the church at Christmas, but the chancel, the font and even the window-ledges belonged to worshippers who had staked their claims years ago. People at St. Joachim's were like Mother in that—or Tennyson's Brook that went on for ever. She put up a gallant fight, but it was no good. There were too many like her; you could pass her in the street any day and never know her next time you met her. Indeed, again and aga people stopped her in the street and addressed her as Amy or Edna or Jane, and then laughed a little and said they were sorry it was a mistake. . . .

She even tried to learn bridge but that was hopeless, and when she went to a whist drive she trumped her partner's ace, and his expression frightened her so much the shameful tears came pricking through her eyelids. After that she realised that of all sad words of tongue or pen the saddest are these " it might have been," and drew into her shell and stayed there. On an average she changed her address every six months. No matter how hopefully she settled down in new quarters there was always something—a noisy wireless or someone overhead banging a typewriter or a sewing machine, and once it was someone practising to be a pianist, or the landlady found that, thanks to a further increase in rates, she'd simply got to raise the rent. So Alice would put her belongings into her old-fashioned black dome trunk and depart for pastures new, that proved just as arid as the ones she had just left. The trunk itself—without which Mother had never travelled, and had red tape strappings on the under side of the lid for all the flotsam and jetsam without which old Mrs. Hunter's generation never appear to have left home—was always a bone of contention with the landladies, who objected to it on the score of size the moment they set eyes on it, and made it perfectly clear that if they had known that accepting Miss Hunter meant accepting that sort of monstrosity she would have found a " Full Up " notice on the door. The room was furnished and not very large—these rooms all appeared to have been turned out to a single pattern—and so, it seemed, had the landladies who reiterated one and all that no, the landing was not available, the L.C.C. would object in case of fire. Usually poor Alice squeezed it into a corner and covered it with one of the late Mrs. Hunter's more dressy occasional tablecloths, the one in white and purple satin with an elephant embroidered in gold thread, howdah and all, and, since she was an inveterate hoarder, it was invaluable for concealing all those bits and pieces, all worthless in themselves, that she couldn't bring herself to part with, just in case one day—you never knew. She and the trunk had been at eight addresses in five years, and her identity card had scarcely room for all the information that had to be crowded on to it.

It was when she was at Ennismore Avenue that she learned of the Legacy.

At first she couldn't believe it. Of late years she had amused herself by day-dreams. When she got into a bus to go to Kensington High Street she would make-believe she was en route for the docks to sail to darkest Africa or China or New York ; when a plane flew overhead she would start pretending that next week she was going to Paris—by air. She used to collect coloured folders for journeys she had never made and now never would. Or she dreamed she was popular, she had a telephone that rang so often she had to tell the exchange to stop incoming calls. " We must have Alice Hunter," the non-existent hostesses remarked to one another, " she's so amusing, such a sport." " Do you suppose we could get Alice ? " she pictured them inquiring one of the other. " It's short notice—but—it would make all the difference if she were there." At other times a house caught fire or a child threatened to fall from a balcony. The street was filled with white-faced people all staring upwards ; eyes glazed, voices were hushed in sheer terror. At the window the stricken victim stood wreathed in flame. Would the engine never come ? Ah, not in time. But see, what is this, whose is that fearless form bounding through the flames, now standing at the window, leaning out to cry in ringing tones, " Spread the blanket. We're coming down " ? " Who'd have thought it ? " marvelled the neighbours. " It only shows you never can tell." Alice Hunter, interviewed by a string of eager reporters, said quietly, " It was nothing. Anyone would have done the same. My hands ? Oh, no, they're not really painful. Nothing that time won't cure."

Some element of common sense triumphing over loneliness had prevented her ever indulging in a fantasy about a legacy. Only too often she and dear Mother had gone over the family tree, prepared in 1906 by Great Aunt Penelope. Mother remembered quite a lot of the relations. Oddly enough, they'd all had a kink or a weakness—the men drank or were failures or in some way unsatisfactory—three or four, Alice was assured, had proposed, but Mother didn't believe in cousins intermarrying. As for the women—the percentage of spinsters was extremely high. And by now, Mother would add dryly, giving her daughter one of her piercing looks, it must be higher.

" If I'd married," said Alice once, " what would have become of you ? " For Mrs. Hunter wasn't one of these independent women who believe that if you want a thing done well you should do it yourself. She knew that the best managers supervise someone else doing it.

" If you'd married, my dear, supposing you'd ever been able to attract a man, I should have taken Potty Bellenger," said Mother, who came of a generation when nicknames were the order of the day. " Naturally, he didn't want a grown-up stepdaughter. . . ."

" But, Mother, you never even hinted——"

" I hope I know better than to cast off my own child," said Mother.

" I could have got a job, learnt shorthand or something."

" Shorthand ? My dear Alice, have you no sense of what's owing to your mother ? "

Sometimes she wondered whether, supposing she had got married, would Potty Bellenger really have proposed ? He seemed to get along so remarkably well without marriage. " If I'd been a man," Alice reflected, " I wouldn't marry anyone. I'd flit like a bee from flower to flower."

Anyway, what it all added up to was that there wasn't a relation who would leave them a stiver. Most of them were dead anyway, and those who weren't dead had gone to live abroad and were dead in another sense. The only one living was Miss Agatha Wells, who was practically as old as Mrs. Hunter, and had been in a nursing home for years.

"Poor Agatha!" Mother used to say. "She was never quite *compos mentis*."

"Didn't she have a disappointment of the heart?" asked kind Alice. "Someone who died on the way out to India?"

"When we were young," said Mother, "all gels of good feeling who hadn't got themselves a husband by the time they were thirty had someone who died on the way out to India. You're more fortunate. You can say it was the war—the 1914 war, of course."

"Of course," agreed Alice, grateful that Mother hadn't said the Boer War, as she might have done in some of her moods.

And now it appeared that Miss Wells had died at last, and in her will left her money to Mother or, should she have predeceased her, to Mother's daughter, Alice. She had died in Bath, and it was from Bath that the lawyer, Mr. Finnemore, wrote to say that he would be glad to have Miss Hunter's instructions, either through her own man of affairs or direct. Alice sat for a long time staring at the paper as if she feared that the mere act of lifting her eyes would cause it to disappear. After a time she laid it deliberately on the table and went over to the window. She stared out while she counted 500. Then she turned her head quickly. The letter was still there and it still said the same thing. Now that she could accept the legacy as a fact Miss Hunter's heart began to beat like a piston. Faster and faster it went till she felt dizzy. She was reminded of the occasion—oh, years and years ago, when she really had been quite a gel, and she had been lent a bicycle and began to descend a hill. The machine went faster and faster and she knew that presently it was going to turn over and she would perhaps be killed. Afterwards, when it had turned over, though she wasn't killed, only ruined a pair of stockings and torn a great rent in her coat, Mrs. Hunter had said, " Why not test the brakes before starting downhill ? " and Alice had dropped her eyes, not daring to confess she had forgotten the brakes' existence. Well, that's how it was now, only this time there really weren't any brakes. She felt so dizzy she had to sit down, her eyes still on the letter and when she looked up she found her landlady, Mrs. Brownlow, on the threshold.

" Is anything wrong, Miss Hunter ? " asked Mrs. Brownlow crisply. " You don't feel faint or anything ? I've often wondered if you suffer from high blood pressure."

" Oh, no," said Alice Hunter faintly. " No, I'm sure I don't. It's just——"

Then she noticed the letter in her hand and made a futile attempt to conceal it.

But a hawk had nothing on Mrs. Brownlow when it came to seeing things that would much rather remain invisible.

" Not bad news, I trust."

" No, no. No, of course not." She rose spasmodically and jerked over to the window. " They're making a lot of noise rebuilding those houses opposite," she suggested. She hadn't noticed the noise really, but she had to say something to distract her landlady's attention.

Mrs. Brownlow had drawn her own conclusions. Poor old so-and-so, she looked properly upset, and seeing it couldn't be anything to do with a man it stood to reason it must be money. She had caught a glimpse of the letter, an official sheet, no doubt from a lawyer. Everybody's income was shrinking and nothing was paying like it should; but Mrs. Brownlow had no intention of letting her lodger add herself to the list of non-payers. Oh, she hadn't a doubt what had happened. The old geezer, whoever he might be, who looked after Miss Hunter's affairs, had written to tell her of a drop in income; and drops in income generally meant delay in payments, and after all everybody's human and no one's in the business for their health. So she said composedly, " That's a good thing, isn't it? As a matter of fact, I came up to say I find myself in a bit of a tight place."

Up came Miss Hunter's head; her eyes widened with alarm. Was it possible that Mrs. Brownlow had somehow managed to open the letter and scan the contents and then reseal it so skilfully that she, Alice Hunter, hadn't noticed? Or had she witch-like qualities (quite a number of landladies had, in Alice's experience) and knew about the legacy and meant to try and borrow something—bite her ear, as that amusing major Mother had met at Bournemouth used to say? He'd seemed quite taken till he realised Mother lived on an annuity, and the only " real " money was Alice's from a dead-and-gone godmother—but that was irrelevant.

" The fact is," Mrs. Brownlow continued, her sharp little eyes taking in every change in poor Alice's expression, and, as it happened, misinterpreting them all, " my sister's eldest girl, the sister that lives in the north that is, is coming to London to work and my sister's written to know if I can have her here. Well, you don't like to refuse your sister, but, of course, the house is full, and—well, the long and the short of it is I'm afraid I'll have to ask you for this room, Miss

Hunter. Deirdre, that's my sister's girl, is coming at the week-end, so if you could make it convenient to go then . . ."

" Well, of course," said Miss Hunter, " I'll probably be going to-morrow. This news——"

She wondered why she hadn't thought of it at once. Naturally she wouldn't want to stay here when she was an heiress. In fact, she wouldn't stay in London at all. She'd go to Bath and see Mr. Finnemore, and she'd start a new life in new surroundings. She hated London, had always hated it for that matter, and now she'd make a clean sweep. " Yes," she repeated, standing up. " It will be perfectly convenient." And, with a courage she'd never have had in the ordinary way, she pointed out a few of the room's defections—some paper peeling from the ceiling, a weak place in the carpet, a cracked window-pane. Mrs. Brownlow was furious.

" If you wasn't satisfied I wonder you stayed," she said.

" No," agreed Alice with a courage that staggered her. " I wasn't satisfied, but till to-day I couldn't afford anything better."

Mrs. Brownlow began to think that perhaps she was mistaken. The letter *had* contained good news.

" I'm sure," said she in a sycophantic voice, " I'm glad of your change of fortune."

But to Alice Mrs. Brownlow already belonged to the past. She remembered how years ago, during her High Church phase, she had learned to pray for a happy death. It was like that now. A happy death to past humiliations, to poverty, to a sense of being superfluous to life. An heiress, as she saw herself to be, could never be superfluous.

After Mrs. Brownlow had reluctantly left her, she began to hurry round the room making mental notes of what she would take with her. This happened every time she moved house. She would spend hours, literally hours, wondering if this time she shouldn't dispense with this or that ornament, that garment she hadn't worn literally for years, a little cushion, a pair of slippers. . . . But in the end she always took them on the ground that they might come in useful. The fact was, she was so poor she couldn't bear to part with anything ; and she had no great intellectual treasures to compensate her for the mean way in which she was compelled to live. To-day, however, she felt as though a door had opened in front of her. Recklessly she discarded the Box of Buttons—for years and years she had never thrown any garment away without first removing the buttons ; the odds and ends of wool belonging to dead and gone jumpers (One day I may have another jumper just this shade, she would argue with herself, returning the little twist to her work-box), the collection of Christmas cards also going back for years and years that she was always going to make into scrap-books for the poor when she had time—and a scrap-book—and a pot of paste. There were old letters and receipts older still ; there were picture postcards and envelopes that could be patched up and used again ; there were odd stockings that might in an emergency be paired together and worn " in the house "; there were little glass bottles that had held aspirin and cascara sagrada tablets and sodamint that she could never quite bring herself to throw away ; and little cardboard boxes and bits of brown paper and ends of string. What she'd have done without the trunk one simply can't imagine. She had a magnificent turn-out, recklessly scrapping everything, as if with all this flotsam and jetsam she severed the links binding her to the drab, uneventful past. (As for what the dustman would say when he called on Monday and found these boxes and rubbish that would fortunately be Mrs. Brownlow's concern.)

When she had the room looking like a salvage dump she found a cheap writing-pad and a pencil and sat down to make notes. She was a great note-taker ; she never went out without first scribbling

Public Library
Toothpaste
Matches
Cornerboy
Stamps

or whatever trifles she intended to purchase—on a bit of paper. Now her list grew under her shaking fingers. She was so afraid she might forget something, though how she could do this when she had only the one room—comfortable divan room, bathroom on same floor—(she'd never risen to h. & c. basin)—cooking facilities (a gas ring)—was difficult to understand. Still, it gave her a sense of confidence. And to-day in addition it gave her a sense of delight. The list completed, she began systematically to empty her drawers and cupboards, laying everything out on the bed, and putting a tick against each article or garment as it was brought from its hiding-place. She was about half-way through when it occurred to her—and really, what a wool-gatherer she was becoming, *Anno Domini* she chaffed herself, happily—that she hadn't yet answered the lawyer's letter, so she put the list down and routed out the typewriter she had bought through an advertisement after Mother's death, day-dreaming of surprising the world with a wonderful novel, (My dear, have you read *Love Lies Bleeding* by A. Hunter ? So penetrating ! So witty ! How that author knows the human heart !)—and wrote to Mr. Finnemore that she had received his letter, and proposed to come to Bath in person (underlined); that, having previously had no affairs, she had not acquired anyone to look after them, that she was sure they—meaning he and she—could manage everything perfectly between them, that she was giving up her London apartments, and perhaps he could recommend an hotel. She proposed to settle in Bath, having, she assured him sedately, no London ties. She added that she would bring all the requisite documents, birth certificates, self and mother, baptismal certificate (self), burial certificate and copy of death certificate (mother), identity card, Post Office Savings Book, ration book and cheque book (all, naturally, for self), and her mother's prayer-book, which would, she concluded blissfully, settle the matter of identity. (When Mr. Finnemore received this letter, he not unnaturally remarked, "Old Miss Wells wasn't the only one who was *non compos mentis*, it seems. Must be a family failing.")

Then she signed and sealed the letter, and went down to the post with it, carefully locking her door and taking the key with her. Landladies and servants, Mother used to say, are Never To Be Trusted. And it is wrong to Put Temptation In Their Way. Mother had a habit of speaking in capitals that was impressive till you got used to it, when it became a whale of a bore, and she certainly lived up to her beliefs. You might have expected landladies and servants to detest her in consequence, but they were far more respectful to her than to kindhearted, frightened, would-be friendly Miss Hunter. "What's she trying to nose out?" was their reaction when she assumed interest in them and their lives. The pillar-box was at the corner, so she was soon back again, and went on ticking off the items on her list. This carried her on till the evening when she had a boiled egg (and HOW fortunate she had kept it, it seemed to set the seal on this exciting day). When she had eaten it and cleared away the debris and decided she wouldn't have the wireless to-night—a programme about Central Europe and then someone speaking on recent developments in science, which was very clever and no doubt reflected credit on the scientists but somehow always seemed to add one more factor to the insecurity of existence—she decided to go to bed. Of course, before she could do this she had to clear the coverlet of the piles of clothes, etc., she had amassed, so she had a nice time putting them all back in their original drawers and cupboards and when the room was as neat as the proverbial New Pin she got into bed with a teacupful of warm milk and lay awake for hours and hours dreaming of a future that should compensate utterly for all the dreary, unrewarding past.

CHAPTER TWO

DURING THE NEXT twenty-four hours Miss Hunter contrived to avoid a tête-à-tête with the landlady, who was devoured by curiosity and wondering how she could undo the harm she had wrought and keep this erstwhile boring elderly woman under her roof. For there could be no doubt about it, the news in the mysterious letter had been good, not bad, She had a pass key and even stooped to entering Miss Hunter's room when the tenant was out, and looking quickly round for a trace of the communication, but Miss Hunter had thought of this possibility and she carried the letter, together with a carbon copy of her own reply, which she had made to prove that she was a good business woman and so impress Mr. Finnemore with her potentialities, everywhere she went. She thought Mr. Finnemore would answer by return of post but, of course, lawyers don't do that kind of thing, and by the time his reply was typed, signed and posted, urging the legatee to make no rash move, warning her that Bath was very full and assuring her that all their business could very well be carried out by letter, she had opened her grizzled wings and flown.

Mrs. Brownlow, realising that she had meant what she said, was in constant attendance. Perhaps, she suggested, she could help in some way—labels now. Had Miss Hunter got any labels? There should be stick-ons as well as tie-ons, everybody knew how careless the railways were nowadays—she had some labels downstairs that would be the very thing—but Miss Hunter said she had all the labels she needed, thank you.

"I'll send the girl for a taxi," said Mrs. Brownlow, showing her Bevans in a broad white grin. But Miss Hunter said she had arranged for a car to collect her things—drivers of hired cars never made trouble over luggage as taxi-drivers did. Why, they (taxi-drivers) had been known to refuse to handle baggage on the ground that, should they sustain any injury in consequence, they wouldn't be liable for industrial injury payments. Drivers of hired cars, explained Miss Hunter, as though she hired such cars every week of her life, expected to help.

When the time for the car arrived Mrs. Brownlow pointed out anxiously that the trunk was still unlabelled.

"You can't take that in the carriage with you," she said.

"I have the labels in my bag," returned Alice quickly, "I shall tie them on when I reach the station. I think that is safest."

Mrs. Brownlow realised that she had lost. "I'm sure," said she, drawing herself erect and looking for all the world like a long black needle with a little billiard-ball trimmed with straight iron-grey hair atop, "I'm sure I was never one to be curious. All the same, it does seem to me *sinister* when a person can't even let it be known where she's going. I mean——"

Miss Hunter's patience, which had been brittle for some days, here snapped completely.

"I am not in the least interested in what you mean, Mrs. Brownlow. I never have been. As for not being curious—all I can say is you know remarkably little about yourself if you really believe that. I have never known anyone more so. In fact"—here her imagination took full control and rushed her on like a runaway horse—"one of the reasons why I have had so few letters during my stay here is that I don't care to have my correspondence examined in detail by a third party before I receive it."

Mrs. Brownlow blew up. She said she'd a good mind to call the police, there was a law of libel, wasn't there? As for herself, it was only her kindness of heart that had made her keep Miss Hunter as long as she had. Other people—*ladies* insisted Mrs. Brownlow significantly—had been satisfied enough. And people with nothing to hide didn't go having their letters sent to accommodation addresses. "We all know what that means," flared Mrs. Brownlow. Alice, a little afraid of the storm she had called up, nevertheless stuck gallantly to her guns.

"If I should be asked," she stated, "I shall NOT say I have been comfortable here. Nor is the service at all satisfactory. *Two* of my teacups have been broken, and I have missed some of my sugar——"

Here fortunately the car arrived and Miss Hunter went into the hall to meet the driver and warn him that there would be some heavy luggage ; she looked a little apprehensive but he made no ado at all about the trunk, and got it down the stairs and into the car without any help or fuss. As Mrs. Brownlow's girl had chosen that day to walk out of her job without notice and hitch-hike to the seaside with a friendly lorry-driver, this saved a lot of trouble. And though the landlady, looking pointedly in the opposite direction, tried to hear where the car was going she didn't succeed. So that, so far as Miss Hunter was concerned, she might have been setting out for the North Pole.

That very morning Miss Hunter had endured agonies of apprehension. The car would forget to come, there would be trouble over the trunk, the car, if it did come, would break down, the driver would be insolent, she would open her bag and find she had left her purse behind, she would lose her tickets, miss her train, find there were no seats available. But none of these things happened. Everything went like clockwork ; the car arrived at Paddington a good twenty minutes before the train went out, porters were affable and reassuring, everyone seemed satisfied with the tips she distributed, she got a corner seat in an empty carriage, the sun came out—and as the train drew away from the station, taking her and the trunk that was practically decorated with labels, Alice Hunter's heart rose like a bird, and she knew that her whole life was going to change from this very day.

And how right she was !

She had congratulated herself too soon. The train had only just drawn clear of the platform when her privacy was invaded. The intruder came marching resolutely up the corridor, slid the door open and walked in. If people are made in pairs you might have said this was Miss Hunter's *vis-à-vis*. Not that they were particularly alike in appearance, except that to the casual eye most elderly women look pretty similar. But Miss Hunter knew her at once ; she had seen her like in a dozen boarding and lodging houses. A utility suit, a little creased and bulged by the shape of the wearer, a sensible anonymous hat, black shoes and lightish rayon stockings, dark fabric gloves. You saw such people everywhere ; St. Joachim's Guild had been full of them, and their history was much the same as hers.

The stranger seated herself opposite Miss Hunter. She wore a utility dark-grey costume (they both called it costume), a blue hat with a little wing—Miss Hunter's had a ribbon—black lace shoes—Alice's were brown but they looked much the same—she carried *The Daily Sketch* where Alice carried the *Mail*, she had the same sensible sort of handbag, the same sort of face innocent of anything but a dab of powder. She even spoke in much the same voice.

The first thing she said startled Alice. " You don't mind me coming in, I hope ? "

Alice felt herself turn crimson. The fact was she did mind, thinking, Surely there are plenty of other carriages—and most of them, as she had seen, were empty.

She said untruthfully, " No, no," in agitated tones, and the newcomer explained, " Never like travelling quite alone. Sounds absurd, of course, but the things you hear nowadays . . . You're not safe, at any age, and though they point out there's a communication cord how can you be sure you'd be able to reach it ? "

" Dear me," said Miss Hunter, who had never visualised anything so dramatic. " I hadn't thought . . . But surely one would never attract attention—I mean, train brigands would look for people in fur coats and—and crocodile shoes. (Crocodile shoes, they'd told her at Burtons, where she always went for hers, were nineteen pounds, one shilling ; they blamed it on to purchase tax.)

"You can never be sure," said her companion. "When I was with Lady Rivers—she had a thing about travelling—we kept a scrap-book of assaults on women, and it was surprising how often they weren't rich or young or beautiful." She laughed dryly. "Rum Old Girls, Lady Rivers used to call them. She said there's a preponderance of lunatics in the country these days—in the world generally, come to that."

Miss Hunter agreed. "All this atom bomb mania!" Meaning that only lunatics would have wanted to discover or invent or whatever the right word was anything so dangerous and inhuman as an atom bomb.

"Quite. What Lady Rivers meant was that you can't expect lunatics to act logically. Suppose you have a homicidal mania." She looked at Miss Hunter intently as though she might even suspect her of possessing this horrid trait. "What you want is blood, isn't it? It doesn't have to be blue blood or young blood or hot blood—just blood. Well, you and I have blood just like anybody else."

Involuntarily Miss Hunter glanced up at the communication cord. The stranger was right. For someone on the dumpy side, with short arms, it might be difficult to snatch it at the requisite moment.

"So," wound up her companion placidly, "I always walk through a train till I see a carriage with someone else in it. Now," she continued, warming to her task, "suppose Someone Doubtful got in and Trouble Ensued, one of us could pull the cord while the other engaged the villain. A sound argument, don't you think?"

"Very sound," agreed Alice. "I never thought——"

"Perhaps you don't travel a great deal."

" As a matter of fact, I haven't to date, but I'm hoping——"

The newcomer ran a thoughtful eye over Alice's general get-up.

" Going after a vacancy ? " she inquired.

Alice's eyes nearly popped out of her head. " A vacancy ? "

" A situation, if you prefer it that way. Oh, you needn't mind telling me. I'm on the same lay myself, and we Old Girls can always recognise each other."

" You mean, you are a lady's companion ? "

The other nodded. " Freke's the name," she said. " Laura Freke. I know every kind of employer there is. The old lady whose own children can't put up with her but assure you she's the easiest creature on earth ; the old gentleman who wants someone with a little nursing experience—he always turns out to be a screw loose ; the woman who has a delicate daughter who needs a little bright companionship—she's worse than the old gentleman ; the busy Committee woman who spends her time improving the lot of the downtrodden and never remembers that charity begins at home. Of course, some of them are all right, and no one knows better than I what a nuisance a companion is. Housekeepers don't see why they should wait on them, and wouldn't dream of being civil ; if there's a nurse on the premises she assumes the companion's there to push the bath-chair and listen to her—the nurse's—love-affairs. Nurses, you'll find, probably always have found, are perpetually pursued by men from Liverpool to London ; I can only suppose they spend all their spare time making up love stories for themselves. The only kind of employer I've not yet come across," wound up Miss Freke, " is the sort you read about in *Jessica's Companion* and *All For Love*, who die at the end of the book and leave their money to their companions. I've been on this lay for twenty years and all I've ever got out of it has been a work-box and a brooch nobody else wanted, and a choice of the dear departed's older clothes. They never offer you her fur coat, of course, or even her handbag, not if it's a good one. And I dare say your story's just the same as mine."

It was quite extraordinary, reflected Alice, that the fact of becoming an heiress had apparently had no outward effect at all. Cain had been surprised not to find a mark on his forehead—or perhaps it was the other people who had been surprised—to show he was a murderer, different from everyone else. On the morning after getting Mr. Finnemore's letter Alice had looked at herself very carefully in the glass and had been a little shocked to see that she looked no different from the morning before. When she went to the local shops she hesitated at each counter, anticipating some staggered comment, but no one paid her any attention except the people waiting behind her, who began to call their orders over her shoulder by way of a hint.

Miss Freke, however, was waiting for a reply. When Alice continued to sit there, rapt and amazed, she drew herself up and observed, her voice more staccato than before, "Hope you don't mind my talking to you. Makes the time go quicker, I always find."

"I don't mind a bit," said Alice, genuinely sorry at having apparently hurt this touchy person's feelings. "I was thinking how fortunate I was not to have to look for situations." She saw an ominous gleam come into the stranger's eye and she added resourcefully, "You see, I'm quite sure I wouldn't get them. For one thing, I've no experience. . . ."

"You mean you're a capitalist?" (She really was the most extraordinary woman.)

"I suppose you could say so. I've been living by

myself since my mother died. I have a little income, not very much, but," she essayed a very small joke, " it keeps me out of the poorhouse."

" H'm," was the surprising woman's retort. " I sometimes wonder whether creatures like you and me won't be happier when we're in it. Shan't be straining every nerve to keep up appearances. And for what? I ask you, for what? "

She seemed to expect an answer, so Alice obligingly tried to find her one. " To keep respectable, to maintain one's self-respect, I mean," she hazarded.

" Have you kept yours? I haven't. I've been kicked around a good deal in the last twenty years. And I don't believe it's been all jam for you. I know what it's like to be a poor gentlewoman. The fact is, what you want in this world isn't gentility but money. If I were an experienced cook or a trained children's nurse I should be three times as well paid. As it is, I'm regarded as an object of charity. People don't mind what they put over on you, because they know you daren't resent it; it's your living. Mind you, I don't say they're wrong. It's our fault, yours and mine."

Miss Hunter looked thoroughly startled. " I'm afraid I don't understand."

" Because you've never thought about it. Sometimes, when I see my bedroom, and I know what the cook's and the housemaid's are like, I begin to see red. And then I take myself to task. 'Why should you have as good a room as they?' I ask myself. Life goes by the law of supply and demand. When things are in short supply they're valuable. Cooks, for instance, and shorthand-typists and miners. People like us aren't in any sort of demand at all. The fact is, we're cheats."

Alice Hunter felt her head whirling. " You must

speak for yourself," said she. " I've never consciously broken any of the food laws, any laws at all."

" Never even given crumbs to starving birds ? " inquired Miss Freke. " That was against the law at one time, you know. But I didn't mean that. Trouble is we were born in a world of privilege. We thought we'd a right to exist. We were wrong."

Miss Hunter cast an anguished look at the communication cord. There could be no doubt about it, this woman was crazy. She ought to have been warned the instant she appeared. After all, it isn't natural in an English gentlewoman to wish to share a railway carriage if there is any chance of having it to yourself. And all that talk about maniacs. Nice women don't think of such things. Psychologists would have a word for her, though Alice wasn't quite sure what it would be. And, as if that wasn't enough, here was this fantastic rigmarole about cheating and having no right to exist ! Why not, indeed ? She said the words aloud, " Why not ? "

" Because we no longer live in a world of privilege. You have to give something in exchange for what you get. You and I may not get much, but we get all we deserve. We have a room apiece, one anyway, and we have our rations, which are subsidised by the Government, and enough money to buy clothes, if they're not very decorative. We don't have to beg our bread at the street-corner, we don't do anything useful. And it's partly our parents' fault, because they were so selfish they wanted our lives as well as their own, and partly ours, because we were too stupid to see we were simply going to be part of the national scrap-heap when our parents didn't want us any longer. And you can stop looking at that communication cord, because I'm as sane as you are, probably more so. No, our difficulty is we've nothing to contribute to the national sack. We're untrained. We're not married—that is, I'm sure you're not."

"No," agreed Alice.

"Even that would have been something," said Miss Freke.

"My mother——" began Alice.

"You shouldn't have let her."

"She was left a widow many many years ago. . . ."

"Suppose you'd never been born ?"

Miss Hunter repressed an instinctive wish to say her mother would probably have been quite pleased if she hadn't. Instead she observed primly, "I was. And I suppose one owes one's parents a duty."

There, she thought, that would put Miss Freke in her place.

Not a bit of it. "Very parochial outlook," said Miss Freke. "You owe yourself a duty, society a duty. How were you fulfilling that looking after your mother ?"

"She wasn't very strong."

"There are nurses for invalids. I'm not sure it's not black-legging staying at home, taking the easy way out. . . ."

"Easy ?" Alice couldn't repress that embittered comment.

"Easier than fighting your way out or you'd have fought. Oh, I'm not blaming you any more than myself. I was fooled just the same way. Mine was an aunt. She brought me up, did everything for me, she said. Now I owed her something. I was caught in a thicket, a thicket of gratitude, just the same as you ; mind you, we could have got out, both of us, I see that now, but we'd have been scratched and when we did get out we mightn't have liked the prospect much. But it was simpler not to fight. I tell you this, if life ever gives me another chance—not that I deserve it, but there is such a thing as luck—I shall take it. I shan't care who pays the bills. I've paid plenty of bills myself, which I'd never run up, and I expect the same's true of you. Law and good behaviour and gentility, they can all go hang for me. What's so genteel about being some other woman's dogsbody? That's what I've been all these years, knocking about from pillar to post, waiting by the deathbeds, always with a hope in the back of my mind, Perhaps this time—a legacy, I mean. But of course not. And after all, why should they? If you want things in life you have to go and take them. The plums of life won't drop though long you stop. But by the hand outstretched they may be fetched. I've stood under those fruit-trees till I've got a crick in my neck and my eyes are bloodshot, and I've never had a plum. But if ever I get inside an orchard again the owner of it had better look out. I'll strip every blessed tree, and pelt him with his own windfalls. It's what I should have done years ago. I'm no more of a fool than most other people. I could have learnt something, gone abroad, seen a bit of life, been in a position to make terms instead of always having to accept them. How about you? Content to live on a pittance for the rest of your days and thank God on your knees every night that it's there?"

"I'm certainly very grateful for it," said Alice with some spirit. "I may not have had a very gay time, but I don't want to exchange with you, particularly not you."

"Why?" demanded Miss Freke on the instant. "Do you know anything about them?"

"Them?"

"The Miss Turnbulls? The Misses Turnbull I ought to say. Oh, yes, I'm out on the long, long trail. Gentlewoman, active, willing, offered comfortable home and pocket-money for assistance in delightful country house. Must be fond of gardening and dogs. Will you walk into my parlour said the spider to the fly? Gardening and dogs sounds country, doesn't it? You see yourself in shabby but well-cut tweeds in a big garden cutting roses; or in shabby but well-cut brogues taking out a couple of terriers. 'This is Miss Freke,' you hear your jailer saying. 'I don't know what we should do without her. Pompey simply adores her.' So down you go—in your utility suit that was never well-cut and your shoes that have just been resoled with something more like cardboard than leather, and you find gardening means cutting the lawn and weeding the paths and perhaps helping in the vegetable garden; and dogs are one peke or two or three. And, once you're in, you find they've forgotten to mention that you're also required to be fond of making beds and washing-up and doing the shopping and polishing and possibly collecting for National Savings or delivering the Parish Magazines. And, when anyone the least interesting does come to the house, they ask you if you haven't got some friend in the neighbourhood you'd like to go and see, or tell you brightly this is a chance for you to have a bit of time off—once you've made the cake and cut the sandwiches and set out the tea-tray. You know," she leaned forward and her fierce brown eyes burned into Alice's paler startled ones, "I sometimes think that if I had a chance of making a life for myself I wouldn't be ashamed of it on the Judgment Day, I'd take it, whatever the cost. Yes, if it meant poisoning the Misses Turnbull, or pushing them over a cliff or down a flight of stairs, provided I could be sure I wouldn't be found out, and that they'd left me provided for. But it wouldn't be any good, I dare say," she added, leaning back against the cushions of the third-class carriage, "either I'd be found out or else the will would be invalid. You see, I'm not really any better than you. Full of sound and fury signifying nothing. And we'll both die in a ditch and most likely be buried by e parish. Or have you taken out an insurance?"

"I certainly shan't be buried by the parish," retorted Miss Hunter. "And I don't think you ought to talk like that. It gives the wrong impression."

Miss Freke laughed mirthlessly. "Are you afraid I'm going to try my prentice hand on you? My dear, what would be the use? You're no gold-mine."

Alice suddenly felt her heart explode. She couldn't and wouldn't stand this any longer. Who was she to be spoken to in this contemptuous fashion, she who had a lawyer's letter in her bag at that very moment, proving herself an heiress?

"I'm afraid appearances are sometimes deceitful," she said, trying to keep her voice calm. "I'm by no means the poor impoverished creature you imagine."

Miss Freke didn't seem impressed. "Do you do it, too?" she said. "Yes, I suppose we're all in the same boat."

"What are you talking about now?"

"Playing at make-believe. I'm not a companion. I'm a famous author and I want to do a book about poor numskulls like Laura Freke and—what did you say your name was?"

"It's Alice Hunter."

"And Alice Hunter. That's why I'm wearing these rags and travelling third-class and lugging my own suitcase on to the bus and putting up with the conductor's insolence, and pretending not to see the porter, because if you don't give them about two shillings they're so rude they give you a heart attack. Really I'm the woman who wrote the Book of the Month last March and my play's coming on at the Haymarket next month. I've got a new dress for it—silver lamé, and shoes from Rayne. My secretary says . . . Oh, drat that telephone. Answer it, Miss Freke. Write to my publishers. Ring up my agents. Get in touch with Linnitt and Dunfee. Oh, yes, I've done it all. I tried this morning. I'm going down to see the Turnbulls because I'm employed by one of the Government Departments making out a schedule . . ."

"I thought Government Departments always went first class," said Alice.

Miss Frake laughed suddenly. "So they do. I suppose if I were clever enough I could believe this was a first-class carriage. Well, you do play that game, don't you?"

"I'm not playing it now. I'm going down to Bath to see a lawyer. I've been left a legacy."

"Who by?" There wasn't any doubt about it. Miss Freke didn't believe a word.

"It's an old aunt, a Miss Wells. She's been living in a—a home there for years."

"Ninepence in the shilling?" asked Miss Freke.

"The will's legal," said Alice sharply. "Mr. Finnemore wouldn't have written to me if it hadn't been."

"Where do you live—in London, I mean?"

"I was in Ennismore Terrace. Why is that so amusing?"

"People who live in Ennismore Terrace—Good heavens, of course I know it. All the Rum Old Girls know it. Near Bradleys, we say—Between Westbourne Grove and Edgware Road would be better. We've all been there one time or another. Are you in one of the Bond Charity houses? I was for a time, while my savings lasted."

"I was in rooms. Nothing to do with charity."

"The Bond Houses were quite nice. For decrepit gentlewomen, you know. But perhaps you weren't eligible. Daughters of clergymen and Serving officers (deceased). My father was a clergyman, that's how I got in. But it didn't last. I tried to work by the day, but nobody wants companions who aren't on the premises. If you live on the premises, you see, you don't have any Trade Union hours. I suppose you're going to move into Knightsbridge or Mayfair now you're a woman of means ? "

" I'm not going to stay in London. I'm going to start a new life in Bath."

" Know anybody there ? "

" No one. But the lawyer will advise me. I gave up my room at once. Mrs. Brownlow, my landlady, was very curious to know my whereabouts."

" But you didn't tell her ? "

" I intensely dislike vulgar curiosity."

" You take care you're not too pernickety to get to Heaven when your turn comes," Miss Freke warned her. " Why shouldn't she be curious ? She has to work hard enough, doesn't she ? What else has she got to amuse her but her lodgers' affairs ? Ever thought what a possibility it would be to run a lodging-house and fill it with people with skeletons in their cupboards ? It would keep you for the rest of your days."

" Until one of your lodgers made a skeleton of you."

" Odds are they wouldn't have the courage. It must take a lot of nerve to commit a murder. I've never tried, though I've been tempted more than once, but I was always afraid I might be found out. Oh, you don't have to worry about the Turnbulls. They'll be safe with me. I shan't murder them. You want some experience before you take a risk like that, and how on earth are people like you and me to get it ? " She smiled, and pulled off her hat which she threw on to the seat. " Do you know what one of my favourite dreams used to be ? I'd hail a taxi and be driven to one of the big hairdressers—Dover Street or Gresham Street—and I'd put my head into the hands of the best man they had—oh, figuratively, of course—and I'd say 'Turn me out looking like Mme de Montespan. I don't care what it costs, I don't care what you do to me, but next time I look in the glass don't let me see these greyish-white wisps which I wind round a pencil every night and pin into place. Let me look windswept or curly-cue or whatever the latest thing is. I don't mind looking absurd, so long as I look striking.' And then I'd go to what they called a beautician nowadays, and I'd say, 'I've been looking at this face for more than half a century and I'm sick of the sight of it. I may have to live alone but at least I'll live with somebody new. Colour it, change it, massage it, pound it—let me take a stranger home with me.' Don't you feel like that?"

"Would you not be afraid of looking ridiculous?"

"Anything would be better than looking as though you'd been picked off the white elephant stall at the Jumble Sale. Do you know what I regret most? That I didn't have these ideas twenty years ago. Go on telling me more about yourself. An only child?"

"Yes. I often wished I had a sister."

"She might have been mother's pet. Did you always live at home?"

It was such a treat to Alice to find someone willing, nay, eager to listen to her life-story, that she swallowed the bait, hook, line and sinker. She coloured a little as she began, but quite soon she, who'd always been awkward and shy, became enthralled. Soon she and this woman she hadn't met an hour ago were like a pair of ardent Beggar-My-Neighbour players. They slapped down their cards with such zest . . . "My early life was hard," said one.

"No harder than mine," retorted the other.

"My mother was delicate. . . ."

"My aunt was lame."

"My mother was unfortunate in her investments."

"My aunt was unfortunate in her vicar."

When they had been at it for some time Miss Freke asked curiously, "Was it really true what you told me at the beginning? Have you really come into a legacy?"

"Of course. I can show you the letter. I've got it in my bag here."

She opened the sensible black bag and took it out. Miss Freke read it with frank envy.

"It doesn't say how much."

"It was enough to keep Cousin Agatha in a home for years. And those places are never very cheap."

"I wonder if there's any property."

"He doesn't *say* so."

"Might be a fur coat—or, a diamond ring. I'd like a fur coat. Wouldn't you?"

"I never even thought of having one."

"I have. Often and often."

"They're very heavy to wear, I believe."

"Just carry it over your arm, walking down Bond Street. And silk umbrellas and stockings, instead of cotton. How old are you?"

Miss Hunter coloured to the roots of her greyish hair. "I—I——"

"I'm sixty-three. I might have another twenty years. There was old Lady Rivers, my last bully. She died at 84, and she could stand up to anyone."

"Why did she die, then?"

"How do I know? Perhaps Heaven thought it had inflicted her on her family long enough. Perhaps the nurse had come to the end of her tether. I'll never be surprised to hear she's going to marry the heir—the nurse, I mean. Not that he's any chicken. Sir Philip

Rivers—a widower. And don't ask me if he's handsome because I've never set eyes on him. If I could prove there was any funny business I might be made for life."

"You shouldn't talk like that," said Alice feebly. "Some people might think you meant it."

"I do mean it. Still, she's probably far too clever. And I was a fool. I let them see I didn't like her. No one would listen to me. Anyhow, it was pneumonia after a fall, and that generally carries the old ones off. Let's assume you're going to inherit ten thousand pounds. . . . What would you do with it?"

"I should buy a little house, I think. And settle in Bath. I've always wanted a house of my own. . . . Isn't there something you've always longed for?"

"Yes," snapped Miss Freke. "I've always wanted a bank account. It enrages me to see these chits of nineteen or twenty pull out a cheque-book and casually write out a cheque, and all I can do is go into the Post Office and ask for a withdrawal form." As she spoke she had a vision of herself hesitating in Marshall and Snelgroves, Selfridges, John Lewis, John Barker and Peter Robinson, when the assistant asked, "Will you be paying by cheque or cash?" "I never pay by cheque," she would retort. "I was brought up in a more strait-laced fashion than would be popular nowadays. Don't pay for a thing unless you've got the money in your purse," my mother taught me. "I shall pay cash." Sometimes it had happened she had seen a real bargain, say a coat that had been reduced because it was autumn weight and this was high summer. If she had possessed a bank account she could have ordered the coat and left a cheque, but it took some days to draw the necessary amount out of the Post Office, and by that time the bargain would be snapped up by someone else.

"But surely you could have opened an account?" murmured the perplexed Miss Hunter.

"What do you suggest I should have used for money?" inquired Miss Freke. "Have you any notion what companions are paid? Once you're living-in your board and lodging assumes a tremendous value. 'You must remember how the cost of living has gone up,' they say, 'and of course you'll have no expenses under my roof.' Some of them go so far as to explain that the servants (the *other* servants is what they mean) don't expect a companion to tip. On the other hand, if you live out and go in by the day, then they expect you to find quarters at pre-war rates. Oh I've never had enough money to open an account. Besides, you need references, and if you say, you're a companion living on what a companion is paid and what, over the years, a companion has been able to save, and suggest opening an account on that you don't get much of a welcome from a bank manager."

Miss Hunter was quite distressed by these acid revelations, but consoled herself by reflecting that some people automatically look for spots on the sun, and other people either managed to open an account or were quite content without one. She felt it was rather unjust of Providence to provide her with this particular companion on a journey undertaken with such hope and delight. She looked nervously at her watch and then out of the window. "How much longer to Bath?"

"We've nearly an hour yet," said Miss Freke. "You know, if you do decide to buy a house there are various considerations you oughtn't to overlook. You've got to be careful. Once it gets round that you've got a house you'll find all your poor relations descending upon you. You'll be running a Government hotel with no tax-payer to meet your losses before you know where you are."

" I have no relations," insisted Alice. " Miss Wells was the last."

" And in any case (was it jealousy or sheer common sense that made Miss Freke so clear-headed ?) you won't be able to touch the money for an age."

" Why not ? "

" Because it takes lawyers a year at least to clear things up."

" My aunt had been dead nearly a year. It's all in the first letter, the one I showed you. You see ? Mr. Finnemore says they've been trying to locate me. If I weren't such a bird of passage . . ." She smiled a wintry smile, but there was in it a hint of if-winter-comes-can-spring-be-far-behind ? that filled her companion with envy. . . . " Anyhow, it sounds as though I could borrow on my inheritance right away. And I've always wanted a house of my own."

" What psychologists call compensation," nodded the astute Miss Freke. " I was companion to a psychologist's wife once. If she'd been anyone else's wife you'd have said she was as mad as a hatter, but that man could explain anything away. She was a kleptomaniac, actually, so calling her a lunatic is being kind. I never had a more arduous job. I had to go round with her wherever she went and when I caught her lifting things from the counters I had to get hold of them and put them back without being seen."

" Did you manage it ? " asked Miss Hunter in frank envy. She'd not only have been seen, she'd most likely have been arrested for stealing.

" Oh, it required tact, of course." (She said that in the offensively airy way of women who tell you of course they've got rice and dried fruit and evaporated milk in their store cupboards, at a time when you yourself know they can't be had in any shop.) " But after a while I used to persuade her there were only a few shops worth visiting and they soon got to know us there, and they realised that anything she took would be returned."

" I'm not surprised you couldn't stand that situation very long," suggested Miss Hunter.

" I stood it, as you put it, for nine months. Then one of the shops suggested that they would rather be paid for anything Mrs.—well, I mustn't mention her name, it's a household word—had picked up. And naturally that didn't please her husband at all. He took it out of me—he was as mean as they come—and I sometimes wonder if that wasn't why she took to kleptomania in the first place. ' I employ you to see that my wife does not—er—yield to this unfortunate impulse,' he said. Well, I told him, ' It's a funny thing she needs so much compensation.' Next thing I knew I was out on my ear, and no compensation at all. She's in a home now," she added, " and her husband's getting his own compensation."

" Really," said Miss Hunter, " I never knew before how much I have to be thankful for."

" Having a private income? Yes, you are lucky. The time's coming, you know, when that sort of thing won't be allowed. And quite right, too. I'm all for the abolition of privilege. Still, coming back to your house . . ." She sounded as if she intended the words in their literal meaning, and Miss Hunter actually shivered. " You oughtn't to live alone, you know. That's how we old girls go queer. If you haven't got any relations you'll need a companion yourself, and by companion I don't mean a pussy-cat. Do you believe in Providence? "

Actually Miss Hunter did, but not to the extent Miss Freke implied.

"Well, I do," that lady continued in vigorous undaunted tones. "I believe it was Providence that put me on the train to-day instead of yesterday, as I'd originally planned. I kicked against the pricks all right when I was held up for a day, but now I begin to think there may have been some pattern in it. You know, I don't believe I'll go and see the Turnbulls right away. They might snap me up, for we're a dying race and a good thing, too. I dare say they're quite well off and could easily afford to pay a displaced person a living wage, instead of getting a decayed English gentlewoman for her keep; and you and I have a lot in common. . . ." But nothing, thought Miss Hunter with a sudden gleam of humour, compared with what she intended them to have.

"Oh, I don't think I shall be advertising for a companion yet awhile," she murmured with that wintry smile that now seemed to suggest spring had retreated a couple of months at least. "I'm very good company for myself."

"I know," nodded the odious Miss Freke. "Go walking round and round your room, chattering away like half a dozen magpies. Dare say you talk to yourself in the street, too. Dangerous practice. I was companion to a woman once who did that. Her daughter got me because she was afraid Mamma would be certified, and so long as she had someone with her no one would know she was still talking to herself."

"But did she? After you came, I mean?"

"Oh, yes, m'dear. Mad as a hatter, but of course they couldn't have put her away because of the money. It was all hers. Three children she had. You never saw such a trio of human crocodiles. I wouldn't sleep happily in my bed at night if I thought that our dear mother was in an asylum. Why, the poor old lady never even knew who I was. Sometimes I was her sister, Gladys, and sometimes I was Mr. Churchill and she was advising him about the Second Front. Still, she died in the end. They gave me a good reference, and a little brooch none of them liked. What I want," she continued with unabated energy, " is a situation with someone of my own age and outlook, who knows what it's like to be an unwanted female of uncertain age—though why uncertain, when it must be obvious to the meanest eye, I've never understood—who's ready to share what she's got with me in life and see to it I don't starve after she's gone."

" But—but . . ." poor Alice felt her head was in a whirl, " you might die first."

" In that case I shouldn't worry about the inheritance. But I come of a very long-lived family."

" I thought you said an aunt brought you up."

" My parents were killed in a railway accident when I was two. But if they hadn't been they'd probably be alive now. The aunt lived to be over eighty."

" You'd have thought she would leave you provided for."

" As yours has done? Ah, but mine wasn't loco. However, that's enough about aunts. They're an odd race by all accounts, and perhaps you and I are spared something by not being able to join it. How about this notion of mine? You want waking up, you know. Life don't last for ever and there's a lot to be done. What about travel? I'll put a girdle round the earth in thirty minutes. Well, we shouldn't be in quite such a hurry as that, but I've always wanted to go up in an aeroplane."

" Have you?" Alice felt quite faint. " How extraordinary! I never have. I've always wanted my own little house, that was mine. No one to say ' Your room will be wanted next week,' or suddenly double the rent or complain if you used a sewing-machine after supper. To be independent." She glowed and Miss Freke saw with surprise that once she might have been quite a pretty girl.

" You be careful," she warned her. " All these new orders. You'll find half your lovely new house requisitioned for a dustman and his dependants if you're not careful."

" I should only have a small house, naturally."

" Any house is too large for one person. Two people now . . ." She smiled persuasively and looked nearly as much like an alligator as Mr. Arthur Crook in similar circumstances.

Alice Hunter felt that any minute she'd be pressing the woman to join her. It went through her hazy mind that she might be the devil in disguise. If he could tempt so inexorably—she didn't know very much about temptation herself—no wonder so many people fell. Desperately she tried to change the subject.

" This train," she said, " seems to be going very fast."

" It's an express train," Miss Freke pointed out.

" Even for an express it seems very fast. And it's beginning to wobble."

" Oh, nonsense," said Miss Freke. " It's you, my dear woman."

At that moment, Miss Hunter's fat black bag fell off the seat with a plonk. She stooped to recover it and Miss Freke's suitcase suddenly crashed out of the rack ; and her handbag bumped on to the floor where it stood by its prototype from Kensington High Street, like two comfortable dark toads.

" Hey, what's up ? " exclaimed Miss Freke, getting to her feet and immediately being flung off them by the motion of the train. " I believe you're right. I believe . . ."

She made a dash for the sliding door and her sentence

remained unfinished. For at that instant it happened. The train, that had become out of control, crashed into a stationary train just outside Yarborough Station, two or three carriages were telescoped, Miss Hunter uttered one sharp cry as something—a piece of window-glass as it happened—cut her hand so that the blood began to flow in the messiest fashion—then something also hit her with a crash on her neat felt bonnet and, as the Victorians liked to say, she knew no more.

CHAPTER THREE

Sister March of the Yarborough General Hospital greeted the doctor on night duty with becoming respect and told him that the old woman in the corner bed in No. 4 ward had died about an hour before.

"Out of a very nasty world," said the doctor cheerfully. "How about the train victim?"

"Miss Freke? She's very low still."

"Not come round?"

"I doubt if she ever will. She had serious concussion and a bad injury to the hand and she's no chicken."

"These old birds sometimes outlive all the chickens," the doctor warned her. "Any relatives?"

"So far as we can discover from her luggage, there's no one. She seems to have been going to Bath to see about a job. Companion to two women called Turnbull."

"Perhaps it's a merciful dispensation she won't get there. Gosh, what a life. How old do you suppose she is?"

"Somewhere in the sixties, I'd say. I wonder if

there's anyone we could get in touch with about the funeral arrangements and so forth. Wonder if she'll come round before the end, be able to tell us anything ? "

A junior nurse who had been hovering now came a little closer.

" Yes, nurse ? " snapped the sister.

" It's the patient in Room 8," said the nurse deferentially. " She's conscious."

" And then they say the age of miracles is past," said the doctor. " Well, before she lapses into unconsciousness again, for heaven's sake, sister, get something out of her."

" You'll be seeing her yourself, I suppose," said sister, and the doctor, who was young and knew there's no room for passengers in the modern world, said he'd be coming along in due course.

The sister went along to Room 8. " Well, dear ? " she asked. " Feeling better ? " The Yarborough was a small cottage hospital and everyone was informal and pleasant. A home from home some of the locals called it.

" Where am I ? " asked the patient. " This looks like a hospital."

" That's right, dear. You've had a nasty accident."

" I've been trying to think. Am I in Bath ? "

" Not yet."

" It was the train, wasn't it ? It began to go too fast, and then something fell on top of me. . . ."

" Quite a lot of the carriage," said the nurse. " Now don't talk too much. Tell us who you'd like us to get in touch with, about your illness, I mean. Have you any brothers or sisters ? " They knew she hadn't any husband or children, of course. There was a ring on her wedding finger, but it was a little silver decorative affair, set with turquoises, picked up somewhere for about a couple of pounds, thought sister. No man ever gave her that.

" No. No, there's no one."

" Alone in the world ? " Sister frowned. " Still, you've got some friend, I expect. Who were you going to see ? "

" I was going to see my lawyer. He lives in Bath. I'd come into money."

Bats, thought sister. Come into money, indeed? They'd been through her handbag and found the letter from Miss Eliza Turnbull.

" Perhaps you would send him a telegram, explaining I've been delayed. I shall be coming to-morrow."

" Well, not quite to-morrow, I'm afraid," smiled sister. " We shan't be able to spare you so soon."

" But—it's urgent. He's expecting me. I wrote."

" We'll let him know about the accident."

" Yes, please. That's most important. What time is it ? "

" Nearly time to go to sleep again."

" Please don't talk to me as if I were a child. I'm sixty-four. I was to have seen him this morning." She looked puzzled. " No, I mean to-morrow, of course. It was this morning the train crashed."

" Dear me, no," said sister. " You've been here much longer than that. Now, don't try and sit up and get excited. You've been quite ill, you know. You don't want to bring on——"

" Please tell me how long I've been here ? It's very important."

" Three weeks."

" Three weeks ? " She was appalled. " But I don't remember . . ."

" No. You had concussion, so we couldn't bother you. Now don't get upset about it. People who're concussed often suffer from loss of memory, and, even if you had remembered who you were, you wouldn't have been well enough to move. It was very lucky really we happened to have a room vacant. Now, tell us the name of your friend and we'll get in touch. I expect quite a lot of people are worrying over you." But she didn't really believe that, of course, for if that had been true there'd have been enquiries long before this.

" She wasn't my friend. She was just somebody who got into the same carriage. I'd never seen her before. What happened to her ? "

" Happened to who ? "

" The—the woman in my carriage."

" There wasn't exactly anyone in your carriage when you were taken out. I mean, it was all smashed to matchwood. You were very lucky to be alive."

" You mean, she was killed ? "

" There were a few casualties. It was a nasty smash, you know."

" She hadn't any relations either. Poor Miss Freke ! "

The nurse started a little. Brain *was* affected then ? She'd been afraid of this.

" Now you're not to worry," she said. " You'll be nicely looked after here, and—what was the name of the lawyer you were talking about ? "

" Mr.—Mr.—oh, I had it on the tip of my tongue. It'll come back in a moment. Something to do with a fish. Mr. Codd ? Mr. Hake ? No, nothing like that. Oh dear, I shall forget my own name in a minute."

The nurse laughed in a friendly way that was intended to be reassuring. " Well, you haven't done *that*, Miss Freke," she said.

" Freke ! I'm not Miss Freke," cried Alice. " That was her, *her*. The other one in the carriage. Why do you look at me like that ? I'm Miss Hunter—Alice Hunter, I always have been. And I was going to see my lawyer about a legacy. A legacy. That's right. My old aunt died. In an asylum really, though they never called it that. A home they said. People always do, don't they? Relations, I mean. Otherwise people, other people, might think it was in the family. And I don't think she was violent. Just eccentric really. That's it, eccentric. She didn't always remember who she was, and of course that made things awkward—with shops and so forth. So I dare say it was quite a merciful release, though I do wonder . . ." Her gestures were getting wild, the effort of recollection was being too much for her, " who she thought she was when she died. Do you believe in life after death, nurse? I do, of course, but I know it's supposed to be very old-fashioned."

"Now you're not to talk any longer," ordered sister in severe tones. "You'll get yourself into a fever, and the doctor's coming along in a minute."

"Oh, yes . . . I'd like a word with him. And I'm not in a fever. I was just wondering what would happen if—if Aunt Agatha tried to tell St. Peter she was Joan of Arc or Mrs. Pankhurst."

Sister went away after that and saw the doctor and told him the old woman was quite dotty. Kept talking about another old woman called Freke who had been in the carriage with her.

"Was there one?" asked the doctor.

"No. She was lying there with a suitcase on top of her and her bag on the floor. Not a sign of anyone else. It's lucky there weren't many people on the train. There'd have been quite a high death roll."

"Who does the old girl think she is?"

"Hunter. Miss Alice Hunter. And she was going to Bath to see a lawyer."

"Well, she *was* going to Bath. She was going to see about a job, did you say?"

" There was a letter in her bag. I wish you'd come and take a look at her."

To Dr. Ogilvie the sick woman repeated her claim to be Miss Alice Hunter, and nothing he said could shake her.

" I want you to let my lawyer know where I am," she insisted.

But when he asked for the lawyer's name she still couldn't recall it. " But, of course, there's a letter in my handbag. I brought all my papers. That will prove who I am. I can't imagine why you thought I was Miss Freke."

" Your identity card says so," the doctor assured her.

" My—oh, but that's absurd. Oh, of course, I see what's happened. You've got the wrong bag. There were two of us in the carriage, you know, Miss Freke and myself, at the time of the accident. And the rescuers picked up her bag and brought it here with me. What happened to her ? "

" I really don't know what you're talking about," said the sister rather tartly.

" You must have made a mistake. She must have died and been buried as me, though that implies great carelessness. I suppose the funeral took place locally, since she had no relatives ? "

" I've told you, Miss Freke, nobody was killed in the accident. Though for a minute you were reported dead. In fact you were actually taken to the mortuary. But you were the only serious casualty."

Alice considered this for a moment. " Did the train catch fire ? " she enquired.

" Of course not. Why on earth should it ? "

" I thought perhaps she'd been destroyed in the flames ; Miss Freke, I mean. Though that would be queer, too."

" Very queer indeed," agreed the sister, whose

patience was virtually at an end. "Queer all her luggage disappeared, too."

"All *my* luggage, you mean. Hers is here, at least I suppose it is. I had a dome-shaped trunk with my initials on it, at least my mother's initials, and they were the same as mine. Amy she was christened and I'm Alice."

"I don't know anything about a dome-shaped trunk," said Sister March.

"Then where is my luggage?"

"There's a suitcase and a flat brown box. Oh, it's all there. You needn't be afraid it was lost. It's got your name on it, as large as life. L.M.F. What does L. stand for?"

"I don't know. Lydia, I should think. Or Lucy or Lilian or Lettice. What's it to do with me?"

"Oh, well," said the sister, apparently under the impression that she was making a soothing remark, "we're not responsible for our names. And now do try and keep calm."

But keeping calm was the very last thing poor Alice Hunter proposed to do. She wouldn't answer any of Dr. Ogilvie's questions, but began all over again her rigmarole about mistaken identity, two women in a carriage, a possible false death certificate, and a re-assertion of the fact that she was Alice Hunter of London on her way to Bath to see a lawyer about a legacy.

"All in good time," said Dr. Ogilvie. "You can't go to Bath yet. It 'ud be suicide."

"I must let Mr.—Mr.—the lawyer know I've been detained."

"He must know it by this time," the doctor offered. "Two or three more days won't make any difference."

"They will. You don't understand. I—I'm the victim of a gross deception. At least, I think I am," she amended, realising that so far she had no proof at all of the monstrous suspicion shaping in her mind.

" You'll feel better later when you're stronger," said the doctor.

She had some ado to keep the tears from her eyes. " I thought I knew most of the dreadful things that could happen to people," she muttered. " But I never dreamed of this."

The doctor, moved perhaps by her obvious misery, let her unburden herself for a while.

" It's perfectly clear what's happened," she said. " When the crash occurred I was knocked unconscious. That was Miss Freke's chance. She must have picked up my bag, with all my letters and proofs in it. . . ."

" That's rather a serious accusation to make. After all, you had only to claim them next day."

" But don't you see, she thought I was dead? Nurse says everybody did, and I was actually driven to the mortuary. If she saw me being driven away, all she had to do was to claim my luggage and leave her belongings in their stead."

The doctor was trying to find a polite way of asking why anyone in her senses should want to be old Miss Hunter, when the sister put in brightly, " Miss Freke's been telling me about a legacy." (Though you might have thought the doctor had gleaned that much for himself by now.)

" Yes," amplified Alice, " a legacy. But not to her. To me. I mean, that's why—she's gone off to claim it."

" But if it's yours—it's not so easy, you know."

" If she can persuade the lawyer she's me and I'm dead . . ." Oh, it was no good. Her head was going round and round. And round. She knew perfectly well what she was talking about, but she could see she wasn't making the slightest impression on her audience. They simply thought her potty. It had been a mistake to mention Aunt Agatha. Still, the doctor meant to be kind.

" What's the name of this lawyer ? " he asked.

" That's what I can't remember. Oh, it'll come back to me, of course."

" It will, if you don't worry too much. And when it does you can write."

But after they had both gone poor Miss Hunter beat her clenched fist on the hygienic eiderdown. Because she knew now she'd been lying here for three weeks, and that meant that the real Miss Freke had three weeks' start of her. She might try and convince herself that the confusion was capable of an innocent interpretation, but if so where were Alice Hunter's luggage, and handbag, and identity card ? When a junior nurse looked in presently she asked for her bag and it was handed to her. As she expected, it wasn't hers at all. The last time she had seen that had been just before it fell off the seat on Miss Freke's side of the train. This contained a ration book, an identity card, a note-case with a little money, ten pounds actually, and there was another pound in silver—and a Post Office Savings Book showing a balance of £170. Was that all there was ? Alice wondered, appalled. She remembered hearing Miss Freke say, " I've never had a cheque-book of my own. Never had enough money to open an account." So all that stood between her and destitution was less than £200 ! There was no insurance card, because the woman was past sixty, and though Miss Hunter had a vague notion that employers had to pay even where slaves were immune she couldn't be quite sure, and anyhow quite a lot of employers did nothing about it. Lady Rivers had presumably been one of those who thought this social health service a lot of new-fangled tommy-rot, all right for the young and for men with dependants perhaps, but sheer nonsense for ageing women.

It was some time before it occurred to Miss Hunter that, unless and until she could establish her own identity, she—and not Miss Freke—only had this meagre sum between herself and destitution.

" I must be calm, quite calm and collected," she told herself, putting the bag away. " If I'm not careful I shall begin to wonder if I really am Alice Hunter, if the others aren't right and my name *is* Freke and I *was* going to Bath to see the Misses Turnbull." It was galling to discover that she could remember their name easily enough, while that of the all-important lawyer slipped away whenever she tried to approach it. " After all," she consoled herself, " I can easily get my identity established once I am out of this place. Mrs. Brownlow will recognise me, and there are tradespeople and oh! one of these days I shall regard it as quite an adventure." But suppose that creature had been able to persuade Mr.—Mr.—X (call him that for the moment) that she was Alice Hunter and suppose she'd actually got something on account, would she, Miss Hunter, be able to reclaim that sum? And now it was quite intolerable to think of the real Miss Freke lording it in Bath on the money of a woman she supposed to be dead.

" But I'm not dead," announced Miss Hunter in fierce tones to the amazement of the young nurse who came in at that instant to put her to rights. " As she and others will soon learn."

" Of course you're not dead, dear," said the young nurse, kindly. " Living miracle, that's what you are. I don't mind telling you we all thought you were going. Sister's ever so pleased. She says you'll be getting up soon. And I expect you're longing to have visitors. I know I should, lying alone in this little room all day."

" I am not expecting any visitors," said Miss Hunter shortly. " I—the fact is, I am quite alone in the world."

" If you were going to be here longer we'd get Miss East to put you on her list. She's ever so kind. Visits patients who haven't got anybody, like you, or whose friends can't get away or can't afford the fare. Mind you, she's a bit heavy on the blessings of suffering, but you don't have to listen."

Miss Hunter was feeling exhausted and distressed. She made a bad mistake.

" I hope you won't dream of putting my name on Miss East's list," she said. " I am perfectly capable of looking after my own affairs."

" Well, she's away till next week anyhow," said the young nurse, and when she had gone downstairs she said to a colleague, " There's an awful warning for you. Pickled Old Maid in aspic. Silly, I call it. You don't have to be peculiar because you're not married. My Aunt Jen isn't married, and she's as much fun as a circus."

It was forty-eight hours later that Miss Hunter remembered the lawyer's name. It was quite absurd the way it happened. It chanced that there was smoked haddock for supper that night, and at sight of it the invalid looked as pleased as Punch. This was one of the dishes she had always enjoyed so much when she lived " on her own." It was so simple to cook ; you just dumped the haddock in a frying pan with some milk and water and let it cook slowly. Then you put a bit of margarine (butter before the war) on the top, and ate it very hot. Some people liked what they called the gravy, but she always poured that away. A nice bit of crusty bread and some butter and you had a meal fit for a queen. It was the first time she'd had it in hospital, and she was so obviously pleased to see it that the young nurse on duty put her head round the door after a while to say, " More finny ? "

Miss Hunter shot up in bed as though someone had put a bullet in her. " That's it," she exclaimed, " that's it. I knew it had something to do with a fish. The name of the lawyer, I mean. Finnemore. I ought to have remembered. I always enjoyed reading Fenimore Cooper as a girl."

The nurse rescued the tray and observed to her friend, when she had left the room, " You know the one in eight, the one they say's dotty ? "

The friend said, " Yes."

And the nurse said, " Well, she is. Can you see any connection between Fenimore Cooper and a smoked haddock ? Well, she does."

Miss Hunter, however, wasn't in the least concerned with what junior nurses might think. The miracle had happened, she had remembered the lawyer's name. Now she could write to him, and it was only a matter of days before the whole tangle was smoothed out.

Writing the letter was much more difficult than she had anticipated. For one thing, her cut hand was still very painful, and she could not hold a pen at a normal angle ; the nib sprawled over the paper and she knew with dismay that no one would recognise her signature. She missed her typewriter terribly, and at the thought of that abominable woman banging away on it, ruining it (for all typists know it is death to a machine to let someone else operate it), she nearly had another black-out. The second and worse feature of the case was that, set down in black and white, the story sounded too fantastic for any reasonable person's believing.

"DEAR MR. FINNEMORE" (she began),

"A railway accident has prevented my calling on you as I had intended; I am at present at the Yarborough Cottage Hospital, but the doctor here tells me I shall probably be able to leave quite soon when I shall continue my interrupted journey to Bath. I have been suffering from concussion and for some time did not know who I was and could give no account of myself to the authorities here. Fortunately my memory has now returned and I know everything about myself. What really troubles me is that I am listed at this hospital under the name of Freke, and all the papers and possessions that were brought in with me bear this out. I mean, my identity card, ration book, etc. The truth is this. I travelled down from London with the real Miss Freke and on the way I was foolish enough to tell her why I was going to Bath. I showed her your letter and we exchanged some information about ourselves. Then the accident occurred and I was seriously injured, so seriously that at first I was taken to the mortuary. Naturally when they examined my things they took for granted that I really was Miss Freke, and I have only just been able to enlighten them. Now this is where the real trouble comes in. This woman—the real Freke—must have deliberately stolen my papers and luggage, including my typewriter, and come to Bath in my name. She is not unlike me in appearance and, of course, as you have never met me you would not notice the difference. She has all my papers, which by this time she has probably shown to you, and even raised an advance on my inheritance by some hard-luck story. On the way down she told me she would have no scruples about taking advantage of anything that came her way. Of course, she must have thought I was dead or she would never have taken this risk. As soon as I am able to travel I will come to Bath where perhaps you could make some arrangements for me to stay. I understand there are a great many hotels and perhaps you could get your secretary to book me a room, say, at the end of the week. Please do not take any further action in connection with this wicked woman. I shall, of course, insist on any loan she may have had being returned. I am sure she is liable for criminal prosecution and I shall brief you to represent me. In fact, I should like you to take up the matter with the police as soon as you get this letter. You remember what Shakespeare says: that he who takes my purse steals trash but he that takes from me my good name takes what does not enrich him but makes me poor indeed. Not that this is true in my case of course, since my purse contained twenty pounds in money, and taking my name has certainly enriched this woman to the value of my aunt's legacy. It is abominable that in these so-called civilised times such a thing can happen and the kindest thing would be to say she is out of her mind, but I am afraid this is not true. She is no more out of her mind than I am, just a wicked woman and a thief, and I rely on you as my legal representative to see justice done."

This letter, which Miss Hunter drafted with great care, took her all the rest of the day to prepare. She wanted to copy it that same evening but nurse said sensibly, "You won't be going out from here for some days yet, so what's the hurry? And you want to make it look nice and shipshape, don't you? You shall have your writing-pad to-morrow morning and do it then."

" Time," said Miss Hunter with a snatch at her receding dignity, " is of the essence of the affair."

" The post's gone out for to-day anyhow," said the nurse in the same maddeningly cheerful tone, " so it wouldn't help you to write all that screed out this evening. You can do it to-morrow and you may want to make some alterations, or perhaps you'll have thought of something else."

Miss Hunter's brow furrowed. " I think I have everything in," she said.

" And so I should hope," sister told the doctor, who didn't mind how much time he put in for children or expectant mothers, but frankly thought these old girls were only a drag on the community anyway, and though he wouldn't have gone so far as to recommend a lethal chamber he made no mystery of his hope that this was the last generation of what, in his youthful arrogance, he called useless mouths.

" Pages she's written," sister continued. " Goodness knows when he'll have time to read that—or patience either."

" He probably won't," said the young doctor. " My godfather's a lawyer. He says there are times when he thinks these crazy old women are a tribe to themselves. Of course, that knock on the head she got would account for anything. Does she still insist she's got no friends or relations ? "

" There's this lawyer in Bath."

" Well, she's got his name, that's one thing, so when she's fit to go out he can take her on to his plate and do whatever he thinks best."

And that was all they said about Miss Hunter that night.

The next morning, after breakfast, Alice slipped out of bed and examined the contents of the shabby box-trunk that bore Miss Freke's name. Sister had been at it, looking for nightgowns, hairbrush, etc. It came as a real shock to the old maid to realise that she had been using someone else's hairbrush and toothbrush since her arrival. As for the clothes, they were, of course, none of them hers. A dull green woollen jersey—a drab dress, celanese underwear in useful buff shades—no, none of them hers, but all of them the sort of things she might have bought. Her jersey was a cardigan in brown instead of green, her dress was dark blue, the stockings were as like as two peas, except Miss Freke knew how to darn. There was no doubt about that ; these were far better darned than Alice's own. She used cheap writing-paper, too, another of Alice's economies. The defrauded creature crawled back to bed and began to copy out the letter.

CHAPTER FOUR

MR. FINNEMORE was a thin old gentleman who looked as if he were made of matchsticks, with a white paper mask for a face, and a little silver hair carefully plastered each side of a brittle skull. His was a small business, for his son had been killed in an accident between the wars, and, though he had taken a partner, this man hadn't lasted. There was a new young man recently taken into the firm, a great-nephew, but he was already wondering how soon he could get out. There was no future in Finnemore's for any up and coming young fellow, and the sooner the Government, whom he heartily supported, took authority out of the hands of doddering old boys like Uncle Corny the better for everyone. Mr. Finnemore, of course, knew that the present generation has no staying-power, no ambition, no sense of what they owe to their predecessors. He clung obstinately to every bit of business and young Finnemore was little better than a clerk. When Miss Hunter's letter arrived the old man read it with growing irritation and perplexity. " Really," said he, " a most extraordinary document. Of course, the woman is as mad as a hatter."

" Which one, sir ? " asked Peter Finnemore, who felt that even a lunatic would cheer up the proceedings.

" You remember Miss Hunter who came in at the end of last month about a legacy ? "

" The Snapping Turtle ? " said the young man. " Rather ! "

" The writer of this," the speaker tapped the assembled sheets with an impressive pair of lorgnettes, " asserts that the woman was an impostor."

" I wouldn't put it past her," said Peter. " That one would take the watch out of your pocket when you weren't looking."

" Have your years in a law office not yet warned you that there is a law of slander, sir ? " inquired the old man.

Peter Finnemore repressed a desire to recite, " You are old, Father William." Instead, he observed interestedly, " You can't dismiss the claim without investigation, though. At least," his frank glance wavered a little under the old man's icy regard, " I imagine you can't."

" When you are as old as I am," said his aged relative, sending a shiver of dismay through Peter's veins, at the thought that he could ever look like this old wreck, " you will realise that the world is to a considerable extent peopled by old women of both sexes who should be certified. I shall pay no heed to this whatsoever."

Peter Finnemore read the letter through. " I say,

sir, are you sure . . . ? " he began. " I mean, how does she know about the typewriter ? "

" Oh, I have no doubt at all that she did travel down with Miss Hunter as far as Yarborough where the accident took place. After all, how else would she know my name, though it is significant that the letter bears no address beyond that of Solicitors, Bath ? And now, how about that lease for Lady Ferrers ? "

The following day the pseudo-Alice Hunter marched into Mr. Finnemore's office in connection with a deed he had required her to sign. Mr. Finnemore being, miraculously, engaged for the moment, Peter Finnemore said unguardedly, " You remember the lady who shared your carriage as far as Yarborough ? Well, the governor had a letter from her saying she's Miss Hunter. Sort of Tichborne Claimant case all over again, though, of course, the issues aren't so great."

" This woman—what was her name ? something quite extraordinary and yet quite apt—oh, yes, Freke—you say she's written ? "

" No end of a yarn, explaining how she was left for dead, and . . ."

" Yes, that is perfectly true. When the crash came she was knocked unconscious. I made inquiries for her, naturally, but was told she had been killed in the collision, and, as the doctor was anxious to make the necessary arrangement for the survivors, I did not pursue the matter. She had already assured me that she had no relations and had been working as companion—she didn't supply the address—to some elderly woman who had recently died. I understood she was coming to Bath in connection with a situation."

" Well, according to her, she's Miss Wells' heir, and . . ."

" And ? " supplied Miss Freke.

"Well, that you took advantage of her presumed death," blundered the young man, realising he'd got himself into an impasse.

At this instant Mr. Finnemore, senior, found himself disengaged, and struck his bell sharply to indicate that he was ready to see his next visitor. (It was typical of him that he refused to have an electric bellpush under the desk or under the carpet, but kept an old-fashioned bell on the table, which he struck smartly with the flat of his hand every time he wished to attract attention. It must have been a very good bell in its youth, Peter sometimes reflected, for the spring and the tone were unimpaired despite the heavy service it had rendered.) In bounced Miss Freke.

"Good morning, Mr. Finnemore. Your assistant has just been telling me some extraordinary yarn about some woman who came down in the train with me. Got bumped on the head in the accident and now thinks she's me. Poor thing!"

"The boy had no right to talk of matters that do not concern him," said the old gentleman testily. "Still, since he has raised the point, I may as well admit that there has been a letter. Quite clearly this woman is suffering from delusions—did she appear to you the kind of person who might—er——?"

"Go off her head? I wouldn't say that. Wouldn't like to say that of anyone. For all I know people may be sayin' it of me. But—she used to go round imagining herself the Queen of Sheba and that kind of thing. You know. Spent years being a companion, knocking about from pillar to post, and I dare say she'd have died of it if she hadn't done a bit of castle-building. One day she'd be a wife and mother, and the next a heroine and the day after that she was Miss Ellen Terry. You know."

"I know there are a great many deranged people

going about. Did you glean any specific information about this lady ? "

" She was about my age, came into my compartment, long journey, we got talking. ' I've never been to Bath, do you know what it's like ? ' ' Well,' I said, ' I haven't been either.' ' I'm going down about a post,' she said, ' to two ladies.' Tempest—Tennyson—something beginning with a T. And then out it all came. No money and no friends, and she saved herself by this sort of transformation business. Mind you, it's not uncommon. I've come across it before. Lots of people do it. They say Napoleon . . ."

" I take it Napoleon was not in the carriage with you ? " said Mr. Finnemore at his most forbidding. " No ? Then I think we may leave him out of our conversation. The trouble is that this lady announces her intention of calling here to claim her inheritance. You appear to have been perhaps rather more confiding than is altogether wise with a stranger."

" Dare say I was," acknowledged Miss Freke gruffly. " Poor old thing. Couldn't help being sorry for her. Asked me what I meant to do with the legacy. If it was her she'd buy a house, and if I bought a house—well, she didn't know anyone in Bath, lonely, you can see how it went."

" A regular old woman of the sea," agreed Mr. Finnemore with some bitterness. He hated anything that made him do more than the minimum of work and he had visions of this mad old woman descending upon him and making any amount of trouble. " It is to be hoped that these ladies, whoever they may be, decide not to engage her. After all," he added hopefully, " there has been a—a time lag of three weeks."

" You haven't got there yet," Miss Freke assured him with an outspokenness that made the rare colour stain his parchment cheeks. " She won't be looking for a job if she thinks she's Miss Hunter. She'll make a bee-line for your office, and if you don't let her in she'll go hareing off to the Police Station. I know her kind. You meet all sorts in London lodging-houses."

"Then in some way she must be prevented from visiting Bath," said Mr. Finnemore.

"H'm. Don't know how you can manage that. Woman's a free agent, I suppose, once the hospital lets her go. You know, if they hadn't told me she was dead, on her way to the mortuary they assured me, I'd have hung about and seen what I could do for her. But they'd got her covered up with a sheet and in the ambulance. Where do you say she is now?"

Mr. Finnemore fumbled vaguely for the letter. "Cottage Hospital, Yarborough," he said. "Hopes to be out by the end of the week."

"I have an idea," said Miss Freke. "Suppose I were to visit her there? Or perhaps that would be a little upsetting. I might get in touch with the hospital authorities and consult with them. If she met me face to face that might do some good."

"You mean, she might recognise her own personality? On the other hand, she might reassert her claims and that might be most unpleasant for you. Perhaps, if you do consider that course, my nephew had better accompany you."

"Not made of sugar," asserted Miss Freke grimly. "Been in plenty of tight corners in my day. And you can't say I'm not accustomed to difficult old women. Spent my life with 'em."

"You mean, of course, since your mother's death?" Mr. Finnemore's shocked tone insinuated that naturally she wasn't including old Mrs. Hunter in her category of difficult old so-and-so's.

"Even Mother had her moments," said Miss Freke. "One of the only reasons I'm sorry I'm not married with a spinster daughter is that I'll never be able to pay old scores. Still, let that pass. Y'know, I can see how it happened. Imaginative old girl, worried about the future—she was no chicken, you can take my word for that, and even old dames like these Tempests, Tennysons, no, Turnbull, that was it, won't want to go on employing aged retainers, and I don't suppose she'd get a pension, not till she was seventy anyhow. When I told her about the legacy, well, she stopped bein' a prospective companion and became an heiress. You could see how her mind worked. She was thinking about the legacy at the time of the accident. Crash! Biff! Bang! And before she can get back to being Miss Freke she's pitchforked into darkness, and when she comes round, well, she's still expectin' the legacy."

"It all sounds a little highly-coloured to me," said Mr. Finnemore in his dry-as-dust way, "but from my experience of elderly ladies it is not impossible. Well, Miss Hunter, if you will be kind enough to take the journey and see what effect your presence has on this lady, that might solve our problem. But I think these—Turnbulls, if that is the right name—should be warned of her—idiosyncrasy. Delusions can be dangerous. She might suddenly imagine herself a member of the family . . ."

Miss Freke chuckled unexpectedly. "Make off with the family diamonds? She'd need more than a train accident to persuade the police she really thought they were hers. By the way, you're sure she won't be turning up here before I can get to Yarborough?"

"I am quite sure she will not. As a matter of fact, the sister at the hospital kindly enclosed a covering note to say that the writer had suffered severe concussion and was not yet in a fit state to travel, but was so anxious for the letter to be sent it was considered best to post it. She says all the evidence points to her bein' a Miss Freke—identity card, ration book, everything."

"Poor thing! I feel as if I owed her something. Yes, Mr. Finnemore, I certainly think I will return to Yarborough. By the way, this document about which I came in to see you . . ."

By the time the resourceful creature had left the office she had raised a pretty little advance on her inheritance, and received an assurance that within a very short time she would have *carte-blanche* with the whole of the late Miss Wells' estate.

CHAPTER FIVE

ALTHOUGH Miss Freke had listened to Mr. Finnemore with outward composure she was inwardly appalled at this development. Her decision to abandon her own identity and take upon herself that of another woman, one with whom she had been acquainted only an hour or so, had been made, of necessity, on the spur of the moment, but not without thought on her part. Years of being companion to women who were either spoilt or stupid (the pleasant employer never seemed to come her way) had taught her to make up her mind at lightning speed. When the accident took place she realised, before the slower-witted Miss Hunter, what was about to happen, and her quick fingers slid back the door leading to the corridor. She had slipped through it and retreated a couple of steps before the impact, so that she missed the worst of the disaster. Shaken she certainly was, but she remained sensible. When she knew that the worst was over she retraced her steps, to find the carriage she had been occupying in a damaged condition and her erstwhile companion lying on the floor with pieces of the compartment strewn about her. There seemed also to be a fair amount of blood spattering everything. Almost before the passengers knew what had occurred a first aid service had been installed; the front part of the train, in which both ladies had been travelling, was the only portion that was affected; passengers farther back were alarmed and shaken, but not hurt. Almost immediately someone appeared at the door of the carriage and a voice said, " Anyone injured ? "

" A lady here, under the wreckage," announced Miss Freke. " I don't think I——"

" That's all right." She was hustled out, only pausing to grab at her handbag before she retreated back into the corridor. The train had been approaching a station and by walking carefully along the line she was able to reach the platform. A young doctor—he looked as though he couldn't have been qualified more than about a week—came driving up in a shabby little car not much bigger than a match-box and walked down the line to the damaged coaches. Miss Freke watched intently. Now they had reached her carriage, now they were lifting something out, something limp and sagging. Miss Freke started to her feet.

" Better take that one straight to the mortuary," said the young doctor, moving on to the next carriage.

Miss Freke felt quite faint. In the midst of life we are in death. What a shame ! Just when she was going to come into a bit of money and have a bit of fun ! There was no sense in it. And not even a relative to inherit in her stead. That nasty Government would take everything. " Everything," repeated Miss Freke, " and they won't know what to do with it. What use is a little sum like that to them ? They like to deal in millions. Now I——" She glanced down and—could it be a sign from heaven ?—realised that this was The

Parting of the Ways. In her haste she had snatched at the bag lying nearest her, taking it for granted it was her own ; but the bag on her knee was black instead of dark blue and there was a monogram A.H. on the flap. Oh, it was perfectly understandable. In the mess and muddle she had picked up Miss Hunter's bag by mistake. Well, that was all right. All she had to do was wait till the rush had passed and then go forward and claim her own bag and restore this one. There was still a good deal of commotion on the line and she still felt a little " swimmy," so she decided to stay where she was for a few minutes more. There was no hurry. Miss Hunter, poor old cow, was dead, and all her hopes with her. It was sad really, no friend, no relative, no one to follow the coffin to the graveyard. A Mrs. Abercrombie, who had been head of the local W.V.S. during the war and was already preparing to instruct volunteers in combating various new gases not hitherto in use, during the coming autumn, disengaged herself from the crowd to say, " What is the name of the woman who was killed ? Was she alone ? " And someone else said, " We found her bag in the carriage beside her, and her luggage. Freke's her name, Laura Freke. She comes from one of the new suburbs outside London." (And how angry Lady Rivers would have been to hear that, only she too was somewhere where, if report is true, there's no more chance of losing your temper or giving orders, either.)

" We shall have to find out her next of kin," said Mrs. Abercrombie. " Was she travelling alone ? "

" There was no one else in the carriage."

Then Mrs. Abercrombie caught sight of the real Miss Freke on the platform bench and she came up asking, " Are you all right ? Have you had treatment ? You must come along and have a cup of tea. . . ."

Then another and much handsomer car drove up and a much older man alighted. " Here's Dr. Kerr," said Mrs. Abercrombie in satisfied tones, as though the doctor was a blancmange she'd made that morning and he'd set quite nicely, after all. She sailed off to speak to him.

That was how it all started. And, after all, Laura asked herself, why shouldn't it work ? Alice had been remarkably confiding ; she had no relations, no friends ; she had given up her room in London and wasn't likely to keep up with the landlady ; she had concealed her destination from this Mrs. Brownlow, and she was coming to see a lawyer who'd never set eyes on her in his life, and who would presumably find one shabby elderly female remarkably like another. Inside the bag was a stout envelope Alice had waved at her in the train ; this held all the requisite documents, and if any are missing, decided Miss Freke between clenched teeth, I can put on a brass face and ask Somerset House, or whoever the right authority may be, to supply me with a duplicate. The more she thought about it the more possible it became. And then think of it. Freedom, the right to snap your fingers at the whole race of Turnbulls, no more sycophancy, no more sleepless nights wondering how much longer you'd be able to go on, how you'd manage when nobody, literally nobody, would employ you any more. No more of being metaphorically rapped over the knuckles, no more regimentation. Get up when you liked, go to bed when you liked, feed at your own hours ; have breakfast at seven or ten, and eat whatever took your fancy and you were able to get. Smash a plate and there's no one to scold ; let the milk boil over without feeling you've more or less sold the country down the river. The thought of freedom was like fumes in her blood, fumes of wine ; she felt suddenly perfectly sure she could carry it off, and how much more enjoyment she'd get out of this legacy than poor, colourless Miss Hunter, who had been half-dead anyway.

She looked inside the bag on her knee ; the documents all bore testimony to the fact that the bearer was Alice Hunter. She had never been abroad or even applied for a passport, she hadn't been photographed for years, not, she had stated, since she was a girl. That meant that no one could recognise her picture in the paper, since no one was going to take a picture of her in the mortuary. If there had been any relation living, no matter how remotely connected, Miss Freke assured herself she wouldn't have given the idea another thought ; but there was no one to defraud. She didn't count the Government, of course. Miss Hunter's little legacy would be a drop in their ocean so minute it wouldn't be noticed. " This may be my chance," she told herself, her hands unconsciously gripping more firmly the bag lying in her lap. " I shall have worked the miracle of which I've so often dreamed. I shall be able to slough my real self, the self of which I've become so weary, and emerge as someone else." It seemed too good to be true. The longer she waited on her solitary bench the more convinced she became that she was going to take the risk. Imagine it, no more Turnbulls, no more interviews with We-Can-Help-You or Lettice Fixit, no more packing her shabby clothes and wondering how long you'd last this time. No more furtive fumblings to know if the bed was made of concrete or was a real mattress, but freedom—a house, a bank balance, a cat if she wanted one. Get up when you liked, lunch at twelve or three, eat bread-and-butter or a cooked meal, take a day in the country or go to the cinema. . . . Such knowledge is too great and wonderful for me, she thought. I cannot abide it.

The young doctor who had ordered Miss Hunter into the mortuary van stopped by the bench to ask if she were all right.

"I am naturally a little shaken," she said, "but apart from that . . ." And then because she could not prevent it and it might even seem odd if she did she broke out, "The lady who was travelling in my carriage. She seemed unconscious. Can you tell me . . . ?"

"Well, I don't know which your carriage was, of course," he said sensibly. "But you can come along to the hospital, if you like. Most of them are only being treated for shock. . . ."

"Her hand was badly cut by glass," murmured Miss Freke, and he looked up sharply.

"What was her name?"

Miss Freke swallowed. "Miss—Miss Freke," she said.

The young man stopped. "Look here, I'm most awfully sorry," he told her. "I'm afraid she had no chance. Knocked out on the spot. Are you a friend of hers? I'm afraid she'll have to be identified."

"I never saw her till to-day," said Miss Freke sharply. "We happened to be travelling in the same carriage. She was going to Bath about a situation."

"Oh, well." He sounded less bothered. "I suppose there'll be a next of kin. You don't know . . ."

"I don't know anything about her, except that she sounded rather friendless." Just in time she stopped herself saying that the poor derelict, Laura Freke, hadn't a relative in the world. That was the way to get yourself hung up to await the inquest, and now that she was embarked on this crazy adventure she wanted to hurry it on.

The next thing to do was to claim Miss Hunter's luggage. Luckily she had been remarkably forthcoming. " A black trunk," she had said, " bearing my mother's initials." She went along to the guard's van and identified the decorative piece of luggage.

It took a breakdown gang four hours to clear the line, and then the passengers who felt able to travel went on by a slow train. Miss Freke went with them, with Alice Hunter's bag and baggage; she had carefully refrained from asking further about Alice, in case someone tried to detain her in consequence. It was getting dark when they reached Bath and she resolved to take no steps that day. At the Station Hotel she demanded a room, and, when they showed her one, she observed coolly that it was no wonder we didn't get all the tourists we wanted, if that was the best they had to offer. They were so startled that this faded lady should show so much malice that they immediately found her a better room, away from the railway line. The next morning she went out and engaged a room at a private hotel—the mention of Mr. Finnemore worked wonders; he was clearly known all round—and then went purposefully to the old man's office. Mr. Finnemore wasn't in the least pleased to see her.

" It's a pity you didn't feel able to take my advice," he said.

Which advice? Miss Freke's heart sank. Was there going to be a complication at the very start?

" The letter I sent you. Dear me, do you mean to say you didn't get it? I made quite sure . . . Now I suppose it will hang about in that establishment where you've been staying. I only hope they're honest people who don't read other people's letters. The fact is I wrote to say there was no need for you to—er—uproot yourself, our business could be perfectly well transacted by letter."

" But I had every intention of leaving London as

soon as opportunity offered," intervened Laura firmly. " I don't say I shall settle at Bath—I don't know the city at all. . . ."

" Very full, very full," said Mr. Finnemore at once.

He began to speak of the dead woman. Miss Freke here adopted a firm line.

" My mother had no communication with her that I can recall. I believe she had been—unbalanced—for a considerable time."

" A sad case," sighed the lawyer. " Never quite sure of her identity, you know. Still, no trouble really except when she believed she was summoned by Providence to extinguish an unbeliever. Yes, that made matters a little awkward. But the nurses were very good, very careful. And, of course, everyone was warned."

" You mean she had homicidal mania? I didn't realise . . ."

" Oh, only intermittent," said Mr. Finnemore in the voice of one who can't believe that the removal of a few people of poor mentality is a matter of any great moment. " Still, she'd exceeded her threescore years and ten. Fortunately, the will was made many years ago, so there can be no question of its being challenged, even if you were not the sole surviving relative." He doodled for a minute. " I think you said you had no legal representative."

" Never needed one," snapped Laura. " Very glad if you'll do anything that's necessary."

Mr. Finnemore looked pleased. " I think you can safely leave your interests in my hands. Although," he frowned, " I assume there is someone, some firm who proved your mother's will."

" The Bank does everything for me, like reclaiming a rebate and all that kind of thing. The—the lawyer (what was his name? she couldn't remember having heard it. He was killed in the blitz, Alice had said, and the bank did everything. I don't understand business, I just signed some papers and the money comes in every half-year) was killed in the bombing."

"Ah, yes. Very heavy casualties, one fears. Well, Miss Hunter, if you ever need a lawyer you know where to come."

She was far better than he had expected from that first letter of hers, much calmer and clearly prepared to leave everything to him.

She had to sign some papers, of course; that was the ticklish moment. She had been carefully copying Miss Hunter's signature as seen on her identity card, tracing it through a bit of tissue paper and going over and over. It was, fortunately, an uncharacteristic signature, and then, of course, Mr. Finnemore had no reason to suppose she was anyone other than the person she proclaimed herself to be. He had the signature witnessed, and as an afterthought said, "What bank do you use, Miss Hunter?" Laura nearly gave the show away then by saying, "I have no account"; then she remembered that Laura Freke was dead, and Alice Hunter's affairs were administered by Pages Bank.

"I dare say there is a branch in this part of the country," she added. "I've no intention of returning to London, so doubtless I could get my balance transferred if I decide to settle in this neighbourhood."

Mr. Finnemore looked dubious. "If they hold your securities they will naturally like to continue to act for you. You could easily arrange to draw money from one of their branches, say ten pounds a week, and your other cheques could be drawn on the original office. I think you will find that will save you a good deal of trouble."

Laura was thinking hard. Here was one of the

danger-spots of her desperate imposture. Miss Hunter mightn't go to the Bank often, but someone there would know her by sight, and if a totally different female marched in and tried to cash a cheque there would be trouble. "I must get the money away from them at all costs," she told herself. "The best thing will be to make the arrangement Mr. Finnemore has suggested and let the next suggestion come from the local manager. Then let him take the initiative and all that will be required of me will be the necessary signatures. He won't question them, because he'll never have seen any others, and, if the transaction is done through one of their own provincial managers, it's not so likely that the head office will make difficulties."

So out of Mr. Finnemore's office she went, and before the end of the day she was established in her hotel and made it clear that she preferred service to conversation and was too old a bird to be caught out by unexplained extras. Here she unpacked Miss Hunter's trunk and agreed with Mrs. Rose (the manageress) that it was a cumbersome affair but it took everything and new luggage was an absurd price. Mrs. Rose agreed to store the trunk, saying mildly, "You don't often see them nowadays. Reminds me of that case where they found a body in a trunk. You could get quite a tidy-sized body into this one."

So everything seemed set for a quiet and secure existence when, like a bolt from the blue, the real Miss Hunter's letter came from Yarborough.

Though she had preserved a cool demeanour while in the lawyer's office Laura was no sooner outside than she felt panic invade her. Here was a development she had never visualised. They had told her perfectly clearly that Miss Hunter was dead; more, she had seen the body, covered with a sheet, piled into the ambulance for the mortuary. She could only assume that the young doctor had made a mistake, and that the mortuary attendant had discovered it. She felt herself shaken with impotent rage. Why should this have to happen ? Of course, if she'd known there was a breath of life in the mess Alice Hunter had become, she'd never have embarked on this perilous course. And now, as she saw it, it was too late to retreat. She couldn't simply disappear, leaving her possessions—Alice's possessions—in Mrs. Rose's rooms. She would find herself without ration book, identity card, anything. And besides, Mr. Finnemore wouldn't leave it at that. She had committed not one but several criminal acts—forgery, false pretences, stealing—yes, that was what it amounted to. Once let the real Miss Hunter put in an appearance and her stand-in was ruined. For, though she might claim she had no friends or family, there must be someone—a landlady, a bank official, even someone at the local church she frequented, who could identify her.

" What on earth am I to do now ? " Laura wondered. She could not even fulfil her original intention of visiting the Misses Turnbull to apply for a situation as companion. Indeed, one of the first excursions she had made after her visit to the lawyer's office to establish an identity to which she had no right, had been to the street in which the Turnbulls lived. A pleasant, even a lordly street, the kind of street that knows how to put companions in their places. She had watched and had seen two formidable females, clearly the Misses Turnbull, issue forth into a waiting car. One went lame, and presumably received an increased petrol allowance on that account ; behind them had followed one of the great army of the unhoused, as Miss Freke liked to call them, an army to which she had belonged for so many weary years. So the situation was filled. She saw the stammering meekness of the companion, and was aghast to think that she had ever filled such a vacancy. Had she appeared such a ninny, so devoid of personality? Why were women such fools? Why did they accept such slavery? "If I were in her place now," thought Laura—and stopped abruptly. Because if she were she would behave in exactly the same way. Untrained women of over sixty were, they had told her at one of the agencies, a drug on the market; if they labelled themselves gentlewomen they were a pernicious drug. They weren't trained for adequately-paid employment and they considered themselves above the bucket and mop brigade, who were incidentally far better paid and had a great deal more liberty. Miss Freke remembered years ago reading a book called *Miss Mole* by a writer named E. H. Young. She had envied Miss Mole her spirit, but it hadn't really made so much difference. The work had been just the same. And how that woman had slaved. And she not forty! "At her age I wouldn't have stood it," Miss Freke told herself in fierce tones. At sixty-three things weren't so simple.

One alternative after another presented itself to her consideration. But the obvious one, of telling the truth and throwing herself on Mr. Finnemore's mercy, never occurred to her. She had the wit to realise that that way disaster lay. Mr. Finnemore would be horrified; more, he would be humiliated, because he had been deceived. You couldn't really blame him, but that wouldn't matter, because people would. They'd begin to whisper that perhaps the old chap really wasn't quite up to snuff now, *Anno Domini*, and there were a lot of up and coming young fellows only too anxious to prove their worth. No, he'd certainly not make things easy; and even if she could get round *him*, there was the real Miss Hunter and all the people at the hospital. And beyond all that was the fact that in just over three weeks Miss Freke had thought herself into the personality of Miss Wells' heir. She had, in a very real sense of the word, buried poor Laura Freke, cremated her, say, and from her ashes had sprung an independent woman who couldn't turn back the page and become that meek grey female following the Misses Turnbull and all the Misses Turnbulls and Lady Riverses of the world down the steps. "All my life," she reflected in amazement, "I have walked behind, never led the cortège. Always I have paid deference, never had deference paid to me. And I can't go back. It would be a failure if I did. I should be starving in a month." Oh, confound Alice Hunter. Why couldn't she do the decent thing and die? Because you only had to look at her and be with her for a short time, hear her aimless unambitious conversation to realise that life and death must be much the same thing for her. Anyway, let her be the companion, live where someone else appointed, count the peaches anxiously to see if one's included for you. She had known independence and what had she made of it? A cautious tremulous woman intimidated by her landlady. Why *should* she inherit a legacy? "I will do something worth while with it," Miss Freke told herself. For she was absolutely resolved that Alice Hunter of Yarborough should somehow be suppressed.

CHAPTER SIX

SHE DID NOT, at this stage, even consider murder. Murder is not a thing that occurs to the average person, except in the abstract. How lovely to murder Aunt Mary—John—that frightful Mrs. Gummidge next door, and those appalling children who bawl all day and run iron hoops under the window. But that's as far as it goes. Suggest putting something in Aunt Mary's coffee, knocking John off with an axe or a poker, thrusting Mrs. Gummidge under the wheels of a passing car or handing the mannerless brats a parcel of poisoned sweetmeats, and horror reigns supreme. Besides, murder isn't easy. Everybody has pointed out the embarrassment of possessing a corpse and the difficulty of disposing of it. But, all the same, Miss Hunter must either be silenced or those in charge of her persuaded that she was soft in the head and her words not to be relied upon. The first thing to be done was to visit Yarborough and learn for herself how far the unfortunate woman had been able to impress the staff of the hospital with her genuineness. And feeling, like Mr. Mell, that there is no time like the present, Miss Freke walked to the station and bought a return ticket to Yarborough.

At the Cottage Hospital poor Alice was making very heavy weather indeed. She had nearly exhausted the patience of all those who had to do with her, insisting, first, that she be permitted to return immediately to London, where she could at once establish her identity, and, second, that she continue her journey to Bath, there to confront Mr. Finnemore and the spurious Miss

Hunter. " When you are strong enough to travel," said sister, putting out a delaying hand. Alice struck it furiously away. " By the time you allow me to travel all the legacy will be dissipated," she cried.

" You haven't even been up and dressed yet," sister told her, rather less patiently. " Why not get up for a few hours to-day ? "

" I ask nothing better," said Alice. " But I've no clothes."

" No clothes ? " Sister felt this was the last straw. If she went on like this they'd get her certified.

" None of the clothes in that box are mine, and poor I may be, but not so poor I'll wear another woman's combinations."

" Then it looks as though you'll spend the rest of your life in bed," sister assured her tartly. " Unless, of course, you'd like one of the nurses to buy you a new rig-out."

" I've no money to waste on new clothes. Besides, I don't need them. I never tried to be smart, I simply ask for my own clothes to be restored to me."

" If you won't wear these and you won't buy new ones, all I can say is that one of these days you'll find yourself in workhouse woollens."

Alice almost spat with fury; she choked and spluttered. Then she demanded, finding her voice at last, " Where's my letter ? And don't pretend you don't know which letter I mean, or that there isn't one. You're keeping it back."

" If you make many more crazy statements," began sister and suddenly Alice giggled. " I'm so sorry," she whispered after a minute. " Do you know just for an instant I thought you said crazy pavements ? "

No crazier than you, reflected sister. The moment of tranquillity passed and Alice blazed out again, " Where is it ? The letter from Mr. Finnemore. Why are you siding against me like this? Has that woman paid you to . . . ?"

"Well, if you're going to talk like that there's no sense my wasting any more time," said sister, rising to her feet with a disapproving crackle. "It's my belief you don't know what you're saying. As for going to London or anywhere else, you're perfectly at liberty to go when you please as soon as Dr. Ogilvie says you're well enough to travel. And if you'll give us the name and address of any friend or relation who will come and take you out, you'll find there's no plot to restrain you. You must know someone in London."

"My landlady . . ."

"Would she come?"

"I dare say not, but she would swear to who I am. And she might convince Mr. Finnemore that he's the victim of a most heartless fraud."

"If she can, so much the better for you. But you can't go anywhere in a nightgown. As for the costume you were wearing, we had to cut the coat off you—you had nasty injuries, you know—but the skirt is here, I think. And there's a long coat . . ."

"That woman's coat. I suppose you think if you can persuade me to wear her clothes that'll count as evidence that I really am her."

That was the position when Laura arrived. A servant came to tell sister a visitor was asking for her.

"I can't see anyone now. Who is it, Anne? If it's about a bed . . ."

"The lady said Miss Hunter."

Sister ejaculated a sharp short laugh. "Oh, bring her in by all means," said she. "Don't keep her waiting or she may dissolve into smoke. And if Father Christmas should turn up bring him along, too."

The servant went out and confided to a colleague that sister was crackers, in fact the place was more like a lunatic asylum than a hospital ; then she went into the waiting-room and conducted Laura into the presence. Sister rose to face a woman in the early sixties, with a firm jaw and an air of one accustomed to looking after herself. No beauty but neat and responsible-looking, the sort of person you'd think twice about engaging for a job in your own household. (This she meant as a compliment ; as a rule you could scarcely endure to think of them once.)

" I hope I have not come at an inconvenient time," began Laura with the gracious air of one on whom heaven has seen fit to bestow a legacy, " but my solicitor, Mr. Finnemore of Bath, has shown me a most extraordinary letter he has just received from a patient in this hospital, and as he is by no means a young man and as the author is clearly a little—a little muddle-headed, we agreed that the best course would be for me to come over in person and attempt to clear up the mystery."

" If you can persuade Miss Freke that she isn't Miss Hunter it'll be a miracle," said sister simply.

" In a sense I can understand how it happened," said Laura.

" How very fortunate. But perhaps you know Miss Freke well ? "

" On the contrary, we met for the first time that day in the train and we got into conversation, and I happened to speak of the legacy. She said, ' Oh, do you play that game too ? ' and I asked, rather startled, ' What game ? ' and she said, ' Oh, make-believe. Sometimes when I'm going on a journey as I am to-day I pretend it's to see a lawyer or look at a house I'm thinking of buying '—having a house of her own was one of her ambitions, she said. She'd been with some titled person, I think, and she was on her way to see another prospective employer. We talked about what we would do if we came into money, and she became quite excited about this mythical house. We were still talking along these lines when the accident occurred. To tell you the truth I thought she'd had it, as they say."

"Dr. Ainslie thought so, too, but one of the ambulance men realised she wasn't dead and they brought her here. She suffered from serious concussion. . . ."

"And I dare say loss of memory often accompanies a blow on the head or whatever it was she had. There was a case in the paper recently—an ex-serviceman."

"Loss of memory is a picnic compared with this sort of delusion," said sister.

"If it is a delusion," returned Laura composedly.

"She won't even dress, can you believe it? Because she says they're not her clothes."

"In that case, perhaps I could see her in her room." None knew better than the cunning Miss Freke at what a disadvantage a person in bed finds himself when confronted by someone alert and fully-dressed.

"I'll tell her you're here."

"Just say a friend."

"She says she has no friends."

"Where does she propose to go when she leaves, assuming she ever intends to get out of bed?"

"She has some notion of going to London, says there's a landlady there who would identify her."

"Did she happen to mention the landlady's name? Was it Mrs. Brownlow?"

"I believe it was."

Laura nodded. "If this is a delusion it's very firmly rooted. I've often thought it must be fascinating to be a mental doctor. . . ."

"Amateurs are always thinking things like that,"

said sister rather sourly. She rang a bell and told the nurse who answered the summons to tell Miss Freke a friend had come to see her. The nurse came back within a couple of minutes with a message from Alice to the effect that she had no friends who could possibly know of her whereabouts, and had no wish to see any of Miss Freke's friends.

"I'll go up in any case, shall I?" said Laura. "Can you spare anyone to come with me? We don't want her spreading a yarn that I tried to strangle her to keep her quiet."

When Alice saw her supplanter come coolly into the room, her eyes blazed, her body shook, she couldn't even control her voice.

"You—you—how dare you come here?" she demanded. "What have you done to me? You're worse than a murderer."

"Now, Miss Freke!" said sister sharply.

But Laura had the situation well in hand. "Suppose you tell sister and myself just what the matter is?" she suggested. "Mr. Finnemore showed me your letter and we both supposed you were suffering from some sort of hallucination, and as he obviously couldn't make the journey himself he thought it a good thing for me to come and get a first-hand explanation. I mean—to tell the truth, I thought for a moment it might be a practical joke, but now I've met you again I can see you're in deadly earnest."

"I wonder God doesn't strike you dead," said simple-minded Alice. "You know perfectly well I'm Alice Hunter and you're Miss Freke, going to Bath to interview two women called Turnbull for a job. Yes, and you'd been with Lady Rivers, who died recently and there's a son, Sir Philip, who will have to supply a reference. You're an orphan and you were brought up by an aunt, and you've never had a bank account, only a Post Office book . . ." she paused, breathless.

"Dear me!" said Laura mildly. "What a lot you know about Miss Freke. Oh, please don't think I'm doubting what you say. I'm sure it's all authentic, and a little enquiry would prove every word of it. Well, I'm here to suggest that the inquiry shall be made. If Lady Rivers is dead clearly she can't help us, but Sir Philip could."

"I never met Sir Philip. I wouldn't know him if I saw him, and he wouldn't know me. Or you either."

"That rather complicates matters. Still, there'd be somebody there. Some member of the household. Were there any other children? I take it Sir Philip is a son?"

"Why ask me? You know much more about the Rivers than I do."

"Another delusion?" sighed the infamous Miss Freke. "Would this Sir Philip—you did say Philip?—recognise you?"

"Of course he wouldn't. He never set eyes on me. Or you either. I told you that a minute ago."

"I'm glad you admit that much. Where does—did—Lady Rivers live?"

"In Mitchelham. Why ask me? You know better than I do."

"Where is Mitchelham exactly?"

"I suppose you're trying to confuse me," panted poor Alice. "It's you who were at Mitchelham, not me."

Miss Freke shrugged. "Well, since that seems a blind alley, perhaps there's someone else who can convince you. After all, you must have friends, neighbours, somebody who will recognise you."

"Of course," said Alice. "There's my landlady."

"Do you mean Mrs. Brownlow?"

"Of course I mean Mrs. Brownlow. She'll know which of us is Miss Hunter."

"Of course she will," soothed Laura. She turned to the sister. "That seems the best way out, don't you agree? Confront Mrs. Brownlow with the pair of us, only, you know," she turned back to the trembling Alice, "you must be prepared to abide by her decision."

"I have nothing to fear," asserted Alice, but when she saw the look Laura exchanged with sister her poor bewildered heart began to beat more fiercely than ever.

"Mrs. Brownlow has a house in Ennismore Terrace—near Paddington, that is."

"You needn't look at me like that. Of course I know it's near Paddington. I lived there, didn't I?"

"And, of course, you know that Mrs. Brownlow suffers from a duodenal ulcer, so . . ."

"She doesn't. At least she never told me."

"Well, you'll be able to ask her when we go up, won't you?"

"I'm not going anywhere with you," panted Alice. "You're quite capable of murdering me on the way, and pretending I fell out of the window by accident."

"My dear," began Laura, putting out her hand. Furiously, Alice struck it aside.

"I am not your dear. I won't allow myself to be spoken to in that way, by you."

"You're making things very difficult," Laura deprecated. "As I was saying just now, we can hardly ask Mrs. Brownlow to come down here; she has her hands full in London, for one thing, and then this ulcer . . ."

"A very pretty plot," sneered Alice. "But I'm not putting myself in your power twice."

"You could take someone with you, I dare say," Laura suggested.

"Someone in your pay, perhaps."

"I really don't know what to suggest since you're so obstructive," Laura sighed. "In another minute you'll be blaming me for the train accident. But you can hardly suggest that the driver was in my pay."

"I really don't think Miss Freke is in a condition to continue this conversation," said sister at this juncture. "She hasn't recovered from her concussion. In a few days' time . . ."

"In a few days' time I dare say I shall be dead, and then it won't matter," said Alice bitterly. "Or were you going to suggest that I should take your place, and apply for a post with Miss Turnbull?"

"I'm afraid it's too late for that," Laura assured her in regretful tones. "She's very comfortably settled with another applicant. I made inquiries as soon as I heard you were, so to speak, all right. No doubt you thought of writing to her . . ."

"Nothing of the kind," contradicted Alice. "And I don't want any more of your suggestions. I shall see Mr. Finnemore myself. . . ."

"Of course, you're a free agent," Laura allowed, "but how precisely will that help you? He's never set eyes on you, has he?"

"How do you know that?"

"Well, why should he? What business have you ever had with him? No, I think my plan about Mrs. Brownlow would be the best. I could write to her . . ."

Miss Hunter nearly threw herself out of bed in her rage. "You write to her! Why, she's never heard of you, and wouldn't know you if she met you face to face. No, I shall manage this myself. Or have you already *squared* her, with my money. MY money. Promised her something handsome if she'll back you up. Ah, but she's not the only one. You can't get away with this, and you must have been mad to suppose you could."

Miss Freke shrugged. " Have it your own way," she said. " But don't forget two can play at the same game. I mean, you're suggesting that if Mrs. Brownlow (whom incidentally I've not seen since I left London) identifies me as Miss Hunter it'll be a plot. But suppose you entice her down to Bath and take her to see Mr. Finnemore and tell him you are Alice Hunter, how will he know that isn't a plot, too? I mean, how will he even know she is Mrs. Brownlow? "

" She'll have an identity card."

" I don't know a great deal about the law, but I suppose it is possible to borrow someone else's. Is there no other person you can think of? You must have friends even if you haven't relations. And neighbours. Or perhaps there are members of the church you attended in London? Are you a Churchwoman? After all, you couldn't bribe half Paddington to say you were Miss Hunter if you aren't. Yes, sister, I'm going now. I agree with you there's nothing more to be done at the moment. And I'm ready to meet you anywhere, in London or at Mr. Finnemore's office or any place you like to suggest. Only, you will remember there's a thing called collusion and I think it's criminal. However, I see there's going to be no end to this until you've seen Mrs. Brownlow and made your effort. You needn't be afraid I shall follow you to London or try and buy up Mrs. Brownlow in advance. I have to settle up my aunt's affairs and I shall be returning at once to Bath."

" To prime Mr. Finnemore, I dare say? "

" I shall have to report the result of my visit here, of course. But he's an honest man. (Too stupid, too conceited, to be anything else, she added in inaudible parentheses.) It will simply be your word against mine, and the whole affair will resolve itself into a question of proof."

"If I produce someone who recognises you as Miss Freke . . ."

"You'll be a remarkably clever woman and deserve six inheritances," said Laura generously. "Well, sister, I won't waste any more of your time. It's perfectly obvious that Miss—this lady—isn't going to avail herself of my services in any capacity. But I do think," she added turning back to Alice and knowing that any suggestion of hers would be rejected outright, no matter how reasonable it was, "you should consult a lawyer on your own account. Have you not got one?"

There was, of course, one danger she could not bypass. Bankers for some reason are always taken very seriously by the authorities, and though it was not beyond the bounds of possibility that a London landlady should be bribed to give false evidence (though seeing the fortunes they must be making at the present time on a sellers' market, so far as their profession was concerned, you wouldn't think the temptation overwhelming) a bank manager was a bird of a very different colour. Sooner or later this was bound to occur to the genuine Miss Hunter and indeed it did, but once again it was a case of the wicked flourishing like a green bay tree. In Mrs. Hunter's life-time the two ladies had lived in a suburb where the deceased lady had felt she was someone. She disliked (and feared) the anonymity of London existence, where she'd be one old frump in an army of frumps. She had never had any opinion of Alice's brains and had invariably paid her visits to the bank in person. Now and again her daughter had accompanied her, but had always remained so much in the background that it was doubtful if anyone ever distinguished her from the furniture of the Bank. As Humpty Dumpty complained, human beings are all so much alike—two eyes, a nose and a mouth and all, roughly, in the same place. Now if Alice had had two eyes on the same side of the nose for instance—or the mouth at the top—someone would be sure to remember her. And after Mrs. Hunter's death Alice only went to the bank once or twice, and then she uprooted herself and came to London. She left her affairs in the hands of the suburban bank, obtaining facilities for drawing cheques from a London office. Even then she usually wrote and asked for money to be sent by post ; Mrs. Hunter had done something only a psychologist would understand and given her daughter a kind of inferiority complex about banks. As for the manager of the local bank, he would be hard put to it to recognise a lady he hadn't seen for five years, assuming he was still alive (as it happened he had been a victim of a V.1 in 1945) while the clerks were perpetually changing. And then, so many nondescript ladies surge in and out of a bank's doors in the course of a week, and, if you get one who hardly ever comes inside and does practically all her business by correspondence, the position is made harder still. Miss Hunter, in fact, had never even set eyes on the manager of the London branch and could not have identified any of the clerks if she met them on her side of the counter.

As for Alice she realised from the start that all her hopes must be pinned on Mrs. Brownlow. It was a pity they had parted on such acrimonious terms, but even Mrs. B. must have a conscience (though the absence of one was one of the accusations Alice had indirectly brought against her during their last famous interview) and she, Alice, would make it clear that all the expenses of the expedition, plus a little *pour-boire* for her trouble, would come out of the Hunter finances.

Oh, Miss Freke didn't stand a chance, and pretty soon she would find herself in prison, for Mr. Finnemore would certainly prosecute, even if Alice hesitated.

So now she said in the same breathless way, " Yes, please go. I hope I shall never see you again. And if you have a grain of honesty in you you'll return my clothes."

At which Laura sketched a humorously despairing gesture to the sister and walked out.

" I suppose," said she hesitantly when the pair of them were back in the sister's room, " she's all right to travel alone? She won't do herself a mischief? "

" Nothing to the mischief she'll do to you if she gets the chance," said sister in grim tones. " Matter of fact, we can't stop her going out. She's not certified. Of course, she ought to wait a few more days; we don't want her fainting on the pavement and us held up in the *Daily Bugle* as an example of how the non-nationalised hospitals treat their patients. But she'll be gone by the end of the week, you mark my words."

Miss Freke went away looking very thoughtful. Years of living in other people's houses and devising such small pleasures and privileges for herself as were possible in the circumstances had trained her mind to work quickly and shrewdly, not to say with cunning. She had some imagination, too, and on her way back to Bath she put herself in the dispossessed woman's place. " If our positions were reversed what would I do? " she thought. Obviously go to London to contact Mrs. Brownlow. But—would Mrs. B. co-operate? Would she come to Bath, and, even if she did, would her word be sufficient? Laura remembered poor Alice's story of that final scene. Here was Mrs. Brownlow's chance to repay her erstwhile lodger in her own coin. Was she going to take it?

Back in Bath she spent a quiet evening completing her plans, and next day she called on Mr. Finnemore to report the result of her visit.

"This woman is quite convinced, or so it appears, that she *is* Miss Hunter," she said. "She is going to produce a London witness to that effect. I thought I had better warn you, as they may descend upon you very suddenly. In the meantime, I dare say you would like to hold matters up till this point is settled."

Mr. Finnemore frowned. Here was another of them, managing women who thought they could teach you your business.

"If this lady considers she has a case against you for fraud, Miss Hunter," said he coldly, "no doubt she will institute the necessary proceedings."

Laura proceeded to take the bull by the horns. "May I ask you one question, Mr. Finnemore? Has it ever occurred to you that perhaps her story is a true one?"

Mr. Finnemore smiled dryly. "It will be time enough to consider that when she has furnished sufficient evidence for a case. In my profession, Miss Hunter, we early become accustomed to deranged ladies imagining that they are legatees, or that they have large sums of money to leave to charities of various kinds, or suffering from persecution mania, knowing that they are pursued wherever they go, their lives threatened. Why, I have had cases where they have actually written anonymous letters to themselves, of a most scurrilous or perilous nature, which they have actually brought to me to support their contentions. Naturally, if such a case is brought you will require legal representation . . ."

"I shall leave it all to you," said Laura. "I've always disliked amateurs. To begin with it's a form of blackleg activity for them to try and muscle in (I think that's the expression) on the field of the professional, and for another thing, they don't know the ropes, so they are almost certain to be defeated on technical grounds alone."

A very sensible woman, thought Mr. Finnemore. Well, with a face like that you had to have something. And she wasn't altogether undowered. She had this legacy and she had Mr. Finnemore's support. No, she could be a great deal worse off.

"I mustn't take up any more of your time," said Laura. "By the way, I'm thinking of taking a small furnished house somewhere in the country for a while anyhow. I've had enough of London life. The new London has no room for people like me, and I've always liked the country. I thought of inquiring at one of the local agents. I'll let you know my address, of course, and if a further visit should be necessary and you will send me a line I will come at once."

And out she went. She had always heard her employers say that earning money involved hard work. Often she had had difficulty in repressing the retort that hard work didn't necessarily involve getting money; but it was quite true. She was working like a burying beetle and the person she'd got to bury and without much delay, and more important still, without involving herself with the police, was that unfortunate bit of flotsam, the real Alice Hunter.

She hadn't won good references from her past employers for nothing. When she was put to it she could move (as she herself expressed it) like a jet plane. And fortune still appeared to favour her. At the first estate agent she visited she was told of a small house that had recently been offered furnished, for an indefinite period. It was remote and not supplied with quite all the amenities a comfort-loving generation has been led to expect; so the rent would be moderate, and there was a local housekeeper who went with the house.

" A reliable woman ? " enquired Laura.

" Something of a dragon, I fear. I have suggested to the owners that the retention of her services should be optional to the tenant, but they won't agree. Partly, I suppose, because they feel Miss Woodman will guard their interests, and partly, no doubt, because they feel responsible for her."

And, if she's useful to them, they won't want to come back to a house in the depths of the country and find themselves without domestic help, amplified Laura. As a matter of fact, it would be an advantage to have a competent woman on the premises.

And being, as has been said and must, in any case, be obvious to the reader, a fast worker, she went out to inspect the house (and the family retainer) and sent a cheque for three months' rent in advance twenty-four hours later.

grunted Alice. But she had no intention of spending money on a new pair.

All the way to London she grimaced and muttered and gestured to herself, going over and over the conversation she would have with Mrs. Brownlow. One or two passengers, passing the carriage as they went up or down the corridor, observed her with surprise and even alarm. One, seeing her fling out her arm and throw up her head in a proud yet beseeching gesture, was quite sure the old girl was off her nut, and even looked through the smaller paragraphs in the evening paper to see if a lunatic was missing from a local home. Miss Hunter, however, was fortunately unaware of this, nor did she realise that two people watched her carefully as she alighted. Because by this time she mistrusted everyone, she wouldn't take a taxi but bought a ticket on the underground. Naturally she didn't look at any of the people round her—all enemies, no doubt—but buried her face in the copy of the *Record* she had bought simply for that purpose. She read about the dollar gap and the various difficulties in which the Ministers (so appropriately according to her) found themselves; she read of a man who had shot four people and then himself, of a fire in which two children and their mother had perished, of a case of gross cruelty to a cat, and of the engagement, for the fifth time, of a well-known actress and film star. All this passed the time adequately, and she alighted at Paddington and made her way to Ennismore Terrace on foot. It was only a short journey, but she felt she could scarcely compass it, her heart beat so tremendously in her breast, her body trembled, she couldn't keep her tongue still. Mutter, mutter, mutter, like a plump elderly witch—all the way to her destination.

At No. 4 the door was opened by someone she had

never seen. That was Check Number One. Not that she had ever particularly noticed the daily women who " obliged " and who were constantly changing their identity, but it would have been reassuring to be greeted by a familiar face. However, she merely asked for Mrs. Brownlow.

" If it's rooms, we're full," said the slattern. (What was Mrs. Brownlow thinking about letting a woman open the door looking like *that*?—a great fat cow of a woman, not even tidy. She had been avaricious and grasping, of course, but she had had an eye for appearances.)

" I haven't come about rooms," she said coldly. " I have come to see Mrs. Brownlow on a personal matter. I believe she is expecting me."

The woman's big pale lips parted. Really, with Mr. Bevan showering teeth on the population, there was no need for her to show those unsightly gaps. She wore a wedding-ring, too. But that didn't necessarily imply a husband. He might be dead or gone off or simply a convention. Believe nothing till you see the proof, was Alice's motto.

" That she's not," said the apparition.

Alice suddenly felt anger warm her icy breast.

" Will you kindly tell her that Miss Hunter is here? " she said, and tried to push her way in.

" She's not 'ere," said the woman in a stupid, gaping way. " Gorn to the orspital. Appendicitis." (Not a duodenal ulcer as the impostor had claimed. But what was one falsehood among so many?)

For a moment Miss Hunter was sure that heaven itself had ranged its powers against her. But a moment later her courage reared its head again.

" Then who is in charge? "

" 'Er sister, Miss Turner's, 'ere. But it's like I told you, there's no vacancies."

" I should like to see Miss Turner."

" She's gorn out," said the woman apathetically.

" Then I will wait."

At that moment a door closed on an upper floor and feet began to descend the stairs. Alice's eyes brightened. Certainly she had always kept herself to herself, but, even so, she must have been observed going in and out of the house. Even if this lodger didn't know her by name he or she would remember seeing her and that would be the first step.

A tall young man with a dark skin came down the stairs. Miss Hunter went forward. " Excuse me ! "

He stopped, startled. " Pliss ? " He was European, but she was too ignorant to recognise his country. An Italian perhaps, all that dark hair and those flashing white teeth.

But so far as she was concerned he was useless. It was only too clear he did not recognise her.

Still, no harm having a try. " We have been fellow-lodgers here for some time," she said.

He looked at her again. " Pliss ? "

" You probably know my face even if we haven't been introduced," she went on desperately.

" 'E's only bin 'ere a week," said the mountainous slut.

" Oh, I see." She stood back. " It's all right. I . . ."

He was so willing to help. " Pliss ? "

" No, no. A mistake. Oh, go, go," she muttered under her breath. " You're no good to me, so why do you block the fairway ? "

The dark man smiled again, then gave it up and walked out. Miss Hunter watched him go. Then she turned back to see the Mountain observing her with great suspicion.

"There's a woman outside," she said, meeting Miss Turner in the hall. "Hurled herself on me like a werewolf. Tried to make out I knew her. Begging. It's a scandal."

"I don't think she's begging," explained Miss Turner. "It's just that she's . . ." She tapped her forehead significantly. "She's been here too . . ."

The second person was deaf, and Miss Hunter had to shout. This attracted a lot of attention, and, after all, she was only going to visit a friend, so couldn't be expected to recognise a one-time lodger. After this Miss Hunter withdrew prudently to the corner where she stared at some periodicals at a newspaper stall until the proprietor came out and looked at her questioningly. She said in confused tones that she was waiting for someone. At last the door of No. 4 opened again and an elderly man emerged. Miss Hunter knew him by sight and hurried across the road to meet him. He was a retired doctor, who spent his time writing in his room on the top floor. He was old but harmless and a bit jiggery-pokery, Mrs. Brownlow used to explain. He seemed to think that Alice was one of his late patients and told her that he had retired from practice with the passing of the new National Health Act. "You can't teach an old dog new tricks," he said. "If you want to get on someone's panel you should go to the local Insurance office, and they'll explain." When Alice insisted that he *must* recognise her he said sharply that if he had to remember the faces of all the women he'd prescribed for his memory would be one of the wonders of the world, and he shook her off. Alice didn't follow him up; she could see how useless it would be. He stopped on the next corner and spoke to a policeman on point duty there, and a minute or two later the man patrolled (there was no other word) in Alice's direction and, stopping at her side, asked if she had lost her way. To her horror, Alice suddenly laughed sharply.

"That's one way of putting it," she said. Oh, she was lost all right, in a fog, a miasma of human misunderstandings, hatred and deliberate depravity.

Then it occurred to her that a policeman might be the one person who could help her and she began to tell her story all over again. By this time being tired, frightened and angry she didn't tell it very well. The policeman, who had been told to be on the look-out for a stolen car, thought she was another of these old dears who was a bit wonky but harmless, of course. He gathered she had lost her identity card and ration book.

"Nothing to get in a flap about, ma," he said. (Ma! She nearly exploded.) "Just go along to the Food Office—you know where that is?—and explain to them and they'll give you an emergency card for a fortnight. And then you'll want a new identity card. . . . You are living in the neighbourhood, of course?"

"Yes. That is, I was until just lately. . . ."

"When you lost the documents?" said the policeman in patient tones.

Alice hesitated. She had lost the documents at Yarborough. "It was in a train," she began.

"Ah," said the policeman, "that makes a difference. What's your present address?"

That stumped Alice. She hadn't got one, of course.

"I was involved in an accident," she said at last. "Suffered from violent concussion. I have been in a hospital."

The policeman nodded. Just what he might have suspected, said that nod. Been in an accident, had concussion, a nasty blow on the head that knocked all the sense out and let all the bees in. Her doctor didn't ought to let her go around in this state. He began to say as much. " Your doctor . . ." But Alice interrupted that it was her belief that so long as you stopped away from doctors you stayed well. She personally hadn't seen a doctor for years and years and years . . . until the accident of course, and look at the trouble in which she was now involved. She wasn't on a panel, she went on, and she didn't intend to be. The same with dentists. Her dentist had retired, and, seeing she had dentures, upper and lower, she didn't have to bother about him, either. Poor Alice! She was rapidly closing every gate against her own escape.

" Where did you say this hospital was? "

Alice remained obstinately mum. Oh, she could see what he was after. Ring them up from the police box round the corner and ask them to send an escort, then somehow inveigle her into the police station and keep her there till somebody arrived.

" Now, you go home and have a rest," the policeman urged. " I suppose you've got a home."

" Yes," panted Alice in absolute terror. " Of course. I have to catch a train. I—the person I came to see has been taken to hospital."

The constable nodded, more amicably this time. " That's right," he said. " You go back to wherever you're staying and go to the Food Office and they'll give you a form, and when you've filled that up you'll get an emergency card for a couple of weeks. We don't let anybody starve in post-war Britain, you know." He grinned at her cheerfully. " And ask about an identity card, too. Of course, they won't give you that right away. They'll have to make inquiries, make sure you're not trying to get two of everything. . . ."

" I see," said Alice. Yes, that might help. Because they could show that a Miss Hunter had been registered at No. 4 Ennismore Terrace. She was too fuddled by this time, not by drink but by exhaustion and fear, to realise that anyone as sharp off the touch as Laura Freke would soon throw a spanner in her works in this direction.

She tottered off in the direction of the station. There wasn't a train for nearly an hour but she could sit there on the wooden benches in full view of a number of people and at least no one could slip a knife into her ribs. And as she thought that she remembered a story she had once read in an American magazine, about a man who had been knifed in a shuttered windowless room, and the author hadn't given the solution. She swayed a bit as she walked. The policeman was wondering if he ought to go after her, when another female popped up. She wasn't the same one, but she came out of the same box, same age, same general appearance. He'd know them apart if he saw them together but if he had to describe them there wouldn't be much difference.

However, the demeanour of the newcomer was composed, if a little hurried.

"Officer," she said, "I wonder if you've seen a lady in a green tweed suit and a brown hat wandering round here just recently? She's suffering from loss of memory, doesn't know who she is, thinks her things have been stolen . . ."

The constable stiffened. "Been in hospital?" he hazarded.

"That's right. At Yarborough. She has no right to be out alone. The authorities stretched a point allowing her to travel up for the day, but—she gave me the slip."

"That's all right, mum," said the policeman, "she hasn't been gone five minutes. Went towards the station." Well did Miss Freke know she hadn't been gone five minutes. She hadn't let the unfortunate woman out of her sight all day. While Alice waited at No. 4 Laura had been on the corner, looking in the windows, buying a copy of *Picture Post*, talking to the salesman. Then, when Alice emerged, she crossed the street into a café, whence she could see Alice talking to the policeman. Her decision to have a word with him on her own account was an impulse that she thought too good to resist. It wasn't likely he would take her, Alice, seriously, but there was no harm underlining the obvious, that the poor old girl was a bit loopy. She, too, knew there wouldn't be a train for nearly an hour, and Alice could only return to Yarborough or throw herself under a bus, and, though scores of people leave the world by this means in the course of a year, it takes a high degree of courage to do it deliberately.

Alice plodded back to Paddington Station, checked up the time of the train and sat down on the rows of seats benevolently provided by the railway company and now the property of the general public. " I won't get in till the last minute," she told herself feverishly. " I'll wait here with people all round me till just before the train's due to start. Then it will be all right." She couldn't say what she feared, but she felt danger over her like a sky. But it was no good. She couldn't sit there patiently till the clock marked the hour. Suppose, for instance, there was a mistake, that the train went earlier than she expected? Three times she got up and looked at the departure board; twice she stopped porters. " No. 11 " they both said impatiently. " It's marked up there." And there was the indicator. Bath, via Yarborough, 4.54. It was now 4.30. She went back to her seat. " Suppose the train fills up? Suppose I don't get a seat? Suppose the doors are locked and I have to find a porter to open them? Suppose—suppose—suppose——" At 4.35 she marched past the ticket collector and found an empty carriage. Now she began to count the instants feverishly. When people came past and peered into the window she first scowled, in the hope that they would move on, then thought it would be safer to have someone, some witness, with her. But there weren't many people travelling, and though a few walked past down the corridor no one came in. It was 4.45—4.50. 4.52. Another two minutes. She found she was praying desperately. Two minutes. Don't let anyone come in. A minute and a half. She stared, hypnotised, at the platform, watching the people as they came along. But she saw no familiar, hateful face, the clock moved inexorably on, the whistle blew, the guard waved his flag—and at last the train began to move and nobody had come in.

They had gone some distance before she began to consider the immediate future. She was going back to Yarborough; her baggage was there, and she was sure she was expected, in spite of her furious denial of a few hours ago. In the morning she would go down to the Food Office and explain her predicament. Sooner or later someone would take her seriously. And then there was Mr. Finnemore. She would insist on seeing him. Her courage grew.

Shortly before reaching Yarborough the train ran into the Marley Tunnel. It was a long tunnel and there were no lights. Surely before the railways belonged to US, reflected Alice, lights came on automatically. Still, in a few minutes they would be running into the daylight again. She lay back with her head against the cushions.

And then she heard it, heard it above the noise of the rippling wheels, Go-ing home, go-ing-home, that was what the wheels said. But this was a different, a quieter noise, a noise so quiet it really wasn't noise at all. A sound, an impression, no more, a soft sliding sound, like a door being gently pushed back. Instantly she was erect and rigid; her scalp prickled, she felt the sweat come out in a dew on her forehead. Desperately her eyes strove to pierce the gloom, but the darkness was complete. " I am suffering from nerves," she told herself ; " there is nothing, no one there. It's imagination." But was it imagination that a cold air was stealing into the carriage ? She felt its breath on her ankles (she had always been very susceptible to cold) ; the paper that she had laid on the seat began to quiver ; she could hear its faint protest as the sheets flapped in the draught. But there was no other sound. The Thing standing there in the darkness was motionless. The tunnel went on and on.

Miss Hunter found her voice.

" Who's there ? "

But no one answered.

" Mustn't faint," she warned her beating heart. " Keep your head. If I can't see It, It can't see me. Can't come across the carriage and set its hands on my throat," she meant. She hadn't the smallest doubt that, if she knew how to achieve it without detection, the infamous Laura Freke would kill her without any compunction whatsoever. " Suppose I offer to give her the money," she thought ; but that was no good. She had the money already and she wasn't going to acknowledge she'd got it by a trick, not she.

The train was driving steadily on ; the wheels still rippled but they had changed their tune. " I-am-here," they proclaimed, " I-am-here." " Mustn't scream, mustn't faint, mustn't pretend I know there's anyone there," Alice told her terrified heart. " The tunnel won't go on for ever. I must be prepared, though." But she had no weapon, not even an umbrella. In the old days a woman could have drawn a pin from her hat, and what a deadly weapon that was. Stab at an eye, a wrist, a throat . . .

The train poured suddenly into the light. Alice

turned her head so sharply you almost expected to hear the neck click. She was alone in the carriage! The draught was easily explained. The communicating door had rolled back, leaving a gap through which the wind could come. Alice's heart beat so fast with relief it almost choked her. " I shall have to take care," she thought. " I mustn't get neurotic, start imagining things. That's what they're waiting for. One sign of anything abnormal and they'll shut me up somewhere." She felt like Ishmael, her hand against every man, or rather, every man's hand against her. The odds were fantastic. How could one simple rather stupid woman hope to outwit the whole malicious gang ranged against her? " It's thinking so much about that woman," she decided. " Well, it's not surprising, but I must stop it. You understand, Alice? Stop it! You've enough to worry about without that." Resolutely she picked up the copy of *Illustrated* she had bought at the station bookstall, and began to read an article on a woman who had made rat-catching her profession. A very strange choice, she reflected. Surely no womanly woman . . .

" Good evening, Miss Freke," said a voice from the doorway. " History repeats itself, doesn't it? This is the second time we've met on a train, just you and I together."

Alice dropped the paper; for a moment she thought she was suffering from delusions, that Sister March and the doctor and all the other people who thought she was mad were right. She looked up. Laura Freke had entered the carriage and was closing the door behind her.

" What sort of a day did you have in London, Miss Freke? What's the matter? Why don't you answer? Or have you forgotten who you really are? Have you, Miss Freke? "

She moved slowly across the carriage.

Alice looked up ; this wasn't a delusion. This was the real thing. This was how it happened in newspaper reports and on screens and in whodunits. And tomorrow the newspaper would carry a story. Woman Found Strangled in Train. Or Woman's Body on Line.

Alice Hunter fainted.

CHAPTER EIGHT

IT DIDN'T last long, her period of unconsciousness, because when she came to herself again the train was still running smoothly and swiftly on the line, which meant, surely, that they hadn't yet arrived at Yarborough. Her enemy was seated opposite her, her hands folded harmlessly in her lap. The wheels of the train kept up their regular cheerful beat. Can't-escape, they said now, can't-escape. And it was true. She knew it. A curious calm pervaded her. She knew it for the calm that, according to the vicar, the Rev. Mr. Anstruther, so often preceded death.

" That's better," said Miss Freke. " For a moment I really thought you'd passed out. You know, you shouldn't be travelling about alone. You're not strong enough. If you'd fainted here while you were by yourself it might have been quite serious. But you're better now, aren't you ? Aren't you ? "

" Why are you here ? " muttered Alice between lips that felt as swollen as if she'd been stung by an army of bees. " What do you want ? "

" I'm only keeping an eye on you, because it's not safe for you to be by yourself."

" Have you been following me all day ? "

" I feel responsible for you. Do you believe in a pattern in life ? "

" I won't answer," Alice told herself. " I won't speak to her. She can't make me. If she tries to touch me or comes closer I shall pull the communication cord." Inevitably her eyes turned upwards.

" Now, now, don't do anything you may regret," said the Enemy's sensible voice. " There's a heavy penalty for pulling that cord, and what on earth are you going to say if you do ? "

Alice saw herself repeating the tactics of the day. And how unsuccessful they had been ! She had impressed no one. Not Miss Turner, the lodgers, the constable, except with a suspicion that she really was demented. Before she could make up her mind the train ran smoothly into Yarborough and stopped. In a flash Miss Hunter was on her feet, had wrenched open the door and fallen on to the platform ; she went scurrying towards the ticket collector. " Let there be a taxi, let there be a taxi," she was muttering. She would go back to the hospital—they couldn't refuse to accept her for one night more—and to-morrow she would go to Bath and see Mr. Finnemore. He was a lawyer, he couldn't afford to risk a grave miscarriage of justice. She didn't dare look over her shoulder to watch Miss Freke coming leisurely along the platform. There was a slight jam at the gate ; someone had to pay an overcharge and there was an argument in process. Alice pushed impatiently.

" It's all right, lady," said the ticket collector. " There's plenty of time." But there wasn't, there wasn't. Every minute she expected to feel a hand on her shoulder. But at last she was through and—oh, wonder of wonders, there was a car with a uniformed driver waiting on the rank. She ran towards him. The man glanced over her head ; from the other side of the gate Miss Freke nodded reassuringly.

" The hospital," said Miss Hunter. " Quickly, please."

The chauffeur opened the door. " Any luggage, madam ? "

" No, no, none. The Cottage Hospital. It's urgent. A matter of life and death." He stood there, smiling in what she called a respectful manner, still holding the door.

" That's all," she said frantically. " There's no one else coming."

But there was. Miss Freke, a cool competent woman in oat-meal brown tweed, walked through the barrier and towards the car.

" Don't let her come in. I won't share the cab. I'll get out."

But it was too late. Miss Freke was there, she had stepped in and put a hand on Alice's knee.

" It's all right, my dear, it's all right. No one's going to hurt you."

The driver closed the door. Alice pounded vainly on the glass window. " Let me out. I won't . . ." She was wrenching furiously at the handle.

" That door's locked," said the chauffeur, getting into gear and driving off into the early dusk.

" Let me out," shouted Alice, but no one heard her, no one except Miss Freke and the driver whom she had primed. The cab drove on away from the lighted roads that led to the hospital, down a long winding lane, and quite soon they were out in open country.

Darkness came on in sudden strides. Alice had noticed this phenomenon when she was in London. At one moment the streets seemed full of a pleasant light, then, as you watched, the world darkened before your eyes. So it was here. They hadn't been in the cab more than a few minutes before it became too dim to distinguish any objects from the window. But at least she knew the hospital didn't lie this way.

" Where are you taking me? " she asked, but her voice was quiet now.

" Somewhere where you'll be safe," said Miss Freke peaceably.

" I want to go back to the hospital."

" You can't. There's no room. You told them you weren't coming back. Remember? "

" I'll go to an hotel."

" I'm afraid it wouldn't be safe for you in your present condition. What you want is a long rest, not seeing anyone. You've had a bad shock. If it's not to have permanent results you've got to be careful. You're suffering from a persecution mania, you know. Oh, yes, you are. You think we're all your enemies. When people get like that they become dangerous not only to themselves but to—well, everybody. There was a case in the paper only last week of a man who thought the neighbours were whispering about him, and he went out and shot three men and four women and a child. And it was all a delusion. Nobody was paying any attention to him at all. That was the root of the trouble, of course. He was being disregarded, and his vanity couldn't bear that, so he began to deceive himself. That's the crux of the situation, you know. So long as you know you're play-acting it doesn't really matter, even though you may be rather a nuisance to other people. It's when you can't distinguish between the play-acting and reality that matters become serious."

Alice leaned back, feeling her mind about as settled as Niagara Falls. She knew who this was, of course; this was the interloper, the impostor, the woman she'd met in the train on her triumphant journey to Bath. Yet—was she the same woman? Her voice seemed different. And—was it the same face? How could you be sure? She found she was asking the question aloud.

"Sure of what?" asked Laura.

"Humpty Dumpty was right," said Alice abruptly.

"Crazy as a loon," reflected the driver.

"You haven't told me where we're going," said Alice. "Are you taking me away to kill me? Is he in the plot? Oh, you needn't shake your head like that. You wouldn't dare bring him with us if he wasn't your accomplice."

Laura found nothing to say to that and the car flew on through the scented dark. Moths flew against the windows and went bumbling off into the shadows; from a nearby wood a bird called. Everywhere were the unending sounds of night, leaves rustling, unseen creatures stalking their prey or beginning their activities when most beasts, human and animal, were preparing for rest. Once a hedgehog waddled across the road in the glare of the headlights and the driver slowed up sharply.

"What's that for?" demanded Alice.

"A hedgehog," said Laura.

Alice broke into peals of loud, disconcerting laughter. "And I used to think you hadn't a sense of humour," she gasped. "How wrong I was. You'd risk all our lives for the sake of a hedgehog, but my life doesn't mean a thing to you. Less than a hedgehog 'neath the taxi's wheel," she improvised.

"Try and keep quiet, dear," urged Laura.

The driver made no sign. On and on they went, under skies of a night grey shot with spears of darkly silver light; the tree-tops were like black cardboard stencilled against the cloudy horizon. Now and again a light flashed past the window, but it was gone too soon for Alice to yell for help. Besides, she was beginning to realise that would be no use. No one would hear; if they did hear, they wouldn't believe a word she said. Sometimes she couldn't believe it herself. This couldn't be quiet uneventful Alice Hunter being carried away in a strange car to an unknown destination. "These things don't happen," she moaned inaudibly, but what she meant, of course, was "These things don't happen to me." They're happening all the time to someone, these or other violent developments, but that's different. They happen to newspaper puppets, not to creatures of flesh and blood inhabiting one's own world.

On and on went the car, past fields almost invisible now, past trees and water and darkness; and she felt the journey was symbolic of her own fate. She was being carried away from all that was familiar into the twilight. At last they ran through a little village, past a signpost, and paused in front of a house standing apart, down a short lane. Here lights were burning and it was clear that they were expected. The front door opened as the car stopped and an elderly woman with a strong lined face came to meet them. At the beginning of the journey Alice had been laying plans for escaping somehow into the dark as soon as the door of the car was opened; but, as the time passed on, a kind of lassitude overcame her. She got out quite quietly, watched her companion giving the driver orders. The strange woman stood by the gate.

"Come in, my dear," said Miss Freke, turning at last. "Oh, Miss Woodman, is everything all right?"

"Yes," said Miss Woodman, who was clearly the laconic type.

"Luggage arrived?"

"And unpacked. I've got you some dinner. Didn't suppose you'd have it on the train."

"No. And I'm sure we're ready for it." She turned back to Alice, saying again, "Come along."

"I'm not coming," said Alice. "I don't know why

you've brought me here, but it's—it's abduction. I don't know where this place is or who that woman is, but I'm not going to stay. This man can drive me back to Yarborough. I have enough money to pay you," she added.

"Now what d'you suppose you can do at Yarborough, without even a toothbrush?" demanded Miss Freke heartily.

"I shall go back to the hospital. And in the morning I shall go on and see Mr. Finnemore."

"I really can't advise you to do that. He . . ."

"I don't care what you advise." Her composure was beginning to topple. "You're a wicked, scheming woman, and I hope you'll go to prison. I hope they give you ten years." She heard a thin screaming sound. A bird of prey, probably, imported to lend horror to the scene. She lifted her head and looked round.

"Stop that," said Miss Woodman harshly. "You'll rouse the whole neighbourhood."

It was not a fortunate remark. Such a consideration had not occurred to Miss Hunter. Now she threw back her head and yelled.

The next instant she was seized on both sides by strong hands and pushed into the cottage. Frog-marched, in short. "You're torturers," she gasped. "You're . . ."

The cottage door closed behind her; she wrenched herself free and ran through an open door. The driver had got back into the car. She beat furiously on the window. "Take me back," she screamed. "I can explain it all. You'll find yourself accessory to a crime, probably murder." The driver let the engine run; he didn't move off, but on the other hand he didn't leave his seat. Miss Woodman loomed up on the right.

"You'd better have your dinner in bed," she said.

Miss Hunter struck her hand away. "I suppose she's

bought you, too. Where is this place? I've never been here before and I won't stay. It's horrible. No taste. Though I suppose that's all you can expect from someone who's been no better than an upper servant all these years. I suppose," she added furiously, "all these abominations were bought with my money. My money." She swept a furious arm and a glass bowl went crashing to the floor. Miss Woodman's mouth tightened; she looked resentful. "You didn't warn me she was violent, Miss Hunter," she said. "She might do herself a mischief, or attack someone else. I would never have undertaken a *violent* case."

Alice, who had been looking round frantically for something else to break, stood like Lot's wife. "You mean, you're a nurse?"

"Not exactly. If you want to know, I am Miss Mowbray's housekeeper but I've agreed to lend a hand, seeing you're ill——" And, for a consideration, of course, though she didn't mention that.

"I—I'm not ill," protested Alice, but she did indeed feel so dreadfully ill her voice carried little conviction.

"Oh, come now! I shouldn't like to think this was the way you generally behaved," said Miss Woodman.

"I—you see, she's cheated me. She . . . Oh, if only I could see Mr. Finnemore. I know I could convince him." She turned to the housekeeper. "To-morrow will you come with me to Bath? I'll pay the expenses, and we can confront Mr. Finnemore. You'll see I'm right. . . ."

"We'll see when to-morrow comes," said the woman grimly.

Laura half-shrugged. "Another delusion," she murmured in soft tones just calculated to reach Alice's ear. "He's never set eyes on her. How could he know? If you could produce someone to prove . . . But, of course, you can't."

"Not yet," said Alice. She wrenched herself free of Miss Woodman's detaining arm. "How long do you propose to keep me here? I suppose you know it's illegal. . . ."

But she might as well have tried to argue with a fog-horn.

The room into which she was taken was small and looked out over some fields that stretched into infinity so far as she could tell. There was very little light, but there was a sense of distance that was confirmed when morning came and she realised there wasn't so much as a shed in view.

The furniture was austere enough for a convent cell—anyway her idea of a cell. There was a bed, a small low armchair with a deficient spring, an old-fashioned washstand, and a dressing-table with a glass. A few hooks shrouded by a curtain were fastened in one of the walls.

"Whose room is this?" she demanded suspiciously.

"This is the guest-room."

"I shouldn't think that woman expected many guests."

Miss Woodman bridled. "Miss Mowbray—the Misses Mowbray, that is, seeing there are three of them—are elderly ladies. They don't have many visitors. So you see there's no need for an elaborate guest-room."

"If it's only for two nights I dare say I can put up with it," agreed Alice grimly.

Miss Woodman said nothing. "And is it customary in this part of the country to starve your guests?" continued Alice, recovering her spirit.

"I'll bring you something up on a tray," said Miss Woodman.

"With arsenic in it, I suppose?" But she was doing herself no good, and she was forced to recognise it.

Miss Woodman merely inquired coldly whether she was able to undress herself.

" I'm not a paralytic as well as an imbecile, whatever Miss Freke may have told you. I shall stay here to-night because I have no choice . . ." For though she was afraid of Miss Freke and this horrid unsympathetic woman who was clearly hand-in-glove with her, she was even more afraid of finding herself abandoned in the dark in this desolate countryside. In spite of what she had told Mr. Finnemore about being tired of London she felt she would almost have exchanged her legacy (or her hope of it, which was fainter than it had been) for a comfortable bed-sitt. in a London boarding-house and the heartening knowledge that Miss Freke had been run over by a bus and killed on the instant.

" Then I'll leave you to it," said Miss Woodman. " I shan't be long."

Alice looked round the little room, and made a dart at the curtains. " Why, the window's shut," she exclaimed. " I thought it was stuffy."

" That window doesn't open," the housekeeper told her quickly.

" You mean you've nailed it up ? "

" I mean, it doesn't open."

She walked out of the room and the instant her feet had gone down the stairs Alice darted across the room to lock the door. But there was no key. She opened the door cautiously but there was no key on the other side either.

" Do you want something ? " asked Miss Freke's hateful voice from the stairs.

" I was looking for a key."

" Oh, I'm afraid there are no keys here. But you needn't be afraid. There won't be any burglars. Miss Woodman and I will look after you."

Alice closed the door and sat down on the edge of the bed. This was the worst predicament yet. Now that they had got her here they had all the power on earth over her. Suppose, for instance, she fell downstairs and broke her neck they only had to say she'd stumbled, been intoxicated, flung herself down in a fit or rage, and hey presto ! she'd be buried as Laura Freke, and that would be the end of that. She still had the feeling that she was overlooking some detail that would change her whole situation, but she couldn't for the life of her discover what it was. Cooler reflection assured her that they wouldn't try to murder her in any obvious manner, because of police inquiries. No, it would have to look like suicide or accident. By this time she realised that they would have to procure her death. There was no other way out of the impasse. The legacy wouldn't do the impostor much good if she had to spend the rest of her life in this out-of-the-way hole. And how much had she told Miss Woodman ?

" If I could get her on my side ! " whispered Alice, hope filtering back into her mind. " If I could convince her ! "

The thought was inspiring. Laura might think it a masterstroke to enlist the woman's help, but it might well prove her undoing. For surely she couldn't have taken the woman on without taking her to some extent into her confidence. Truth is for ever truth, she remembered, and fortunately did not recall the opposing quotation about Truth for ever on the scaffold, Wrong forever on the throne.

The sound of feet on the stairs brought her rapidly to an upright position. No sense intimidating the one person who might be transformed into an ally. She had managed to shed her skirt and jumper and kick off her shoes when Miss Woodman returned, bearing a tray. When she saw Alice she frowned.

"Not ready yet?" she chided.

"I was thinking. I'm not used to the country, you know. There are a lot of queer noises."

"Nothing for you to be afraid of. Now then, quick with that nightgown."

Alice pulled it over her head, contrived to shuffle out of the rest of her clothes under its utility folds, and scrambled into bed.

"How delicious that looks," she said with genuine appreciation. "It's years since anyone's brought me a meal in bed. And I didn't like to have it often, even when I got my own food, because people don't like it if they get an impression you're feeling a little bit off colour."

"I know," said Miss Woodman, a tinge of humanity creeping into her voice. "I've often thought that myself."

"I used to think if ever I'd had a daughter or a companion of any kind I'd arrange for her to feel poorly at least once a week. Not really ill, you know, but just, as it were, convalescent. Trays in bed and the wireless upstairs. It does give you such a feeling of wealth to be waited on."

"Well, now's your chance," said Miss Woodman. "Miss Hunter tells me you've not really recovered from your accident, and you're to be treated like an invalid, so it's a good thing you're prepared to enjoy it."

She dumped the tray on the bed. "Don't bother to bring it down. I'll come up for it presently. Sure you've got everything?" (And if you haven't don't dare ring for it, that severe voice implied.)

Alice replied hastily that it was delicious, yes, she had, such a treat. There was even a table napkin, so whatever you might think about Laura Freke it was obvious that this woman was accustomed to gentle people and their ways. (Yes, even after two World Wars, Alice divided people up into gentlefolk and the rest. She belonged to gentlefolk though only just, her income was *so* small, and Miss Woodman belonged to the rest. Quite suitable really she should be waiting on her, she thought in her muddled way.)

" And now," she reflected, taking the cover off a very nice dish of poached eggs and tomatoes, " two eggs, just think of it, I must map out a plan of campaign." The bare thought made her feel happier. She was a great planner, a shocking loss, really, to the Civil Service. She'd never have bothered about getting things actually built, but her plans would be irreproachable. There was a pot of tea and some delightful thin ginger biscuits, the kind she liked best, and after she had put the tray on the little table and was beginning to think up openings for conversation to win Miss Woodman to her side the woman came in with a glass of warm milk.

Whenever the milk ration allowed, only, of course, living on one book isn't easy, Alice always had a small cup of milk last thing ; and this was a half-pint glass. She drank it gratefully, and quite soon afterwards felt so drowsy she forgot to register dismay that she couldn't secure any privacy for herself, and when the two ladies came up later on she was fast asleep.

" Never even took her teeth out," said Miss Woodman. " That shows you. I swear by that stuff, Miss Hunter. Quite tasteless and sends you off at once. Do you ever suffer from sleeplessness ? "

" I always say the best sleeping-draught is a good conscience," returned Laura, tartly.

" My kind's easier to get," murmured Miss Woodman, taking up the glass.

CHAPTER NINE

DURING THE DAYS that followed Alice stuck rigidly to her vow. Sometimes she thought she couldn't bear it, simply couldn't bear it, hearing Laura addressed as Miss Hunter. And even now it was difficult not to turn her head and look alert when she heard her name. But she managed it. Too much depended on these weeks for her to risk a single slip.

On the third day she observed mildly that she'd like to go out for a little, and Laura said heartily, "An excellent idea. Only be sure you don't get lost. There are no landmarks round here, and no kind of transport at all. It's as quiet as the grave."

"How fortunate you were to find it," said Alice, sweetly, but she bent her head to conceal the trembling of her lips. For the thought of the grave was never long out of her mind. She wasn't a clever woman, but even she could see this state of affairs could not be prolonged indefinitely.

"I'll get Miss Woodman to go with you," Laura continued, and would take no denial. So soon in Miss Woodman came, wearing a very appropriate hat and jacket, carrying the raincoat without which she never ventured out of doors, no matter what the weather, drawing on fabric gloves (even for a walk in the woods, reflected Alice), and the pair set out.

"Have you always lived in the country?" Alice asked presently.

"I was in service in Wimbledon at one time. A very pleasant neighbourhood, though they tell me all the big houses are cut up into flats now."

"I've sometimes imagined I was mistress of one of

those big houses," said guileless Alice. "I've often heard people say it's a mistake to have a guest-room, people will come and visit you, but I always had at least three guest-rooms in my dream-house and they were always full."

"All right, I dare say, if they brought their rations," remarked the unromantic Miss Woodman.

"We lived in a—a sort of suburb of Wimbledon during my mother's lifetime. She made friends more easily than I do. She played cards, too. I remember one of her friends, a Miss Luling, saying to me, 'You're laying up a very solitary old age for yourself, Alice, unless you take up bridge.' At the time I didn't believe her, but now I think it's true. When I was in Romary Street there was a woman who played bridge till two o'clock in the morning. I went into her room once, quite by mistake, you understand, and there were eight people there. It wasn't a large room by any means, and the eight people practically filled it. When I opened the door they all looked up at me over their cards, just their eyes, I mean, the rest of their faces were hidden, but I felt as if I'd got into a den of wolves. And anyway," she added, "I'm no use at cards. I did try after Mother died, but I didn't seem able to pick up the knack."

"A great waste of time in any case," said Miss Woodman decisively. "Give me a piece of knitting of an evening and I'm perfectly content when it's time to go to bed. Something attempted something done has won a night's repose."

"Yes," said Alice naïvely, "I learnt that at school, too."

When the pair came back Laura was waiting for them in the hall. "Had a nice walk?" She flashed a conspiratorial glance at the housekeeper.

"Very pleasant," said Miss Woodman, as though the

question had been addressed to her. " It's mild without being damp."

" You must have another walk soon," said Laura, who somehow didn't seem pleased about it, not as pleased as you'd expect, that is.

It cost Alice a good deal to stick to her original resolution, but she had been well trained in the school of patience, and she regarded Miss Woodman as a man suffering from diabetes regards insulin. She didn't like her, but she was her one hope.

The weeks piled up. Alice received no letters and wrote none. She had abandoned the thought of Mrs. Brownlow as an ally; better put all your eggs in one basket and then you can keep an eye on them.

" Miss Freke seems to be coming along very nicely," remarked Miss Woodman one day. " I should think she'll soon be all right going about on her own."

" I wouldn't dare risk it," said Laura, simply. " She may seem calmer, but you know what they say about the calm before the storm. If she would admit that she is Miss Freke, then I should have more hope."

" It's very good of you taking all this trouble and going to so much expense on her account," continued Miss Woodman. " You haven't known her very long, have you? "

" I feel as if fate threw us together. I can't turn her adrift now."

" You mean, she goes with the money? " Miss Woodman hazarded.

Laura started. It was a crude way of putting it but the truth could hardly be more succinctly expressed.

Sometimes on their walks together Alice tried to draw out her companion to talk about her own youth.

" I've been chattering away like a magpie and you never say a word," she confessed. " My mother used to tell me I talked too much. She said no man marries a talkative woman, but I don't think that can be true, unless marriage brings out a woman's latent conversational powers. Because you must have noticed that when two or three are gathered together, as the prayer-book says, it's always the wives who talk the most, and the spinsters who slip in a word here and there when there's a pause."

"I've always tried to do my duty," was Miss Woodman's uncompromising reply. "Are you like your mother, Miss Freke? How do you remember her so well?"

"She only died a few years ago," said Alice, unguardedly. "And do you know, for a long time I felt quite guilty because I hadn't died, too. It seemed so selfish of me. Mother hated selfish women. She was always pulling me up. Selfishness leads to extravagance, she used to say."

"I don't think anyone could call you extravagant," Miss Woodman consoled her.

"I've never had the chance. Do you know what I used to want more than anything on earth? You'll think me quite crazy when I tell you. It was jewellery. Whenever I had a little time to myself I used to stare into jewellers' windows. Suppose someone came along and offered you one thing out of everything you can see, which would you choose? I often played that game. The difficulty was there was so much."

"Did your mother have much jewellery?" (Alice didn't notice that her companion was talking to her as if she really believed she was Miss Hunter.)

"She had at one time, but she sold it before she died. She said there was no sense wearing it when we never met anyone, and I shouldn't have any use for it. Just a temptation to burglars and servants, she said. Do you know, the only thing of hers I have is this ring."

She tried to twist it round her plump finger as she spoke. It was a quaint ring, quaint rather than valuable, turquoises in an antique silver setting. "My father gave it to her when they were first engaged; of course she had real diamonds for her proper engagement ring, but this was just a token." She had been turning it this way and that as she spoke and now she actually contrived to get it off her finger. "It's got their initials inside. A.W. from M.H. Mother was a Miss Wells, the same as Aunt Agatha. Father's name was Maurice. I remember Mother used to pronounce it in a French way—Maurice with the accent on the second syllable."

"You've never told me much about your father."

"He died when I was fourteen. He was always a quiet sort of person, and of course he didn't pay much attention to me. No one could be expected to notice me when Mother was about."

There was a short pause, then Alice yielded to an uncontrollable impulse.

"Miss Woodman," she said, "you've known me for nearly ten weeks. Do you still believe that woman's story about me? I am Alice Hunter, I am, indeed. What does she mean to do with me? She can't keep me here for ever. Suppose I got away and got to the village, what would happen?"

"Someone would bring you back," said Miss Woodman, sharply. "It's no good, Miss Freke. Until you make up your mind to be sensible and accept facts you'll never get away."

Alice looked at her in a heart-broken fashion. "I believed you were beginning to be convinced," she cried. "Oh, how can you go on believing her story? Do I look like someone who would make all this up?"

"Now, now," said Miss Woodman, "that'll do. We

can't have a scene here, you know. You wouldn't like Miss Hunter to get you into a home. You're much better off here."

"She wouldn't dare put me in a home. She's got to keep me under her eye, from now till the day I die. That's what frightens me," she added in a rapid mumble, "she'll get tired presently, tired of me, I mean, not of my money. And then what will happen?"

"You'd better come straight home," said Miss Woodman, "and don't let anyone else hear you talk like that. Why, you're practically accusing her of planning to murder you."

That evening Alice couldn't sleep, and had to have recourse to the sleeping-draught Miss Woodman had given her on her first night. "I hope you didn't leave the stuff in her room," said Laura, sharply. "We don't want a scandal!"

"I don't think she's got any idea of taking her own life," said Miss Woodman.

"These deranged people. What's the matter? Why do you look like that?"

"It's a funny thing," said the housekeeper, slowly. "You'd never think she was deranged to hear her talk. She was telling me the other day that when she was living in Bridgmont Road by Notting Hill Gate she went to Purley for her meat, and Williams for her groceries. Now I was in service in Bridgmont Road before the war, and the lady I was with went to Purley, though she got her groceries at the Universal Stores. It's funny, isn't it, that she should know about Purley?"

"Not in the least," snapped Laura. "She's heard me speak of him. And then it's stamped on the ration book, I dare say."

"When you change your retailer they stick a bit of

paper over the original name, at the Food Office," Miss Woodman reminded her.

"Do they? Yes, of course. Then she must have heard me mention the name. It's quite probable I said this meat we get from Young's isn't a patch on what Purley used to send. There's nothing very mysterious about that." She managed a hard little laugh. "You look as if you thought you'd made some wonderful discovery."

"There's another thing," continued Miss Woodman, not in the least discomposed by her companion's scorn. "That ring she wears. Do you know what initials are inside it?"

"How on earth should I?"

"To A.W. from M.H. They're the initials of the late Mr. and Mrs. Hunter."

"Did she think that up herself? How cunning these mad people are."

"If she is mad," conceded Miss Woodman.

"If?" Up came Laura's head with a jerk. By a trick of the lamplight—there was no electricity at The Cottage—an enormous shadow appeared on the wall behind the housekeeper's head, a menacing shadow, full of power. "If I were superstitious," thought Laura, "that would have given me quite a turn." And to show that she was perfectly unmoved she repeated, "What do you mean by If?"

"I was just thinking—suppose she is Miss Hunter?"

"Suppose? That's absurd. "I've told you——"

"That you're Alice Hunter. I know. But so has she. It's a problem, isn't it?"

"Her whole existence is a problem, but I don't see any solution to it."

"Not a satisfactory one," agreed the other. "But then no solution could be satisfactory to everybody, could it? You see, I've been thinking a good deal during these weeks. Mr. Finnemore's never so much as seen her; not that it would help a lot, if he did. Still, he never has. This Mrs. Brownlow who was in hospital hasn't been asked down."

"I understand she's convalescing in the country," snapped Laura, who knew nothing of the kind. "She's been very ill indeed."

"If Miss Freke was to go and see her. . . ."

"You mean, you think Mrs. Brownlow might be able to convince her she isn't Miss Hunter?"

"I mean, I think she ought to have a chance to say—perhaps—she is."

The silence lasted so long that it seemed to harden like concrete, and Miss Freke's first feeble attempts at speech made no impression whatever on the solid surface. During those minutes she couldn't believe her ears. This was something she had never considered.

When she thought the silence had lasted long enough Miss Woodman said coolly, "Now, don't get me wrong. I don't want to make trouble. You say you're Miss Hunter and there's no reason why I shouldn't believe you. It must be nice to be independent after all those years. I've always thought there's nothing like a little money of your own to make you feel life's worth living. Always being in someone else's house, at their beck and call p'r'aps, well, sometimes you do begin to think at least in the grave if they ring bells you won't hear. We've got a lot in common, really, haven't we? The Colonel's lady and Judy O'Grady, though I don't think you're quite the Colonel's lady, if I may say so."

"What on earth *are* you trying to say?" demanded Miss Freke in a voice that she hoped sounded commanding. But of course it didn't. It came out like a croak.

"Just that it must be nice when you're getting on—and I'm no chicken myself—to feel you've got a little financial security. Work palls after a bit, doesn't it? and it's nice to be the one that gives the orders for a change, isn't it?"

Her eyes stared straight into Laura's. "Poor Miss Freke!" she said gently. "We'll both have to take great care of her, won't we?"

That was the first time Laura thought of murder.

CHAPTER TEN

MISS HUNTER—the real one—was looking out of the window of the living-room when she heard a sound she instinctively associated with London: she was no countrywoman and she still thought of Piccadilly Circus when she saw cars, and the Great West Road when she heard a motor bicycle. This was a car, a very small one, but still a car, and it was so surprising in this forgotten corner of life to hear anything linking it to reality that she simply stood staring, like someone in a fairy tale who sees a toad turn into a prince.

"A car—here?" she thought. "Where can it be going to?" For she had walked up the lane, accompanied by the indefatigable Miss Woodman, and knew it for a blind alley, ending in a thicket, that in its turn gave way to alleged impenetrable woodland. She'd never gone any farther. Both Miss Freke and Miss Woodman said they had no bumps of locality and they didn't want to be food for the crows before they need be.

"It would be nice to walk in the woods," Alice said one day when they were out, but Miss Woodman assured her sensibly, "*You'd* be lost in no time. You've no notion what they're like. Nobody comes back. They say they're full of skeletons."

" Who says so ? "

" Why, people round about." Miss Woodman sounded a little testy.

" I didn't know there were any people round about. I've never seen any."

" There's a village at Great Moreton."

Alice began to laugh. " Is that our postal address ? "

" Yes."

" I wonder what Little Moreton's like." She stooped suddenly and picked up a big stone.

" She's mad all right," thought the alarmed housekeeper. " What are you doing with that ? " she asked aloud.

Alice chuckled. " Looking for Little Moreton," she said.

" Come along and act sensibly," Miss Woodman adjured her sharply. " Besides, there are snakes in the wood."

" It's surprising where you can find snakes," said Alice in earnest tones. " Practically anywhere. Railway carriages, for instance."

Miss Woodman wasn't going to listen to any more of that nonsense. Mind you, she didn't really think Alice was cracked. But it was what her mother had told her—how long ago ? " A girl's got to think of herself, Bertha. Never you forget that." She was thinking of herself now. Those fears that sometimes rode her in the dark hours were retreating rapidly, fears of being too old for the job and not having enough to live on. People like her were never able to save a lot, and the Government pension might be all right for those with married children to whom they could go as paying guests, but a single woman had overheads such people never dreamed of. So it was worth a good deal to her to keep in with Miss Freke and share her ill-gotten gains. If anyone had told her that this is what is known technically as blackmail she would have been horrified. She had spent her life being paid for obliging and this was simply obliging in another form. She really did see it like that. Already she was planning the letter she would write to her erstwhile employers, explaining that Miss Hunter had an invalid friend given to fits—that sounded better than saying she was out of her head—and she, Bertha Woodman, had considerable influence over her, so much so that Miss Hunter had begged her to stay on and she'd decided to accept. The Mowbrays wouldn't be pleased, of course, but generosity had never been their strong suit, and at all events now they wouldn't have to wonder whether they ought to make up the State pension to what their housekeeper would consider a living wage. (If she'd only known it the Mowbrays would probably have thrown a champagne dinner with delight at the news; they were all terrified of Bertha, so terrified they didn't dare give her notice.) But as it happened the letter was never written. Because, as the cinema would probably have said, Death Won The Race.

But Bertha hadn't considered that eventuality on this particular bright morning.

It was a month since the momentous conversation between the two women in whose hands Alice's fate lay, and so far Bertha had made no further reference to it. She seemed perfectly satisfied with her position. But Laura wasn't deceived. The woman was biding her time, and by prolonging the suspense was strengthening her own case. For Laura was inwardly afraid. She had reached a stage where she could neither halt nor retreat; she must plod ahead, and one day, round a corner, she would find Miss Woodman waiting for her, presenting her terms. And no matter how savage they were, Laura knew she could not reject them. It would be a case of unconditional surrender. As Alice would have remarked: " Oh what a tangled web we weave, When first we practise to deceive!"

Clearly this state of things could not continue indefinitely. For years Laura had thought of herself as a slave, but she had had a minimum of freedom even then; she could take her luck in her hands and walk out of a job, and no one could stop her. But now, like Abraham's ram, she was caught in a thicket. But, unlike the ram, she had no intention of dying as a sacrifice. No, that portion she reserved for another.

On the morning when the unexpected visitor came to The Cottage she was busy in her room, laboriously typing, laying plans of which she spoke to no one; Bertha was in the kitchen, which was at the back of the house, and Alice was reading a novel by Angela Flower in the parlour. So it was that she was the only member of the trio to hear the little car come chugging up the lane. In her own rather mutton-headed way she was not without courage and, though she couldn't as yet see a way out of her present impasse, she had by no means given up hope. She knew, of course, that Miss Freke, with Bertha's assistance, had spread the rumour that she was daft. Once or twice when they had been out they had met other dwellers in this remote spot, and heads had turned quickly each to each, voices had whispered, and, though she couldn't hear what they said, she knew perfectly well they were telling one another that there was the poor crazy woman who didn't even know who she was. Not that she attracted a lot of attention. People in country districts don't find zanies either rare or exciting. She was just a poor old so-and-so, who was lucky to have friends to keep her out of an asylum. No romantic story was connected with her, at no time had her appearance given ground for romantic speculation, and they forgot her as soon as she was out of sight. But the seeds had been well enough sown for them to accept the story Laura had put out without any hesitation.

When the car stopped at their own gate Alice drew the curtains aside and looked out with interest. A young man was alighting, a young man, as it happened, remarkably like Miss Flower's heroine. Miss Hunter ran to the door. The hall was empty ; upstairs Miss Freke was laboriously typing. " My typewriter," thought Alice bitterly. " It'll be ruined for me now." In the kitchen Bertha was running the tap. Nobody heard the parlour door open or Alice emerge. She had the front door wide and was down at the gate all in a flash. The young man had just set his hand on it and he looked at her in surprise.

" Oh ! Good morning," he said, " I have a letter for Miss Hunter. I wonder if she's in."

" I am Miss Hunter," said Alice.

The young man looked troubled. " I'm afraid there's some mistake."

" There is, but that's not my fault. I'm sure I've done my best to put it right."

He knew then who she was, this poor woman with a complex about being somebody else.

" Is—er—the other Miss Hunter in ? " asked the young man.

Alice stood blocking the gateway like a determined little bull. He couldn't very well push her aside, and he couldn't start bawling at the top of his voice, like someone shouting to be rescued. The story would be all over Bath in forty-eight hours, don't ask him how, but in this part of the country, and probably everywhere else for all he knew, winds, trees, the very dust on the roads, seemed to pick up rumours and spread them as birds spread the seeds of plants and berries on their flight.

" You mean Miss Freke ? Yes, she is. She's typing.

Listen, you can hear it." She leaned forward and put her hand on the young man's arm. "You would think a person who says she's had a typewriter six years—well, nearly six—would type faster than that, wouldn't you? Mind you, I know it wasn't a new machine, but it had been reconditioned. It really isn't fair to the typewriter."

Politely Peter Finnemore listened. He knew exactly how the woman in the room upstairs was working. She was looking along the lines for the appropriate letters. It was the way he typed himself. Every now and again she found three or four close together, or else remembered their position on the keyboard and there was a little rush of click, click, clicks, and the another pause while her eyes scanned the keys. There might be something in what this old girl said, he reflected, but then most likely Miss Hunter had never mastered the art of speed-typing. That didn't seem to him surprising; he was quite sure he never would himself.

"I don't know who you are," Alice continued.

"I've come from Miss Hunter's lawyers."

"You're not Mr. Finnemore."

"Well, actually, yes." He smiled. Such a charming smile. "That is, I'm his nephew—his great-nephew, in fact, but he prefers it the other way."

"I can't think why you want to spend your life in a lawyer's office," said Alice, unexpectedly. "Helping people to cheat other people. That's all it is."

Peter Finnemore chuckled; he couldn't help it. He'd heard worse definitions of his profession.

He said, "My uncle's sent me out with a document that requires Miss Hunter's signature. He didn't think it would be necessary to bring her all that way, and as I had a call in this direction. . . ."

What Cornelius Finnemore had said was, "I cannot stand that woman in my office again. Take that rattletrap of yours and get her signature ; you can do it after your call at Bayleys to see the house. And for goodness' sake don't let her inveigle you into conversation, unless she's prepared to pay for it at the current rate."

Peter Finnemore, delighted to get out of the old bustard's presence for a bit, cranked up The Matchbox, as his Austin 7 was known locally, and went off.

" If she can spare the time," he now said to the real Miss Hunter, with a display of charm that would have sent Miss Flower's heroine off her head with delight—but she interrupted him.

" It's a question of whether you can," she retorted in her rather unexpected way. " Spare the time to right an injustice, I mean. Because I *am* Alice Hunter and one day I shall be able to prove it. But, of course, I do need an ally. They scarcely let me out of their sight. I'm trying to win this housekeeper person round. If I could get to London again I feel sure I could establish my identity." The undying flame burning before the tombs of numerous Unknown Warriors all over Europe had nothing on the flame of hope resolutely flaring away in Alice's solid bosom. " Or if someone could make her talk about the past she'd soon trip herself up. Ask her what my mother looked like. She wouldn't know. How could she ? She never set eyes on her. Or get her to describe the assistants at Williams'—that was my grocers. Or the name of the man who left the milk. He was Percy and he had red hair. She might make one or two lucky guesses, but she'd be bound to be caught out eventually. But that's the worst of the law. They never do the sensible, straightforward thing. They have to go round corners, like a cat that always takes the longest way home, or so they say. We never had a cat, Mother didn't like them. Now that would be another point. Ask her for the name of the last tabby we had. She might pretend she'd forgotten, but it wouldn't matter what name she said because there never was a tabby. It all seems as if it should be so simple, but that's the trouble. It's just because of that nobody believes me. Nobody thinks these things can happen, though they accept them all right in films and books."

She looked as if she was prepared to spend the day at the gate, but at that moment Miss Woodman came looking for her and found the front door open. She came hurrying down the path.

"Now, Miss Freke, you know you're not supposed to hang about in the cold like this. Without even an extra woolly on. You'll have pneumonia before you know where you are."

"I've never had pneumonia in my life," said Alice, coolly. "And as for not knowing where I am, it would have been more to the point if you'd said before anyone else knows. Because they will, one of these days. I don't believe justice will always be defeated. One of the poets—I forgot which, I have so many other things to remember just now—said Murder may go unpunished for a time, but tardy justice will defeat the crime."

"You'd better go quietly indoors," said Bertha Woodman, firmly. "Murder, indeed! Who's talking of murder?"

She didn't realise then that quite soon everybody was going to be, using everybody in its normal restricted sense.

She turned to the young man. "I don't know what you wanted, but we don't buy at the door."

"I——"

"And I thought we had to buy petrol with dollars. And then you can go careering round the country trying to make people part with money they haven't got. What's the matter? Miss Freke, I said go indoors."

"I'm going," said Alice cheerfully. "Only you'd better be careful. That woman won't like it if you upset her lawyer. He might even begin to ask questions and discover the truth, and that wouldn't suit her book at all. It makes the devil blush, you know. Not that I've ever seen *her* blush."

"Have you come from Mr. Finnemore?" asked Bertha, bluntly.

The young man tried to explain.

"If you'd rung the bell like a Christian it would have saved a lot of time," Bertha assured him. "And surely you could see you were talking to a sick woman."

Alice stuck valiantly to her guns. "Not nearly so sick as That Woman's going to be when she's found out."

"My uncle thought he could save Miss Hunter a journey," Peter explained.

"Men," muttered Miss Woodman, hustling Alice up the path. "Always trying to think for somebody else, and generally doing it wrong. How do you know Miss Hunter wouldn't rather have come into Bath? Now you've upset Miss Freke and we shall probably be days getting her calmed down."

"I'm not the least upset," said Alice, undaunted. "He——" But she wasn't allowed to finish that sentence, for Laura, hearing all these voices, now came hurrying through the hall to demand what on earth was going on.

"There was no need for Mr. Finnemore to send specially," she said, with what seemed to the gentler Alice a strange lack of grace. "A letter——"

"There is a point to be explained. And then the document requires witnesses."

"Miss Woodman can witness it for me, and no

doubt you are competent." She whisked the young man off with such resolution that Alice was reminded of the old-time pantomime with Nellie Wallace disappearing through a trap-door.

Bertha Woodman had tightened her lips till they were like a crack in a concrete slab. " Whatever came over you, going out like that ? " she said. " What were you talking about before I came ? "

" Myself," said Alice. " It's not often I get the chance."

" I don't doubt you talked a great deal of nonsense."

" I don't believe he thought so," said Alice. " Wouldn't it be wonderful if he took my side, and tried to help me ? "

" Have you been asking him ? "

" I just told him the facts. He looks a sensible sort of young man."

" He can't have much sense if he paid any attention to what you said."

Alice looked at her with dismay. " You said that just like That Woman does. I thought you were beginning to be a bit shaken yourself. Do you really believe in your heart of hearts she's Alice Hunter ? "

" I'm a housekeeper, not a private detective. Why on earth shouldn't I ? "

" You listened to me so sympathetically. I was beginning to hope——"

Miss Freke came out into the hall accompanied by the young man. " Thank Mr. Finnemore for taking the trouble," she said, " but it's perfectly simple for me to come into his office if he wants a document signed, and it's not very convenient having people at the house just now. I have trouble enough."

The young man sounded horribly embarrassed. " It's very good of you," he muttered.

Alice leaned over the staircase. " It's not good of her at all. She simply hasn't any choice. It's like No Cross, No Crown. No Miss Hunter, no stolen treasure."

Bertha Woodman's hand closed furiously on her arm ; with the other she covered the reckless mouth.

" If you're not careful it won't be possible to keep you here," she said in threatening tones.

" Nothing would please me more," retorted Alice, pulling free from the other's restraining grip. " Don't hold me like that. I believe I could have a case against you for assault." She tore up the remaining stairs, barging Miss Woodman against the banisters, so that the breath was driven out of the woman's body. Alice dashed into the bathroom and locked the door. As Peter Finnemore walked down the path, privately resolved never to step through that gate again, she leaned out of the bathroom window and bawled, " Don't believe what they tell you. It's a trick, a plot. But they shan't defeat me." Miss Woodman banged on the door.

" Miss Freke, be quiet at once."

Miss Freke—the real one—came into the garden and turned her malevolent sallow face up at the gesticulating figure.

" I could have you certified," she threatened.

" Try," shouted Alice, secure in the knowledge that they couldn't break down the door. " That 'ud cook your goose for you." She saw Peter getting back into his car. " Remember, I'll pay all the expenses to get justice done," she screamed after him. " I shall have the money when I get my rights."

They seemed to Peter like three madwomen, and of the three he preferred the one they called Miss Freke. She was desperate and possibly dotty, but she hadn't got the rat-trap mouth and stony eyes of the other two. And if there was a shadow of doubt, if, say, she really was Alice Hunter, what an appalling situation for her. It haunted him all the way back.

In The Cottage the two women held a consultation. Alice had been summarily pushed into bed and the door locked, for, of course, there was a key, though Miss Freke had no intention of letting Alice have it.

" I can't imagine how you think this will do you any good," said Laura, through white lips. " You'll simply have persuaded him you're completely insane."

" Then why don't you look more pleased ? " demanded Alice. " That's what you want everyone to think, isn't it ? Shall I tell you why you don't make any move ? Because you daren't, because you know that would be the way to uncover the truth."

She drew the sheet over her head. " I'm tired and I've nothing more to say at the moment. I'm going to sleep, and by the time I wake up perhaps that young man will have come back with a posse of policemen. A posse," she repeated, smiling. It made them sound so very important calling them that.

CHAPTER ELEVEN

PETER FINNEMORE drove back in a very thoughtful frame of mind. His uncle greeted him with characteristic impatience.

"You young men!" he scolded. "No sense of time. All this work waiting to be done." He waved a bony arm at a pile of correspondence. "Did you see the Bayley property?"

"Yes, sir. Mrs. Bayley is coming in to see you to-morrow about some of the clauses in the proposed lease. She wants them toned down."

"Toned down?" The old man stared. "Do you mean to say it isn't signed?"

"Oh yes, she signed it all right, but——"

"Well, if it's signed there's nothing more to be done about it."

"That's what you think," said the young man, irreverently. "Mrs. Bayley looked as if she was going on and on, like the dormouse's tail."

This literary allusion escaped Mr. Finnemore. "Stuff and rubbish," he thought. "Once a document's signed there's nothing you can do about it, except tear it up, and that wouldn't happen, because the document was now in the possession of the firm.

"And Miss Hunter?" he next inquired. "You saw her?"

"I saw them both," said Peter.

"Both?"

"Both the Miss Hunters."

"Are you stark staring mad? There's only one."

"Oh, in law, yes. But there are two ladies at The Cottage claiming to be Miss Hunter."

" So long as you got the right one's signature—I take it you did ? "

" You mean, the one who came here ? Yes."

" That is Miss Hunter."

" I—suppose so. Did it ever occur to you, sir, that there might be something in the other woman's story ? It's a tall tale, I admit."

" My dear boy, there are times when I wonder if we shall ever make a lawyer of you. Don't you know that our first duty is to make things easy for our clients, who are always right, except when they come in conflict with ourselves ? For heaven's sake, don't start stirring up mill-ponds."

" Not much of a mill-pond at The Cottage," said Peter. " You know, it's like a Chekhov play."

" These foreigners ! " grunted the old man. " Pinero was good enough for us."

" Made my blood run cold. Those two rounding up the poor old dear who thinks she's been defrauded."

" Upon my soul, sir," exploded the old gentleman, " I cannot imagine how you ever faced German troops if the sight of a couple of determined old maids can make you turn pale."

" Even Germans are human beings," murmured Peter. And then the telephone rang and Mr. Finnemore's attention was distracted to more important events.

Not much of a mill-pond at The Cottage, Peter had said, and in the parlance of his contemporaries, how right he was. After Miss Hunter was bundled into bed the two women whose livelihood (futures anyway) largely depended on her staying in that state of life where, not Providence, but Laura Freke had chosen to call her, put their iron-grey heads together to consider a future policy.

"We can't take all these risks," said Laura, decidedly. "One of these days she'll convince someone her absurd story is true, and they'll start making trouble. All we want is a little peace."

And the money, of course, but that was so obvious it wasn't necessary to mention it.

They had laid the foundations pretty well. All the neighbourhood knew that the newcomer to The Cottage was a bit loose in the upper story, had delusions and might at any minute think she was Princess Elizabeth or even Helen of Troy. All the same, it would be unwise to let her go about unchaperoned. The world, even nowadays, contains plenty of philanthropists, nosey people at best, only too anxious to redress wrongs, real or imaginary. Once let a member of this dangerous class get hand-in-glove with stammering desperately-earnest Alice Hunter, and not only would the fat be in the fire but Laura Freke would probably be in jail, and though, in that event, she wouldn't have to bother about finding the rent or the housekeeping money, it wasn't a solution that appealed to her in the least. If you'd asked her, she would probably have said she wished she had never embarked on this dangerous adventure, but it wouldn't have been true. Now that she had handled money she could never go back to emulating the meek spinster in attendance on the Misses Turnbull. She had tasted blood, as Miss Woodman would have put it, and no less fiery diet would satisfy her again.

Well, then, they must ensure that no one could take poor Alice seriously. She was a bit queer, anyway; Miss Freke had thought that from the start. Well, people who talk to themselves and imagine they're Gracie Fields or the current Miss Blackpool can't be called normal. But that weakness might be exploited. This precious pair were in a very strong position, in that neither of them had a particle of compassion. And it isn't necessary to use physical force, not in a brutal manner, that is, to achieve the objective they had in mind. Like two witches they sat plotting over the fire.

After Peter Finnemore's visit Alice became gradually conscious of a change in the atmosphere. She formed a habit of suddenly looking over her shoulder when she walked down the stairs, because Something was watching her from the floor above. Sometimes at night she would hear the sound of an opening door, just as she had heard it in the railway carriage, and know that the Eye was watching her in the dark. She sat in the little garden under a tree and presently she would begin to freeze into immobility; for the windows behind her were full of eyes, so that she dared not turn her head. But if ever she did she saw no more than a curtain falling into place. Or perhaps it was the wind stirring the folds, and why should she, why should anyone, be afraid of the wind? She would come resolutely back to the house, and as she closed the garden door the sound would echo through the passages and on the staircase. Other doors would close softly, but when she rushed in a frenzy to the morning-room Miss Freke would be seated at her desk, while the normal sounds of activity would emanate from the kitchen.

" Who is in the house? " she would ask passionately. " Who, besides ourselves? "

And Laura would say, " Calm yourself, my dear. There is no one, no one at all. It is just your famous imagination playing tricks with you."

" The house is bewitched," she muttered. " I must get away, get away."

A day or so afterwards, creeping down the stairs, for if she moved very softly there was no echo, she heard voices in the hall. Laura was speaking. " Oh

I have taken steps about that," she was saying. " I'm not lost to all sense of responsibility. The local car hire service have been warned to pay no attention to her, if she should contrive to send them a letter. And in any case, since she is never left alone in the house for a single instant, no car can come without one of us seeing it, and explaining the situation."

" Suppose she got as far as the high road and asked for a lift ? " inquired Miss Woodman. " You can't warn every passing motorist."

" It's most improbable that she should get so far unperceived. Under our new arrangement she is always watched by one or the other. It makes things a little strenuous for us, of course, but it is best, and it may not be for so long, after all."

Alice crept back to her room ; her heart beat so fast she thought it would stifle her. Until now, she told herself, she had not really appreciated the extent of her imprisonment. Hope, that dauntless plant, had kept itself alive even in this frosty air ; one day, perhaps to-morrow, perhaps next week, the miracle would happen, somehow she would get away. She never got down to planning the details, but this couldn't be the end of her life. " Why, I believe she would not even stop short of murdering me," she reflected.

That night Miss Freke put on the radio. " I believe there is an excellent play," she observed. " Shut off from life as we are here, it is nice to feel ourselves in touch with the world."

Had she known the nature of the play ? Alice was sure of it. They had articles on the week's drama in *The Radio Times*. She had never seen a copy of *The Radio Times* lying about, but that didn't mean it wasn't somewhere in The Cottage. The play was very gruesome and very exciting. A rich woman was enticed, by means of an advertisement, to a lonely cottage in the country as a paying guest. Here various misfortunes befell her. The cottage was surrounded by an impenetrable wood, where she ventured and lost her way; coming home by an unfamiliar path she found a ramshackle shed and in the shed a spade bearing evidence of recent use and a woman's hat that clearly hadn't been there long. It wasn't the sort of hat any village woman would wear; and that night in her room she found herself in absolute darkness, her candle burnt out, her match-box empty, while footsteps came stealing along the corridor, the handle of the door rattled, and then a voice, speaking in a low sepulchral tone, whispered, "It's locked, but no matter. There is another way in."

The woman shrieked. Alice sprang to her feet. "Turn it off," she cried. "Turn it off. The B.B.C. has no right to put on such a play. It is enough to send people in lonely places out of their minds."

"But Miss Woodman and I are enjoying it," Laura protested. Miss Woodman sat with them in the evenings now, knitting interminably.

"What are you making?" Alice asked once.

"A very useful object," said Miss Woodman.

And a quotation from the poetry she had read so ravenously in her earlier years flashed into Alice's mind.

The shroud is done, Death muttered, toe to chin.
He snapped the ends and tucked the needles in.

"You're not alone in a cottage in a wood," the housekeeper reinforced Laura's protest. "You're all right with us, you know."

And Laura said softly, "Quite all right. You do know that, don't you? Why, no one could harm you. You're never out of the sight of one or other of us.

That should reassure you; shouldn't it, Miss Woodman. Even when you're in the garden we're watching, even though you may not know we're there."

"I knew," said Alice, in a stifled voice. "You're always there, about my bed and in all my ways. Don't think I don't see through your plan. You mean to drive me mad, really mad, and then you can have my money for ever."

The weeks went on and it was high summer. The sun lay in sheets of gold over the lawn, and the birds went mad in the trees. And Miss Hunter fought desperately to prevent herself from following their example. The persecution was worse now; the only shoes she was allowed were bedroom slippers; if she said she'd like to go out and it wasn't convenient for either of her companions, her shoes would disappear altogether.

"They want resoling," Laura would say. "Miss Woodman took them in." And she would add, "You really should draw something out of your Post Office account and get another pair. I'm sure you wouldn't like to feel you were in debt."

"I haven't got a Post Office account," said Alice wildly. She wondered what they were doing about her banking account. Once, when Miss Freke's bag fell open, she saw a number of notes (stuffed with notes, it was, you might say), and the corner of a registered envelope. Actually, Laura had put her own plan into action. Alice's signature was not difficult to copy and anything odd could be put down to the damaged hand. Anyhow, Mr. Finnemore had accepted her, and the bank, having once agreed to allow money to be drawn on a local account, made no trouble. The capital stayed at the bank in the Wimbledon suburb, and the cashiers at Yarborough saw no reason to suspect a phony signature. But though the plan seemed running smoothly enough on the surface, it was built on a very insecure foundation. Laura had, as they say, bitten off rather more than she could conveniently chew. She hadn't only Alice to contend with, there was Miss Woodman as well. Miss Woodman knew when she was on to a good thing, and her native shrewdness prevented her from doing anything that might render her liable to police action. But her demands were becoming heavier; she wanted more liberty, less labour and more money, always more money. She suggested that if Miss Hunter (as she scrupulously called Laura) wasn't satisfied, she, Miss Woodman, could seek employment elsewhere. A good housekeeper could easily find a situation, and, of course, when her erstwhile owners of the house returned, she could join up with them again.

"I expect you'll be glad to see them," hazarded Laura.

Miss Woodman folded her hands complacently. "I've been giving a lot of thought to that," she said. "I'm not so young as I was, and there are times when I think I'd like to move into a town or a suburb, say, Having worked hard all my life I feel I'm about due for a rest. I'm sure you see my point, Miss Hunter. Besides, you wouldn't know how to manage without me now, would you?"

Oh yes, Laura saw her point all right. She was right in it now, up to the neck. Scylla and Charybdis, that's how she thought of her two companions. Nothing could help her now, she reflected, but death, and not her own death, of course.

Life seemed to be throwing up one problem after another, but she was a woman of spirit. She had already accomplished a good deal; she intended to accomplish more. And if Miss Woodman's power had increased, poor Alice's had deteriorated. She was no more than a shadow of the woman she had been; in fact, there were times when she seemed to accept the fact that all her claims were delusions, that she really was Laura Freke, and uncommonly lucky to be living in a cottage in the country instead of being incarcerated in an asylum. " Time," Laura told herself, " is of the essence of the plan." And, like some plump remorseless spider, she sat in her web, scheming the destruction of the wretched fly.

And then one afternoon, while Laura was sitting by the little fire an unexpected wet day made pleasant even in that princely summer, Miss Woodman made her plans known. She came marching in without so much as by your leave or the pretence of wanting to know anything to do with her duties; she had put on a rather handsome black dress and a large gold brooch; and she sported her best shoes, an ominous sign. She discarded the apron she normally wore and nothing about her, her manner least of all, suggested that she was in a subordinate position. Her first words made it clear that the impression thus created was intentional.

" She's sleeping," she announced casually, crossing to the other side of the hearth and sitting down uninvited. " We don't want her snooping, do we, so this seems as good a time as any to come to an understanding."

Laura tried to stand on her dignity. " Really, I don't think I altogether appreciate——"

" Now there's no sense coming the high-and-mighty over me," Miss Woodman told her coolly. " Of course, if you don't want to hear what I've come to say, I can go and see this Mr. Finnemore for myself. It rests with you."

" What good do you imagine that would do you?" Laura demanded.

" He might be interested in what I had to tell him —about *her*, I mean." Miss Woodman's tone suggested she really didn't care which course she adopted.

" I doubt it," said Laura. " He's already had letters."

" I could offer him more than letters. What about the ring ? "

" A mere coincidence."

" I know coincidence has a long arm, but it's not an octopus. And then he might think it funny that she should know so much about the shops round Ennismore Terrace. And the white poodle at No. 16 and the Scottie at 23. Oh yes, she talks to me a lot. People like her that don't get about much notice everything. And if inquiries were started it wouldn't be very nice for you, would it ? You couldn't have two people in a house claiming loss of memory."

" What is all this leading to ? " Laura leaned back as carefully as if she were made of some brittle substance that might break were it too roughly handled. And, indeed, at this juncture that was how she felt.

" I thought we might come to an arrangement." Miss Woodman had her plans all cut and dried. She knew what she wanted and what she intended to have. But she was shrewd, too. No sense killing the goose that lays the golden eggs. Even so the terms seemed to Laura unbearably harsh. But she had no choice. She was bound to accept them. It wasn't only the money, though that was bad enough, but she was entering into a compact with a woman she feared and detested, who could increase her terms at any time. It's all very well to say that people who are being blackmailed can approach the police, but that doesn't always solve the problem. It didn't in Laura's case.

Having made her bargain Miss Woodman passed on to her next point.

" I don't know if you're aware of it," she said, " but people are beginning to talk."

" Village gossip." Laura sounded disdainful.

" You can't get round it that way," Miss Woodman assured her in sharp tones. " Here you are with someone you say is ill, someone who perhaps hasn't long to live."

That jolted Laura all right. " I never suggested——"

" I only said perhaps." Miss Woodman was as cool as the proverbial cucumber. " Well, suppose anything did happen, you know what would follow like the night the day ? An inquest. People might think it funny you'd never had a doctor to her, if she was as bad as you make out. You wouldn't like an inquest, you take my word. I was in a house once where they had one, and the police came in, and the people had to move. Oh, I don't mean they could prove anything, but—well, nobody cares for anonymous letters and stones through windows with messages written round them."

" What earthly good do you imagine the doctor could do ? " Laura demanded.

" You and me may know it would be a waste of time, but there's the village to consider. Besides, just suppose she was to pass on ? Nobody lives for ever, and you might just as well be dead as moulder here for the rest of your days. If she'd seen the doctor, then there wouldn't be any trouble about the certificate."

" You talk as though you could dictate to the doctor as well as to me," burst out Laura. " Suppose she starts talking to him ? "

" That'll be all right," said Bertha. " I've thought that bit out, too. Now, the doctor we've got to get is Dr. Mack. The regular one, the one everybody has, is Dr. Lee. They say he's very good, very sympathetic ;

that washes him out for us. Dr. Mack's retired really; he came here nearly a year ago and took the Old Vicarage. Lives there with a housekeeper."

"If he's retired," Laura began, but Miss Woodman said quickly:

"Oh, he goes out now and again. Only most people don't want him, see?" She tilted her elbow suggestively. "That's his trouble. By tea-time he doesn't know a migraine from a meningitis. Mind you, I don't say there was any scandal, I don't know. But seeing he's not much past sixty he didn't retire on the score of age."

"Do you know him?"

"I've no call for doctors, I thank my stars. The Miss Mowbrays had their own man all the way from Bath. No, he wouldn't know me from Eve if we met in the streets, except that I'd be more decent-like. That's why we have to have him."

"If he'll come."

"He'll come. You go down and spin a yarn. He likes it to be thought he's preferred to Dr. Lee."

"I still don't understand why you're so eager. . . . To my mind, it's too risky."

"That's because you haven't thought. Y'see, it's all very well for you to say she's barmy. . . ."

"There's you . . ."

"Ah, but someone might suggest you were making it worth my while to back you up. People have such suspicious minds."

"I still think it's dangerous," said Laura flatly. "No sense putting one's head in the lion's mouth. She mightn't need a doctor for years. She seems healthy enough."

"Still, people can have accidents. I haven't told you my plan yet." She leaned back and began to outline it.

Laura gasped. "That's dangerous, too."

"A question of two evils," said Miss Woodman in a hard voice. "Anything else is more dangerous still."

So, not without some further demur on Miss Freke's part, it was arranged. Poor Alice! She was in a tight spot when she only had Laura to contend with, but the addition of this hard merciless woman set the seal on any hopes she may have cherished of ultimate salvation.

CHAPTER TWELVE

PETER FINNEMORE's holiday came in June, and, like a bird winging its way to its nest, he went up to London. He didn't want to go abroad, and couldn't have afforded it in any case. Besides, no town on the Continent could give him anything London couldn't. He had friends there, chaps he'd met in the war, and others he had known earlier still. And London was a place of perpetual encounters. He had absorbed the airman's philosophy of living for the moment. Life at Yarborough with old Great-uncle Corny was dull as tombs; but during the fortnight's vacation anything might happen, the whole course of his life be changed. He would have rearranged the order of the three cardinal virtues, putting hope before charity. Nothing but hope—the hope of something turning up—had kept him at Yarborough so long.

He took his car with him, and got himself a room in a boarding-house near Notting Hill Gate, a ramshackle unpainted sort of a building, not altogether recovered from the blitz. But the food was good and the bed well-sprung and that was all he asked. Most of the other boarders were elderly women getting through the autumn of their lives as comfortably as they could, but there were a few young chaps doing courses or just started on jobs, who couldn't afford luxury any more than he could. And he had his friends and in the evening there were pubs, and he knew a girl or two, and you couldn't be bored or lonely or dull in London, not at twenty-five. And certainly not if you were the sort that had scraped into the Commandos by falsifying your age when you were just seventeen and know life's an adventure and the surface monotony is no more than the brown paper packing on the parcel from Asprey or Fortnum. And feeling that way about it life, of course, didn't disappoint him.

One evening he went into a cinema by himself, being of those who don't feel lost in their own company, and when he came out he dropped off at the local, a pub of some repute called The Sleeping Clergyman. A small red car, so conspicuous you'd notice it ahead of all the magnificent smooth running American models with which London was thronged that summer, was drawing up as he arrived, and a man, as conspicuous as the car, climbed over the side. Peter stopped dead and grinned.

"Well, well," he said, meeting the owner's eye. "I didn't know it could be done."

"There's nothing that can't be done," said the other on the instant. He was the sort of chap you can't forget easily, as conspicuous in his own way as his car, though no one could blame you if you didn't want to meet him in a dark alley by night. He was a square-set fellow in atrocious clothes, with red hair and thick red brows and a face of almost the same red-brown as his suit. Might be anyone, reflected Peter. A commercial traveller, a bookie's tout, a racketeer, Member of Parliament, anything except a meek season-ticket-holder of life.

"I meant the car," said Peter, coming closer. "I thought mine was the original model. I'm planning to leave her to the British Museum when I'm through, but this . . ." His look was so admiring that the owner of The Scourge beamed on him.

"Nice work, isn't she? It's like what your mother tells you when you're young. It's not the dame who looks like a film star who's the most good; get 'em for use, boy, not for show."

They went through the doors of The Sleeping Clergyman together, and the man said, "Crook's the name, Arthur Crook. I——"

"Gosh!" said the young man in a tone of such respect that even Crook was surprised. "Not—not the Criminals' Hope."

"That's the one," said Crook heartily. "Night and day service."

Peter said quickly, "What's yours?" proud of being able to buy the great man a drink. And when the glasses had been filled he said in rather wistful tones, "Your life must be one long excitement."

"Long bein' the operative word," agreed Crook.

"Yes, I hadn't thought of that. I suppose quite a lot of chaps would like to put your light out."

"They try," Crook acknowledged. "No one can say they don't. Adds to the fun really, of course. You'd understand that."

"I?"

"Weren't you in the war? A RAF type. Daresay you had to do a bit of devil-dodging in your time."

"Wouldn't mind being back," Peter acknowledged.

"Cheer up," said Crook. "It's a wicked world. Always something coming or going. London?"

"Bath."

"Lots going on there, they tell me."

"Lots of old women of both sexes." Peter sounded despondent.

Crook sat up so suddenly he nearly upset his beer.

"Don't despise them," he said in vehement tones. "All you chaps are the same. If a fellow don't wear a fur-lined overcoat and a diamond tiepin you write him off a dull dog. Not so. Some of the best cases I've ever known have been among these old women. Miss Martin—Miss Fitzgerald—Miss Pettigrew—talk about the monstrous regiment of women. Leave the out-and-out sharps for the police. That's about all they're capable of dealin' with. The little more and how much it is. . . . And if you tell me there's no mystery in Bath you ought to be seein' one of the specialists at the Throat, Nose and Ear Hospital."

"There are moments," agreed Peter slowly.

"Oh, what a crowded world one moment may contain," exploded Crook, who had a disconcerting habit of quoting from the lesser literary lights when his audience least expected it.

"There is something that haunts me rather. Old Uncle Corny won't listen and he may be perfectly right, but all the same I can't altogether forget it."

"One of your clients?"

"No."

"Then my advice to you is not to touch it with a barge-pole."

"It's too late for that," said Peter. "I've become involved and that gives me a sense of responsibility. If Uncle Corny wasn't so like his name I'd have had a word with the local police, but . . ."

Crook put a hand not much bigger than a ham on his companion's knee. "You listen to your Uncle Arthur," he said impressively. "There's a whole class of the community, and not the silliest class at that, that prides itself on having nothing to do with the police. You join 'em. They're like burrs, the police are. They stick. What's your trouble?"

"Just one of these same old women you were talking

about just now. It may be all moonshine, but—there are damned odd features."

It was Crook's turn to buy the drinks, so he said, "Same again," and this time they carried their tankards by common consent to a table in the corner.

"What's so odd about this old girl?" Crook asked. "Odder than any of the others, I mean?"

"She's convinced she's the victim of an appalling fraud. Oh, I know that's a common enough delusion, but here some of the facts support her case. Tell me, Mr. Crook, if you met a chap in a railway train and there was an accident and he was conked out—only temporarily—would you so to speak adopt him and make your own life infernally difficult and cramped on his account?"

"Not unless it paid me," said Crook simply.

"That's just the point." He took a great swallow from his tankard. "On the surface, it looks as if the old gorgon must be losing money."

"Philanthropist perhaps," said Crook, in the voice of a man who believes in dragons, bogeys and long-legetty beasties.

"I wouldn't say it was that. The poor old soul was chased away directly they heard her talking to me."

"They?"

"There's a housekeeper there, or at least that's what she calls herself."

"And you think they're in a plot?"

"When I said something to Miss Hunter (assuming she's genuine, which I'm beginning to doubt) she said *we* are doing our best. But I've been making some inquiries, just as a matter of human interest, and it seems obvious that our client never met the other one. . . ."

"Call her X," suggested Crook. "Save any misunderstanding."

" Well, she nev met X till they happened to share a carriage to Bath, and it's not as though they found they were soul-m es or any clap-trap of that sort, because there isn't a doubt about it X is dying to get away."

" Thinkin' she may be dyin' in another sense if she stays much longer ? "

" Oh, I don't supp she'd go as far as that."

" When you're my age," said Crook, " you won't be so easily surprised. If you're right and Miss Hunter's keeping this one gainst her will—by the way, you haven't explained why she should ? "

Peter broke into his story ; Crook heard him out without interruption. Then he remarked, " Well, that's one explanation and it could be the right one. It's what they say—*l'audace, l'audace* and *toujours l'audace* (his accent would have defied Mr. Churchill's). Only my way of putting it, and I've said this till it's amazin' my tongue ain't paralysed, is Be bloody, bold and resolute. Well, this dame's the last two, all right, and it could be she'll be the first before she's finished."

Peter looked shocked. " Murder's a serious affair."

" So's impersonatin' somebody else and nickin' her legacy. Of course, if it's all true she's a wicked old woman, but you can't help admirin' her guts."

" I can," said Peter briefly. " I saw the other one—X. She was frightened to death, and this is 1949."

" No reason that I can see to suppose it's a more moral age than any of the other forty-nines," returned Crook coolly. " Taken any steps ? "

" I went round to the house in Ennismore Terrace, pretending not to know Miss Hunter had gone, but I drew a blank there. The landlady had been carted off for an operation—peritonitis it turned out to be—and though of course that was perfectly successful, the way they always are, she died of shock a few days later.

I don't think My One knows that. She talked of getting away and coming to London and imploring this Mrs. Brownlow to come down and get her away."

"No letters?"

"No opportunity of posting them, I'm sure. You know how it is in these remote country places. No pillar-box for a mile and the postman picks up the letters. Well, you can bet your Aunt Fanny's fat cat My One would never be allowed to see the postman, and if she did put a letter out the odds are it 'ud never get farther than the hall."

"For a lawyer," said Crook in dispassionate tones, "you take a lot of liberties. You do realise you haven't got a scrap of proof against the woman who calls herself Hunter?"

"Not yet."

"But you're after it? I see. A bit awkward for you in the circumstances, ain't it?"

"That's just the point. You know, the last thing the poor old soul shouted to me as I was going was that she could pay anyone who got her out of jail. I've been thinking and thinking. D'you believe in fate?"

"I get you," said Crook. "You can't pull the old lady out of the soup, so Providence is goin' to put someone in your path who can. And that someone happens to be me. Trouble is, I live in London."

"There's quite a good train service to Bath."

"Go-slow all the way," they tell me.

"I thought you were interested in these odd old ladies."

"London's full of 'em. Besides, the essence of life is change."

Peter looked very downcast. "You mean, it's not your cup of tea."

"A nice cup, I must say. Let me put it straight. I'm a working man. I'm no Galahad to go round saving potty old dears from worse than death. And if she's really *non compos* she can't hire a lawyer."

"I always heard you were pretty hot stuff at backing outsiders," murmured Peter to his tankard.

"You've got a nerve," retorted Crook, with spirit but without undue heat. "You really are suggestin' I should beetle down and see what's going on."

"Nice place, Bath, if you don't know it," Peter reassured him. "Jane Austen and all that."

Crook groaned. "You're not telling me there's another dame in this?"

Peter echoed the groan. "Forget it," he said hastily. "All the same, it's tantalising."

The shocking thing about that statement, from Crook's point of view, was its truth. It was tantalising. The whole story was so far-fetched, so fantastic, so likely to be instantly dismissed by any sane person as the fabrication of an imbecile, that he felt himself tingling with excitement. It's only on the films that heroines have to be young and fair. Helen of Troy wouldn't have given Mr. Crook a bigger thrill.

Business of an exacting nature kept Crook in London for the whole of the next month. Then his peregrinations took him into the West Country. He didn't precisely have to go to Bath, but even a human atom bomb needs a bit of a holiday now and again, so he drove the long-suffering Scourge into Great Moreton, the nearest town of any size to the Cottage, and that was a miniature model. Naturally he made for the local, and ingratiated himself with the landlord within five minutes of his arrival. He took part in a darts match and staggered everyone by the casual manner of his throwing and the astounding accuracy of his results. Then he settled down to the business of the day—night and day were all alike to him when there was work to be done—which was, first, getting the beer down and second, learning the lay of the land.

It was never hard for him to turn the talk in the direction that suited him best, and pretty soon he had touched on the peculiar household at The Cottage.

"Local mystery," they tell me, he suggested, pushing his tankard across the bar counter and saying, "What's yours?"

Bob Day, the landlord, said, "A mild and bitter, thanking you. That's a queer set-up all right. Not that we see much of that lot here."

"*Crème de la crème*?" asked Crook, his red eyebrows shooting into his hair.

"Ladies," said the landlord as if that explained everything. "Away at the moment, though."

Crook looked disappointed. "I thought two ladies from London were there now."

"Foreigners," agreed Bob Day, to whom anyone outside a radius of fifteen miles deserved that appellation. "Using the place as a private luny asylum from all accounts."

"Whose accounts?"

"There's a woman there, a Miss Woodman, Bertha to her friends, if she's got any, housekeeper to the Misses Mowbray. They all keep themselves to themselves, as they say. Never touch a drop. Don't get it from the grocer either. But Bertha Woodman gets the rations from my sister sometimes. She has the shop at the corner, and it's not much gets past her. Of course, Frostyface, that's the lady in charge of the other one, goes down herself some weeks and then there's nothing doing."

"God bless the squire and his relations and keep us in our proper stations," suggested Crook.

"Summat like that. Still, when old Bertha goes down it's different. They've not been here long, only since the youngest of the Mowbray sisters took some female complaint—too delicate to let on what it really is—and the doctor said she shouldn't be so isolated. No telephone there, see, no electric light even, and if there's a drought heaven help them for water. They wouldn't let Miss Janet go by herself (ever hear of the Siamese twins? well, these are the Siamese triplets), so all three of them went off to Bournehaven; Miss Janet's in a hospital of sorts and the other two live on the doorstep, if I know anything of them."

"And while they're away the foreigners have cashed in on the drought and the housekeeper?"

"That's right. Nobody ever sees the dotty one, though now and again chaps passing, specially of an evening, hear her singing or shouting away. Or hammering on a door or a window. Reckon she's violent. Still, if she can put it over the other two her middle name should be Goliath."

"There were three old maids of Lee," chanted Crook with a suddenness that attracted attention all round. "And there are still three, according to you."

"That's right. Though how long they'll last, don't ask me."

"These loonies go on for ever," Crook assured him. "I should know. They come pourin' into solicitors' offices by the dozen, looking like members of the Witches' Trade Union. Been here long?"

"Came a month or so after Miss Mowbray went off. Been here four months p'r'aps, no, say five. One of them had had an accident, injured the brain, that's the story, and they wanted a quiet place for her. Well, they couldn't have found anything quieter. But it's queer all the same."

Crook looked at him interrogatively.

"I mean, no one ever seeing her, never being allowed out alone."

" Cripple, perhaps," suggested Crook.

" Oh, she goes out, up the lane and a little way into the woods, though never very far, but the housekeeper's always with her. And that's another thing. Bertha Woodman's been at The Cottage as long as we've been at The Heart, seemed set for her century, but now all of a sudden she's saying it's about time she retired." His voice was tinged with scorn. " That's what she says. Retired. Why, what does it amount to but saying the job's got above you and it's time you went on the shelf ? I hope I step straight out of my bar into the churchyard. No shelves for me. Things on shelves get dusty and forgotten."

" Perhaps," suggested Crook thoughtfully, " she's come into a bit."

" Dare say she might if she stayed on with Miss Mowbray. Mind you, there'll be trouble if they come back, two of them, anyhow, and find this Miss Hunter's lost them their housekeeper after twelve years. They're the old-fashioned type of lady, you see, won't eat things out of a tin and never learnt to cook."

" It could be Miss Hunter's offered her more pay."

" That's another queer thing. This other lady, Miss Freke she is, and if one chap round here has said Freke by name and freak by nature, twenty have said it—well, Miss Hunter gives out she's a friend who's been taken bad, but there's no question about it she's no more than ninepence in the shilling."

" Ah, but perhaps the money's hers, and she's paying for the lot of them ? " Crook looked very hard-boiled.

" From all we can learn, and there's not much escapes us in these parts, it's the other way round."

" Mean to say you've never seen the dopey one ? " said Crook.

" No one ever sees her, though my missus heard her once. She was taking a short cut through the woods to see her mother. The old lady lives out beyond The Cottage and don't get much beyond her own gate. Well, she's eighty-five if she's a day and her health's none too good. But if ever a woman enjoyed bad health it's my mother-in-law. Well, as I was saying, the wife was going along through the start of the woods when she heard voices : and there were Dopey and Bertha. The dopey one was chattering away nineteen to the dozen spouting poetry, something about a lost good, and the housekeeper let her run on a bit and then she said, ' Now, Miss Freke, this is all moonshine and you know it. You're making it up as you go along. Do you suppose any sensible person would believe you ?' And Dopey said, ' That young man believed me, I'm sure he did.' My missus never got the hang of who the young man was. ' Well, if he did he hasn't done much about it,' says Bertha, ' and if you want to know what I think he didn't believe a word.' Dopey said something about a robin redbreast in a cage—oh, she's a queer one all right, though, mark you, I don't approve of folk that put robins in cages. It's not even as though they were singing birds. It's against nature."

" And is that all your wife heard ? "

" To tell the truth, she sheered off, not caring much for the set-up. You never know with these queer ones. The last thing she heard was Miss Freke saying, ' One of these days it'll be you in prison, not me,' and then Bertha Woodman began to pull her away towards the house, telling her she should be careful or she'd find herself shut up for good."

" Very comforting," said Crook. " Any more ? "

" I did hear they'd had the doctor to her a week since. Dr. Mack that was. He's an old chap who settled here after the war. Gave out he was injured in the bombing, but injured by the bottle's more like it."

"Come here often?"

"Never puts his nose inside the place. No, one of the ones that drink alone. If you can call it alone."

"Mrs. Mack?" suggested Crook.

"He calls her the housekeeper. He's a fat old chap like a balloon in a waistcoat. Comes from London I did hear tell. Don't know what wind blew him here."

"Still practises though?"

"Goes out now and again, just to keep his hand in. Most of us roundabouts go to Dr. Lee, but some of the old ladies fancy Dr. Mack. More of a bedside manner, I dare say."

"More practice at it, most likely," said Crook, shamelessly.

"Mind you, I dare say he would take on a few more patients if he could get 'em, the right sort, I mean. But he gave out from the start no night work and no babies, so it's no wonder he never caught on. Still, Miss Hunter called him in. Leastways, his car was seen outside The Cottage." He chuckled. "We don't miss much hereabouts."

"I'll say," conceded Crook. "Making a habit of visiting?"

"Just the once is all I heard. Bertha told my sister high blood pressure, might have a stroke any time. Must be kept very quiet, in bed, if possible."

"And, of course, no visitors?"

Bob Day looked surprised. "They don't know anyone hereabouts. Why they came——"

"Could be that is why. Anyone heard the doctor's version?"

"The woman of his——"

"The concubine?"

"She said he came back saying the old lady was

fit for a circus. Thought she was the Pope of Rome or someone. 'You keep away from me,' she told him. 'I know you. You're John Knox,' she said. Reckon she'll do someone a mischief one of these days, if she gets the chance."

Crook put down his tankard. "Someone'll see to it she don't, get the chance, I mean," he replied grimly. He had one for the road and went back to the Scourge. It was too late for visiting to-night, they'd never let him in, not if he said he was the Archangel Gabriel. Probably not much time to lose, he thought. He wasn't a medical man but he knew there are drugs and potions that make people delirious. He didn't know how much the old woman knew, Frostyface, Miss Hunter, call her what you will, but he was ready to bet his reputation she didn't mean the old 'un to come out of The Cottage till she came feet foremost, and here he was right.

It was a night of such tranquil beauty that a man's heart might well turn over. Crook's was turning, too, but not because of the night's magic. He looked down the empty road ahead and then at the heavens where bars of soft, dark cloud striped a sky of night gold. There was a luminous quality in the atmosphere, and the air was soft and pure. The trees stood up very black and still as though they were made of cardboard; but beneath the silence and the calm he was aware of the tremendous activity of the country at night. It was as though under the surface a whole creation toiled and planned, like the creatures in the secret cave of the children's fairy books, making the fairy money, sewing the fairy dresses, while above them the world was sleeping. He had a sense that seldom visited him, a sense of his own impotence. Only a few miles away unspeakable things might be happening. That tale of a mad woman singing and screeching, and hammering on the door unnerved him. He got into the Scourge and drove rapidly in the direction of The Cottage. He only hoped his ears might be refreshed by the sound of turmoil within, but when he reached the house all was perfectly still. The gate was closed, the front door bore an air of impenetrability; the windows stared blank and unlighted. He switched off the engine and sat for a while looking at the house as though he could compel it to reveal its secret. "Or isn't there a secret?" he asked himself, seeking reassurance from a robust imagination. "Is it all as it appears on the surface?" Young Peter Finnemore was a romantic, villagers were gossips, he himself incurably inquisitive. Heaven knew, it all looked simple enough. Two elderly women with a third in attendance, one a bit odd. Only wasn't it even more odd that the housekeeper, who had served her employers docilely enough for twelve years, should suddenly announce her intention of retiring? It looked as if there might be something sinister there. For it would be natural for Miss Woodman to wait for the Misses Mowbrays' return before she gave her decision publicity. After so long it was reasonable to suppose that the old ladies would do something for their henchwoman, and if she wasn't going to wait for them, well, that implied she was, to put it vulgarly, on to a better thing. It all hung horribly well together.

He was still brooding along these lines when a cry fell on his ears, long and melancholy. "Are they torturing her?" he wondered. He turned his head. And began to think there was something dangerous about the whole neighbourhood. For now he could most clearly perceive a great white form materialising apparently against that magical sky. It hung directly opposite him for a moment, then turned, changing shape as it went.

"They'll be putting a strait-waistcoat on me next," reflected Crook. "A damned owl, that's all it was."

He started up the car and began to go back to Great Moreton. He was putting up at the local for the night. Another cry followed him, and he looked over his shoulder, but the owl had disappeared. Still, its cry would carry a long way in so quiet a night, and it could only be his imagination that gave this cry a different, more human quality. The fact was he wasn't made for the country. Put him in any haunted house you pleased in the London area and he wouldn't have turned a hair, but the country . . .

"There's too damned much of it," he said, "and it's all so damned dark."

CHAPTER THIRTEEN

NEXT MORNING, of course, everything looked different and optimistic, as it usually does by daylight. The sun came out, for once there wasn't a fresh Government crisis in the headlines, and the cry he had heard last night had been an owl, of course. Only a loon would think anything else. After breakfast he got out the Scourge and retraced his path to The Cottage. But as he pushed open the gate the sun went behind a cloud, and though he wasn't superstitious this seemed to him an omen of what was to follow. He found himself wondering why anyone had chosen to build a house in this remote place so far from any other human habitation. Instantly sinister thoughts were engendered in the mind, his mind, anyway. He couldn't understand people who love quiet and seclusion for their own sake. Nuts he thought them. If it was quiet you wanted, what was wrong with the grave?

He rang the bell—no electricity, he noted, to judge

from the prolonged clanging that resulted—then stepped back quickly to send a rapid glance over the windows. And so he was in time to see the curtains on an upper floor stealthily parted, and a pale grim face look down on him. He was standing with his back to the door by the time the suspicious eyes focused themselves, but, like the beasts in the Revelation, he appeared to have eyes before and behind.

He waited a minute or two, then rang again. Whoever was within had clearly been waiting on the other side of the door, for it opened an inch or two, and he saw a woman with grey hair unskilfully dressed, wearing the kind of suit that is sold by the dozen in any big stores.

"Who do you want?" said a low harsh voice.

"Crook's the name," he began, and the woman started to close the crack, and would indeed have succeeded but for the toe of a large vulgar brown shoe that the visitor had wisely inserted the instant the door opened.

"There's no one here of that name. You have come to the wrong house."

"Not me," said Crook. "And it's my name I was giving you. I was looking for a Miss Hunter."

"I am Miss Hunter, but——"

"I mean the other Miss Hunter," Crook explained.

"There is no other Miss Hunter."

"No? That's funny. She seemed to think—the other lady, I mean——"

The woman's voice came cold with disdain.

"You are doubtless referring to Miss Freke." But the old girl looked shaken.

"Well, if that's her name. Maybe she's at home now? I understand she don't go out much."

Laura stood her ground. "I don't think you mentioned your business——"

" Guardian angel," said Crook sunnily. " Mention my name in any pub and you'll get a come-back that'll surprise you."

" I cannot imagine how you came in contact with Miss Freke," said the woman icily, " but if you do know her——" She paused. " You don't, do you ? " she said in a cunning voice. " You didn't recognise me."

" Chaps have been good enough to say I can work miracles," said Crook modestly, " but even I have my trade union limits. How come I should recognise you when so far as I know I've never set eyes on you before ? "

" And—you have not met Miss Freke ? "

" Friend of hers asked me to look her up if I was down this way."

" She has no friends." The words burst out before Laura could stop them.

Crook grinned. " You'd be surprised. Well, going to let me see the lady ? "

" This friend of yours," said Laura, " whoever she is, must have warned you that Miss Freke was—well, unbalanced."

The change of tense made him look up sharply. " Was ? " he demanded.

" Yes. I'm afraid you've come too late. Miss Freke is dead."

There was a moment's silence. The occasions when Crook was caught on the wrong foot were few and far between, but this was one of them.

" Too bad," he said, gently, after a minute. " Sudden, wasn't it ? "

" The doctor had told me it might come this way, without warning. Yes, I suppose you could say it was sudden in the sense that no one had suspected the condition of the heart."

" Heart, eh ? "

" Yes. Miss Freke suffered from high blood pressure, and that may have accounted in part for her excitability. And, of course, the concussion from which she suffered at the time of the railway accident, completed the damage."

" Responsible for the heart, too ? " murmured Crook.

" No. That must have been a disease of long standing. But, really, if you want a detailed clinical report on her condition, I can only refer you to the doctor. Dr. Mack at the Old Vicarage, Great Moreton."

" He the chap who signed the certificate ? "

" Yes."

" How long since you knew about the heart ? " Crook asked. " By the way, should I be keeping you standing around ? Maybe——" With an expansive gesture he indicated that there was plenty of room inside the cottage.

" Really, there is nothing for me to add," said Laura, ignoring the tacit proposal. " As I have already told you, the news came to me as a considerable shock. Dr. Mack warned me that the condition was so far advanced that any sudden shock might precipitate a crisis."

" And something—or someone—administered said shock ? "

Laura said very coldly, " Miss Freke died in her sleep."

Crook nodded. " What they call a merciful release."

" Few can have been more so. She was becoming increasingly "—she hesitated, casting about for a suitable word—" unreasonable," she selected. " I question whether we could have kept her very much longer, even in this quiet spot. It involved constant supervision, and if she had managed to elude our surveillance the consequences might have been serious."

"Serious is the word," Crook agreed, thinking, old dame must have been a school-marm in the cradle. "Plenty of talk as it was," he went on in his chatty way.

Laura looked at him with increasing suspicion. Not a gentleman, she noted, always the hardest type to deal with. You would have expected him to take a hint, know when he wasn't wanted. But the elephant had nothing on Crook when it came to being thick-skinned. He seemed as though he'd be perfectly happy to spend the rest of the day leaning against the porch and putting his coolly insolent questions.

"Villagers always gossip," she said disdainfully, "I naturally have no idea what they have been saying."

"You should stand at the cross-roads and lend your ears to the winds," Crook advised her. "You couldn't miss it. Poor old lady. Speaking as a lawyer——"

He could have sworn that at that she turned pale. "A lawyer? Miss Freke had no lawyer."

"Must have had someone to make her will," Crook protested.

"That is a point that had not occurred to me. So far as I know she made no will. In any case, she had nothing to leave. She had been employed for many years in a—a menial capacity in other women's houses."

"And you rescued her from slavery?"

"From an asylum," retorted Laura. "For—you can confirm this at the Cottage Hospital if you are suspicious, though I can see no reason why you should be—that is certainly where they would have bundled her, if I hadn't come to her rescue."

"I know that Maskelyne and Devant had nothing on women when it comes to mystery," said Crook in his barefaced manner, "but—what made you do it? You hadn't known her long, had you?"

"Do you believe in fate, Mr——?"

"Crook. I did mention it."

"Mr. Crook?"

"Nemesis? You know the hymn 'God moves in a mysterious way His wonders to perform'? Sure you do. Well, Nemesis is the same. Sometimes it comes in the guise of Sir Galahad and sometimes looking like me."

She began to be afraid then, though she concealed it gallantly enough. "I am beginning to wonder whether Miss Freke's—champions, shall we say?—were of the same mental calibre as herself."

Atta girl! applauded Crook silently. Pity she was on the wrong side of the fence, from his point of view. "Well," he said aloud, "I mustn't be keeping you. My friend'll be shocked at my news, I'm afraid. Kept it quiet, haven't you? I mean—not a breath in the village."

"Miss Freke died in the early hours of yesterday morning. This is Wednesday. If you have any suspicions you are perfectly at liberty to see the doctor who attended her."

"Funeral takin' place—when?"

"This afternoon."

"No time lost," Crook approved. "Well, I'm all for quick work myself."

He didn't ask any more questions. He could find out everything else he needed to know, and she might give him a nasty clout if he became too inquisitive. But he did say as he turned to go, "Any address for wreaths?"

"I am asking for no flowers."

"Lady still on the premises?" he murmured.

"Really!" Miss Freke looked now as if she were about to blow up. "I cannot see what concern that is of yours."

" You know how it is with buddies." Crook actually sounded apologetic. " Did the dear departed look peaceful? All the bundle."

" To my mind there is a great deal of nonsense talked about the beautiful expressions worn by the dead. For the most part they are—unrecognisable." She spoke with such passion that even Crook was silenced. Anyway, he agreed with her. There is an anonymity about death that made it highly desirable in his opinion for coffins to be closed down at once. Remember people as they were in life, not looking, as some of these old dears did, like a calf's head in the box.

" In any case," Miss Freke continued, " she is no longer here. I thought it best for her to go to the mortuary."

" Amen," said Crook, and now he really did make a move. The doctor had given the certificate, and the doctor could supply any more information he, Crook, needed. Though whether any such information was going to be any help to him now seemed extremely doubtful. Jumping into the Scourge he drove back to Great Moreton and made his way to the Old Vicarage. After a long wait a great fat trollop of a woman opened the door. If Bob Day was right and she was the doctor's inamorata they must have a tight fit of it on the couch, he reflected vulgarly. The woman made no pretence at courtesy.

" We don't buy at the door," she said.

" Lady," Crook protested, " I've nothing to sell. On the contrary. Dr. Mack in? "

" He doesn't see patients at this hour."

" I'm not a patient."

" Then what do you want with him? "

" Representing a late patient, about the only representative she had. Thought he might be able to give me a few details. Her friend's a bit shaken—well, natural enough in the circumstances—I didn't like to trouble her. But as a lawyer——" He paused.

"Ow!" said the woman, reflectively. "Lawyer. Well, I'll tell him you're here. What name?" Crook gave her a card. He carried them for just such emergencies as this.

"Tell him not to hurry himself," he said in his most cheerful tone. "The day is young, and even I have some years this side the grave. Always provided," he added inaudibly, "that old cat at The Cottage don't have a chance of dropping anything in my beer." It was a comfort to reflect that, according to all accounts, she was a teetotaller.

He waited without rancour quite a long time before the Concubine returned to say ungraciously, "The doctor can see you now."

Sleeping off last night perhaps, Crook wondered, following her. Bob Day had described the old man graphically enough and an excellent description it was. A balloon in a waistcoat. Big hands, fingers yellowed with tobacco, big face, huge paunch, fringe of white hair—everything about him a bit shaky, a bit shady too, no doubt. But under it all he bore the stamp of his origins, was what used to be called a gentleman, in the days when the word carried no opprobrious suggestions.

"Good morning, sir," said the doctor. "And what can I do for you?"

"Good of you to spare me a few minutes," said Crook heartily. "I'm down from London."

"A delightful city," the doctor approved. Crook's heart warmed towards him. He could have said with Spenser, if his brow had been high enough to read the fellow—"To mery London, my most kyndlie nurse, etc."

"You've said it. Not surprising really the old lady

went loco when she made up her mind to leave it."

"Old lady?" The doctor looked somewhat at a loss.

"Old lady at The Cottage. Hear she passed out very suddenly yesterday morning, wasn't it?"

"Yes, oh yes." The doctor seated himself with care, and it must be quite a job lowering all that ballast, Crook reflected. "Sudden but not unexpected, no, not unexpected. I warned Miss—er—Miss Hunter she must be prepared for just such an emergency."

"Was she warned—the other one, I mean?"

"Miss Freke? We thought it best not to tell her. In her condition—I do assure you, she was practically certifiable."

"That seems to have come on very suddenly, too," said Crook musingly. "I mean, she was on her way down to Bath to take on a job."

"It is certainly most fortunate for her prospective employers that she abandoned the notion. She was quite unfit—quite unfit. I understand there had been a serious railway accident, she was in hospital for some weeks quite unaware of her own identity—not that that in itself would account for the high blood pressure you understand. That was a progressive condition, and the same goes for the heart."

"Now, tell me," said Crook, leaning forward, very man to man. "Did she have any sudden shock?"

"Miss Hunter tells me not. She was in one of her most difficult moods, however, accusing the housekeeper of attempting to poison her."

"You don't think that's likely?"

The doctor looked horrified. "My dear sir, have you any grounds whatever for making such a suggestion?"

"Not a suggestion," Crook explained. "Like Rosa Dartle, I ask for information."

" I can see no advantage accruing to the woman."

" Not if she was found out, of course."

" I think, Mr.——"

" Crook."

" Crook, you can put that notion out of your head. Of course, the poor old lady was quite unbalanced. She had what I think in your profession is known as a persecution mania. Everyone was against her, she was imprisoned, cheated, starved, spied upon. I really consider it most courageous of her friend to look after her, and I can't conceal the fact that she did show some relief when I warned her that her trial, if I may call it so, was likely to be of short duration."

" Is it true," asked Crook, " that she thought you were the Pope of Rome? Now, you don't think there was a chance she was putting that on? "

" I see no point in such behaviour."

" But that's just it. Loonies don't need points. Still, you haven't any doubt that she did die of heart failure? I mean, you saw the body before you gave the certificate? "

" Miss Hunter insisted. After my previous examination, I should have been prepared to give the certificate without a second visit; it was, after all, only what I had anticipated. But Miss Hunter said that people gossiped, she would be most obliged if I would return with her. She had to come down to me to ask me to call. No telephone. No convenience at all."

" Except looking-glass ones," Crook agreed. " I mean, what you and me might think intolerable could be turned to advantage, supposing you were the kind of person that liked living in a desert."

" I see your point. Poor lady, a fresh shock awaited her on her return. The housekeeper had taken advantage of her absence to leave the house, with no notice whatsoever."

Crook pricked up his big ears. " Any reason? "

" There was a note Miss Hunter showed me. Quite barefaced, saying that after what had happened she preferred not to stay, and she was sure Miss Hunter would understand."

" And did she? Understand, I mean? "

" She said, 'You would have thought she would have waited to see me over the funeral. After all, my nervous system has been as much shaken as hers.' "

" After what had happened," brooded Crook, thoughtfully. " No hint as to what that might be, I suppose? "

" I assume she referred to the scene of the previous night, when she had been accused of poisoning the old lady."

" Not too nice," Crook allowed. " I mean, daft old body yells loud enough to be heard in Piccadilly that X is trying to do away with her; within a few hours she dies. Lots of people adding two and two together and making it five."

" I could have reassured them," said Dr. Mack, with some dignity, mostly injured. " In my opinion there is no doubt of the cause of death."

" Funeral's this afternoon, I hear."

" Yes, I was able to arrange with Benson—a Bath firm—to expedite matters. I've always found him most obliging." He rubbed his hands. Crook had a vision of a rosy, sober little Benson, a little tub of a man in black with striped pants, saying, " Always happy to oblige. Sudden death? Quite in order. Murder? My dear sir, it is the policy of the firm I have the honour to represent to ask no questions. Permit me to draw attention to our trade mark—a fish, its mouth covered by its fin." Lumme, I'm going as daft as the old girl, he reflected. " Well," he said aloud, " it looks like Miss Woodman developed cold feet." Corpse-cold perhaps. What did she know? A lot more than anybody guessed, enough to send her scuttling before the undertaker's men came in. Crook brooded, his great chin on his hands. Could she be involved? But why the heck? No will, Miss Hunter had said, well, the one calling herself Miss Hunter anyway.

" Maybe she's gone back to the bosom of the Mowbrays," he suggested. " It should be possible to find out." Though he didn't say that aloud.

" I am exceedingly sorry for Miss Hunter." He came out of his trance to realise that the doctor was still talking, like a radio you've forgotten to switch off. " I feel she has suffered from the villagers' malicious gossip. I have never previously lived in——" He paused and began again, " small beer is an insipid drink to the man accustomed to wine," he announced pompously. " It is impossible to conduct one's affairs with any privacy in a small place. The first time Miss Hunter called she was in a very distressed state of mind. She had at that time no inkling of the seriousness of Miss Freke's condition, but she was troubled by what that great man, Churchill, called a whispering campaign. I didn't happen to see the housekeeper on that occasion, or I might have formed a better view of the type of woman she was. Of course, living with those peculiar women—I refer to the Misses Mowbray—she would tend to become a little odd herself. Mrs. Jerome, my housekeeper, knows her by sight, though not intimately. She saw her in the village the day before Miss Freke died and stopped to ask how the lady was, which was civil of her. And Miss Woodman, in the most peremptory manner, said if she was so interested why didn't she come to me direct? It quite upset Mrs. Jerome. But that's absolutely typical of village life. Really, I feel a great deal of sympathy for Miss Hunter. A most able woman and quite devoted to her friend. I could see that she could scarcely believe it when I told her of Miss Freke's precarious hold on life, and she implored me not to give her an inkling. So assiduous, too, to know whether a certain dish the housekeeper was preparing at that moment in the kitchen would be suitable, and when I said that nothing she took could affect her condition or prolong her life she said, 'Laura has a great interest in her food. I'm glad she doesn't have to diet,' and most hospitably went to tell Miss Woodman all was well and came back with some sherry, though I understand she is not a drinking woman."

"Nice touch," said Crook, wondering if the mention of sherry would touch a chord in the old gentleman's mind. It appeared that it did. "I wonder," said he, "if I can offer you a glass of port. Usually at about this hour——"

Well, whatever you might say about him you couldn't say he'd joined the Go-Slow Movement, Crook reflected. Aloud he murmured that port was poison to him, but if there was a drop of beer on the premises . . .

It appeared that there was. Mrs. Jerome liked a glass now and again. The old gentleman stuck to port, and chatted about the neighbourhood while he imbibed.

"The Misses Mowbray," said he. "Positive Victorian survivals. What was good enough for Mother is good enough for us. No telephone, no electricity. Quite astonishing."

"No bathroom, perhaps?" Crook suggested.

"To tell you the truth, I have no knowledge. I had never been on the premises or met any of the members of the household until Miss Hunter called me in."

"Got their own pet medico?"

The doctor looked slightly sheepish. " They—what is that old saying ?—keep themselves to themselves. Live like troglodytes, according to the villagers. That, of course, is an exaggeration. They certainly don't live below ground. But they neither pay nor receive calls, and I understand that the woman——"

" The Disappearing Housekeeper ? "

" Exactly. Most apt. I understand all contacts with the village were made by her."

" Regular Castle of Otranto," said Crook. " Who has their medical cards ? Your rival here ? "

That was the wrong touch. " A singularly unfortunate phrase," said the doctor, pouring out a second glass of port and drinking it much too quickly. " There is no question of rivalry. I am retired, but I undertake a few cases in the neighbourhood. As for the Misses Mowbray, I believe they have their own physician in Bath. As a rule they visited him ; one of them used to drive the car—oh yes, they possess a car." The second glass of port seemed to have restored his equanimity. " It's an odd reflection that an ancient car only excites mirth and derision, whereas ancient furniture constitutes an enviable possession."

" All right for them that like worms," said the Philistine Crook. " I reckon I'll get my share soon enough. You know, they can't be absolutely Victorian if they have a car."

" Miss Mowbray's method of driving dates a great deal farther back than our good Queen Victoria. She reminded me of Boadicea in her chariot, her main ambition being apparently to wreak as much damage on passers-by as possible."

Crook, not to be outdone in historical allusion, said something about Jehu, who drove furiously, adding that that seemed to be the only thing anybody knew about him. He finished his beer, waited a minute to see if there was to be an offer of a second cut, and when there wasn't he got philosophically to his feet.

"See you at the cemetery this afternoon?" he offered.

Dr. Mack looked surprised. "I—I hardly think so. It is not as though Miss Freke were a regular patient. I understand she wishes the funeral to be very quiet."

"I shan't take a band with me," Crook assured him.

"A charming situation," said the doctor, brightening perceptibly at the prospect of his visitor's departure. (Referring to the cemetery, Crook supposed.) "Perfectly delightful. Larks singing, trees burgeoning—no one could desire more."

"Except, of course, not to be the fellow in the box," suggested Crook. And taking up his horrible brown bowler he departed.

"Hanged if I see what I can do," he confided to the Scourge, bowling back to The Heart In Hand. "Check up at the registrar's on cause of death."

He was disconcerted to find that the registrar kept strictly limited hours, but the man happened to be on the premises and, seeing Crook on the pavement, sent out a female, the lady who obliged, from the look of her, to invite him in. Crook represented himself as the deceased's lawyer, and was provided with a copy of the death certificate. Death was due to heart failure and what he presumed was the professional term for high blood pressure. "No relative present at death," offered the registrar, "but I understand from her friend that she had none. Very sad for these elderly ladies when they outlive their contemporaries, and perhaps sadder still to think the Government takes anything that's left in the circumstances."

"Speaking as a lawyer, I'd say there wouldn't be anything for the Government to take, not when expenses are met," Crook assured him. He wondered rather how Miss Hunter was going to cope with that situation. But that was her funeral, and he wouldn't be surprised if there was yet another before they were through.

" Because there's some explanation about this disappearing housekeeper. She knows something, and she don't mean to get in touch with the police. Wonder where I can contact her, and when." It didn't occur to him that he might never do so, and, as usual, his optimism was justified, but when that time came things had moved to a stage where she couldn't tell him much he didn't already know.

CHAPTER FOURTEEN

ON HIS return he found Bob Day in the bar, polishing glasses. " Did you see Miss Freke ? " the landlord inquired.

" They are all gone into the land of light," said Crook solemnly. " We cannot see you, Mother, We cannot hear you call. There's nothing left to greet us, But your picture on the wall. Though come to that there wasn't even a photograph. Very sudden but, according to the doctor, not unexpected."

Bob looked incredulous. " You mean, the lady's dead ? "

" The Snappin' Turtle who opened the door to me said so, and the doctor backs her up. Seen the body, too. No surprise to him, might have happened any time. How come you heard nothing ? "

Bob Day rubbed his forehead. " Well, now, that's queer," he acknowledged. " Stan Haslett does all the burying in these parts——"

" Not this one, he don't," Crook interrupted.

"Fellow called Benson came all the way from Bath yesterday to collect the body."

"You mean, she's not even to be let lay in her own bed till the funeral?"

"Maybe Miss Hunter's afraid of spooks. She's alone there, y'see. Oh yes, that's something else you hadn't picked up. One hell of a row on Monday, off goes our Miss Woodman on Tuesday——."

"Where?"

"Could be Bournehaven."

Bob Day nodded. "It isn't likely she'll cut herself adrift from them just when she's about due for a pension."

"On the other hand she's been talking about retiring, and it seems that that's just what she's done."

The landlord brooded. "That's one way of looking at it," he said at last.

"Not your way?" asked Crook, conversationally.

"Well, I ask you. She's left there to keep an eye on the house when the foreigners come in. Seems as thick as thieves for a while, then without any warning she ups and vamooses and the other lady dies."

"And you'd tie the two together as boys tie two pigs' tails and call it cause and effect."

"I know Bertha Woodman. Terrible respectable she is, never heard her laugh to my knowledge and my sister the same. Careful, too, about money. If she'd been the woman in the Testament she'd have swept the house for a halfpenny let alone a piece of silver, and have borrowed the neighbour's candle to look for it. And if she walks out without a word to anyone, so far as we know, it's because she's not going to be mixed up in something that's not nice."

"The row," Crook began, but the man made an impatient gesture with his big hands. "Bertha's not one to be put out of house and home by a few hard words. No, if she's gone it's because she knew something."

"Good heavens, man, you're not suggesting she's gone to the police?" Even Crook hadn't thought of that.

"Bertha Woodman get herself mixed up with the police? Not likely."

"A minute ago you were hinting there was something odd about the old girl's death," Crook challenged him.

"Maybe there was, but why should Bertha care? What's an old woman to her? But it could be——" He hesitated.

"Murder?" said Crook.

"I never said the word, sir."

"And won't, if you've any sense. There's a thing called slander, and the courts don't like it, they don't like it at all. Mind you, I don't say everything's as clear as a crystal ball. I mean, why go to Bath for the funeral? Still, it's not as if this Miss Hunter was a native, and seeing she's kept herself to herself since she came here she may have wanted to go on being high and mighty up to the end. Dr. Mack seems to have fixed up the funeral arrangements for her."

"When did you say it was, sir? The burying, I mean?"

"This afternoon."

"Quick work," agreed Bob. "You thinking of going?"

"I was. Not that it makes any difference either way. We can't stop it even if we want to. We've no ground for askin' for a delay. A doctor saw the old girl a week before she died and warned Miss Hunter what to expect. He's told me as much, and he saw her after death and gave a certificate. You ain't suggesting, I suppose, that Miss H. has bought up the whole neighbourhood?

Anyhow, if any buying was being done you'd expect her to start with Bertha Woodman."

"Maybe she did," said Bob. "I tell you, that woman loves money like another chap loves his dog or his beer. But even so murder's got an ugly sound."

"Whatever it is it's only just happened. I wonder where she is and if we could persuade her to talk."

As he had anticipated, Laura was the only mourner at the graveside, and she started and looked resentful when she saw him. When the interment was over he approached her to say, "No more news of Miss Woodman, I suppose?" and she demanded tartly, "Why should you suppose there would be? She went off so suddenly."

"And that didn't put any ideas into your head?"

"What do you mean?"

"It could be she knew something."

"If you have an accusation to make you should do so in the proper quarter. As for Miss Woodman knowing something, I am completely at a loss to understand what you are talking about."

"Didn't Miss Freke say something about being poisoned?"

"She was constantly making these wild accusations. We neither of us paid any attention to them."

"But shortly after making one she does die, *and* Miss Woodman disappears. Even at my school they taught us simple addition."

"You are implying a very serious accusation against a woman who is not here to defend herself," said Laura, in freezing tones.

"That's not my fault," protested Crook, reasonably. "By the way, did she take her gear with her?"

"Miss Woodman is not a snail that can carry its

house on its back. She is going to send for her things in due course."

"Tell me one more thing," begged Crook, as the woman moved forward with the clear intention of ending the conversation. "Why do you think she went? She must have had some reason, even if she didn't put it into the letter. I mean, something happened."

"Why should you suppose——?"

"Well, she said it—after what has happened. Keep the letter by any chance?"

"Had I known you were going to make all these inquiries I should certainly have done so."

"But you didn't? H'm." It could be, he was telling himself, the lady's not being quite straightforward about this. Maybe there was a bit more in the letter than she happened to mention. Anyhow, what about being sure? "Now, lookee," he said persuasively, "you will understand if she ran out on you at such a time there can only be two reasons. Because she was afraid of trouble, not of her making and didn't want to be involved, or else she was up to the neck already and felt the water was still rising. You pays your money and you takes your choice."

"I am as much at a loss as you can be, I assure you," said Laura loftily. "Her—defection—came to me as a complete shock. I know, of course, she was put out by my insistence that the doctor should be called in——"

"What's that?" asked Crook sharply.

"Yes. She said he had been to see Miss Freke a few days earlier and had given us an adverse report, and it would be enough to let him know what had occurred, and he would supply a certificate without demur."

"But—you weren't happy about it?"

" I could see no reason for not calling him in," returned Laura. " If Miss Freke died from natural causes—and I have no reason whatever to suppose anything else—then there was nothing to lose and everything to gain by having the doctor up to see the body. You don't have to tell me how people talk in a small place. I have had plenty of experience since my arrival here. I certainly didn't propose to provide the smallest quantity of fuel to feed that vicious flame."

" I'd say you were right at that. Pity you didn't have the other chap, though. There seems to be some feeling against poor old Mack. Well—how did Miss Woodman take it when she saw you weren't to be turned from your resolve ? "

" She said, ' Please yourself, but he won't like it, and it isn't necessary.' I told her I had every intention of pleasing myself, and went down to the village. Miss Woodman was right in one thing, Dr. Mack would have been delighted to hand me the certificate without stirring out of his room, but I insisted."

" That's what I don't understand. Why ? Unless you'd something to make you think it wasn't a natural death."

" Rumour gets about here like dust in a sandstorm. Miss Freke had made a specific accusation against Miss Woodman that she was being poisoned. It's true that no one else was present, and there was no earthly reason to suppose that accusation would ever go beyond ourselves, but—the fatal word had been used. Poison ! "

Crook eyed her narrowly. " You don't think there might have been a grain of truth in it ? Come clean, Miss Hunter. Is there a chance ? "

" What reason would she have ? " But now her voice was fearful. She smote her hands together. " If she hadn't gone away I'd never have entertained such a thought. But—why did she go? It was only *after* I insisted on calling in the doctor."

Crook was watching her, a big impassive lump of a man, but his mind worked quickly enough. If there was anything wrong, he was reflecting, would she have called the fellow in? It was taking an almighty risk. Ah, but it was a question of choosing the lesser of two evils. Must have been a hard choice, like the blackamoor finding himself with a crocodile on either side of him. "Which is the least?" he had faltered. For she was right. Once the story of the poor old girl's death was out the tongues would start wagging. No, it was a risk either way and her horse had come in at long odds. Not that she was completely secure from slander. The locals would tell each other that Dr. Mack was no better than an old sot anyhow. Still, officially she was all right.

"Any reason for wanting Miss Freke out of the way?" he asked slowly. "I mean, wouldn't she have been out of a job?"

"She was only temporarily employed by me," said Laura in a sharp voice. "Her permanent employers were the Misses Mowbray."

"She's been spreading the yarn she was going to retire."

"Then I suppose they were going to pension her off."

"You should tell that to the villagers," Crook warned her. "Their version is that she was leaving one employer for a better one."

"It's not my habit to listen to village gossip," flashed Miss Freke.

"You could do worse. As Bob Day says, it's not much gets past them. And she never did talk of retiring till you came along. Never mention it to you?"

"Will you kindly tell me why you are asking all these questions?" demanded Laura, suddenly icy again.

"Representin' the dead woman."

"But you never saw her." The cry burst from her pale lips.

"Introduced through a third party," mumbled Crook.

"Surely that is very—irregular?"

"Lots of irregular things about this case. Housekeeper goin' off like that for one. That's the worst of amateurs. Haven't had enough experience to know that when you're in a jam your best course is to sit tight and challenge the other side to smoke you out."

"She may have gone to Bournehaven to see Miss Mowbray. There was a train she could have caught from Yarborough."

"Walking to Yarborough?"

"I don't know. There's a car available at Great Moreton. She could walk in there. Or there's the bus. It was market day and they run three buses. She'd know that, of course."

"Know where Miss Mowbray's staying?"

"At the Ocean Hotel. I think, as she was their employee, I should let them know. She always said she had nowhere else to go, and she used to talk about where she'd live when she did retire. I asked if she meant to live alone, and she said I couldn't understand what it was like for someone who had always lived in other people's houses to have her own place at last, no matter how small. But she was wrong, of course. I know very well."

"How come?" asked Crook.

"Personal experience," snapped Miss Freke.

Crook looked somewhat surprised. "I thought——"

"You've never been an unmarried daughter," Laura

went on, taking no notice of his attempted speech. " It was always my mother's house, and after that a landlady. Never anything of my own. I lived for the time when I should be independent. So, you see, I understand very well how Miss Woodman felt."

" Retiring on her savings, perhaps? "

" How can I tell? I'd only known her a few months, but presumably Miss Mowbray would make some provision. And there's a Government pension, isn't there? She must have been insured all these years, and she was certainly over sixty."

" Maybe you'll hear about that from Miss Mowbray. Thinking of runnin' over to Bournehaven, by the way? Someone ought to go." His eyes sparkled.

" I had thought of that," said Laura swiftly. " I have every intention of informing them in person."

" Staying long? " asked Crook idly, picking up his hat and preparing to depart.

" That will depend on the youngest Miss Mowbray's health. I have The Cottage on a three-monthly tenancy. I have renewed this once and the second period comes to an end next month. It is of course very remote."

" Nice place for ghosts," suggested Crook casually.

" And now that that poor woman has gone to her rest there's naturally nothing to keep me here." Laura disregarded an interjection she regarded as flippant and in poor taste. " I have a little time before my lease is up. And now," she continued briskly, " I hope I've told you everything you require to know. If you are thinking of starting a suggestion that Miss Freke's death was not due to natural causes let me remind you of your own warning about the law of slander."

A girl of spirit, thought Crook, getting into the

Scourge and driving off. There was no rancour in his mind, but he was absolutely convinced at this stage that there was something fishy about this very timely death.

The next step was perfectly obvious—to unearth Miss Woodman—and this in due course and with remarkably little delay (all things considered), he proceeded to do.

There were three buses from Great Moreton on a market day, leaving at 9.30, 11.30 and 2 o'clock. If Laura was to be believed, her housekeeper had been on the premises when she, Laura, went to fetch Dr. Mack shortly before 10 o'clock, so that put the 9.30 bus out of court. And when she returned the note was waiting for her. Therefore, it seemed pretty clear Bertha must have caught the 11.30. Crook wandered into the village shop, kept by Mrs. Throstle, Bob Day's sister, and began to dig for information. Mrs. Throstle said she couldn't help, because she always kept the shop open till 1 o'clock on market day and went in herself on the 2 o'clock bus. This was mainly used by those who didn't set much store on marketing, but liked to get to the cinema once a week. She was quite sure Miss Woodman hadn't been on that one.

"Who generally goes on the 11.30?" asked Crook, and she thought a bit and suggested two or three names. "Not that it'll be anything to go on if they didn't see her," she warned him. "She never did mix much, and people are mostly friendly hereabouts. If she didn't talk to anyone they mightn't see her. Still, you could try."

So Crook tried, but though two of his witnesses remembered a stranger, that being their way of saying someone who didn't greet anybody, nobody would go so far as to identify Miss Woodman positively.

"How about the driver?" asked Crook, in his resourceful way.

But the luck wasn't with him this morning. The old driver had recently died and the new one came out from Yarborough and confessed that a lot of the faces were still unfamiliar. Crook hadn't even got a photograph of her, and descriptions of one elderly unobtrusive female are very likely to fit half a dozen others.

"Any other way of getting into Yarborough?" Crook inquired.

"There's a local hire car. You could try them."

But he drew blank here also.

"How about the station?" he said, refusing to accept defeat. "There is one, I suppose?"

"Oh yes. Not many trains run but there's one about mid-day every day of the week, except Sunday."

"You are an up-and-coming borough," Crook congratulated him.

The booking-clerk remembered a lady dressed in dark clothes who booked to Bath on the mid-day train.

"Only just made it," he said. "It was a slow train, stopping all the way. The only fast train of the day is the early morning one."

Crook had another idea. "Direct line from Bath to Bournehaven?" he inquired.

The clerk said there was a good train service, adding casually, "The lady asked me that."

Crook clapped his great hands together. "Why in tarnation couldn't you say that at first?" he asked the startled and somewhat indignant clerk. "Now we are going places." But when he was away from the station he still had to admit he was only at the very beginning of the journey.

It was too late to do anything that night. Bournehaven, that has been described as the Princess Elizabeth of watering-places by a publicist who should have known better, would be full to overflowing in this brilliant summer weather. Besides, if the lady passing as Miss Hunter did propose to go there in quest of her disappearing housekeeper, she, too, would have to wait till the morning.

Having got as far as he could for to-night he wandered down to the bar and here, not greatly to his surprise, he was presently joined by Peter Finnemore.

" What's cooking ? " asked that young man. " I've heard about the funeral from Bob. I rather wanted to put in an appearance but the old man set his Bevans and wouldn't let me go. She wasn't our client, he said, and, unless I could guarantee we should be compensated for time and travel, it was off."

" You didn't miss much," Crook told him. " It's the third act of any play that counts."

" The pity being that so often it's the worst act of the three."

" Now, now," Crook rebuked him. " You and me are in on this act. Tell Bob what you're drinking and I'll put you in the picture."

" Do you suspect foul play ? " Peter asked, bringing his glass over to where Crook was sitting.

" Meaning that you do ? "

" It's very tidy," Peter demurred. " Besides, where has Miss Woodman gone ? "

" Could be Bournehaven. Anyway, we'll soon know. Frostyface is going down in the morning. It seems there's a connection from Bath if you're set on an early start, and I don't suppose she means to spend the night there. What do you make of Miss Woodman ? Strong-minded female, would you say ? "

" She's got a mouth like a rat-trap and I'd say she was quite capable of shutting up that poor old dear in a dungeon with bread and water, to say nothing of the rats, for a week, and never losing a minute's sleep in consequence."

"Capable of poisoning her?"

"I wouldn't care to go as far as that. Anyway, why should she? What does she stand to gain?"

"There we need the evidence of our chief witness and she, poor old girl, is under the churchyard sod. But my guess would be that deceased was going to spill some beans and don't ask me what beans, because I haven't identified them yet."

Peter reflected. "Suppose Miss Woodman had it in for Miss Freke."

"The alleged Miss Freke, or——"

"The survivor. Well, we've got to call her something. Say she had some hold over Bertha, and Bertha thought this was her chance of putting her to sleep, and Miss Hunter discovered the plot."

"Suppose I was the Duke of Edinburgh. Still, I suppose it is possible. Or say Bertha was seen going through Miss Freke's papers, trying to pin something on to her. Say she believed Miss Hunter's story and had got some proof, and Miss Hunter threatened to tell the other one. It's all damned involved, ain't it?"

"You can say practically anything at this stage," said Peter frankly. "Maybe the poison, if there was any, wasn't intended for Miss Hunter at all."

"Meaning Miss Freke knew she was in Bertha Woodman's power? All the same, a corpse is a nasty thing to have about the place, and Bertha hadn't just seen a doctor. It would have meant an inquest. No, I doubt if that gee will run."

"Well, then, how about this? It wasn't a natural death and Miss Woodman knows it. But she can't prove a thing. After all, she does the cooking, and if questions were asked it might be uncommonly awkward for her. And it's an axiom that a person who's done

one murder doesn't stop short of a second, if murder's the most convenient way out, and she thought she might as well go while the going was good."

"Above ground rather than under? You may have something there. Still, her proper course 'ud be to approach the police."

"That mightn't be very convenient. The police are like badgers—dig, dig, dig. They'd want to know when she first started getting suspicious. I fancy she knew something that put Miss Freke in her power."

But Crook was frowning. "That don't add up either. If she had a hold over Miss Freke she was made for life."

"But perhaps only a short life. That's the point I'm trying to make."

"She got out in a devil of a hurry, leaving no address. All her stuff's at The Cottage."

"She'll have to send for it sometime, or call for it, and then she'll be bound to give an address. Besides, I don't see Miss Freke putting herself out to deal with the luggage."

"You have something there," Crook admitted. "And if she'd been goin' to the police, why wasn't the funeral held up?"

"Perhaps the Misses Mowbray can help. If Miss Freke is going down to-morrow it looks as though she has no more idea than we where Miss Woodman may have got to."

Crook got up, almost overturning the beer. "Can't imagine why we're sitting here on our great backsides when there's a telephone next door," he observed inelegantly. "What did she say the name of this hotel is? The Ocean?"

Characteristically, he got through with very little delay, but he had to wait quite a while before the eldest Miss Mowbray could be coaxed to the telephone.

She didn't like the instruments, didn't trust them, didn't hold with them, but sooner than let her next sister take the message she staggered along the hall, poor old trout, and into the coffin-shaped booth.

" Who is that ? " said a precise tinny voice, in a tone that called for the answer, this is the Atom Bomb. Crook restrained himself, however, and gave his name.

" Never heard of you," said the tinny voice. " There's some mistake."

" Here, don't ring off," Crook implored her. " There's a mistake all right, but not the one you think. I'm a lawyer."

" We have a lawyer."

" I didn't say your lawyer. Representing Miss Hunter."

" Hunter? Oh, our tenant. I trust," the voice sounded prim and affronted, " nothing is wrong."

" Everything's wrong is my guess," was Crook's cheerful assurance. " Say, have you heard from Miss Woodman ? "

The voice stiffened. " I heard recently telling me her plans. May I ask by what right you make these inquiries ? "

" It's me or the police," Crook told her. " Though I don't promise it won't come to the police anyway."

" The police ? " Like a poor old poll-parrot she echoed his words.

" The fact is, Miss Woodman's disappeared. We thought maybe you had some news."

" I ? Certainly not. She has not been here, if that is what you mean."

" It was. No hint of future plans ?"

" We have not heard from Miss Woodman for some time."

" Not since she wrote saying she might be goin' on the retired list ? " hazarded Crook.

" I understood from her letter that Miss Hunter had offered her a—a companion's position. Quite unsuitable." Her tone said that showed you the sort of woman Miss Hunter was. " If you are representing Miss Hunter I feel it only fair to say that I regard her behaviour as quite disgraceful—enticing my servant away from me."

" Well, I shouldn't think that holds any longer," Crook consoled her. " Seeing that Miss Hunter herself don't know where Miss Woodman is."

" You mean, she has just left The Cottage ? "

" That's about the size of it. The dotty old lady died and—well, it could be your housekeeper is superstitious. She may have thought one death would be followed by another."

" You are not trying to tell me there is an epidemic in Great Moreton." Here the three pips sounded and the old lady nearly fell off the telephone with shock.

" Hold everything," said Crook hastily. " That don't mean a thing. No, there's no epidemic, not the way you mean. But this old lady died very suddenly and——"

" Are you warning me that my housekeeper may be concerned in the death ? That is absurd. But possibly that explains the telegram."

" Which was that ? "

" The telegram from Miss Hunter, saying she will be with me to-morrow on urgent business. What an extraordinary situation ! I can only suppose that Bertha has changed her mind and decided not to remain with Miss Hunter."

" In that case you'd think she'd write to you, wouldn't you ? Any idea where she might have gone ? All right, lady, hold everything. That's the first thing the police'll ask you."

" I am afraid I can't help." But the voice sounded

agitated now. " You cannot mean that Bertha is in any kind of trouble.

Crook groaned. " See, lady, what d'you think I've been talking about all this time ? "

" Perhaps Miss Hunter will be able to throw some light on the scene," observed Miss Mowbray.

" If she could she wouldn't be coming to Bournehaven. No, she's coming to see what you can tell her."

He rang off and went slowly back to the bar. " The Snappin' Turtle's going to make sure of getting in first," he told Peter. " Say that poor old dear didn't die from natural causes and say someone's going to start wondering aloud just how it all did happen. Frostyface means to be sitting pretty. Take it by and large, it was damn' silly of Miss Woodman to go like that."

" Self-preservation," insisted Peter. " I wouldn't say there was much love lost between those two."

" Like two rattlesnakes. Well, here's to the morning."

CHAPTER FIFTEEN

ON HIS WAY out he stopped to ask Bob if anyone had engaged the local car for the station next day, and Bob said " Yes, Miss Hunter from The Cottage." It was all over the village already that Miss Woodman had disappeared, and the odds on the unfortunate corpse being allowed to remain quietly where it had been lowered until the Day of Judgment seemed pretty poor. Or so it appeared to Crook, who was generally right over things like that. " We'll be holding hands with the police before we're through, you mark my words," he said.

The next morning he was up bright and early and so was at the station when the local hire car drew up and Miss Freke emerged.

He had left the Scourge just out of sight, and she was so much engrossed in her own affairs she didn't even see him. She had no luggage, he saw, and she looked elegant but unfashionable, wearing a hat with a veil such as London women sported two or three seasons ago. There was a pink rose in the front, and he thought that if she wanted to be conspicuous she was going a very good way about it. But why, he thought, should she wish to attract attention? She looked quite different from the thin, scaly old maid who marched down to the village for the rations. He even believed she'd got some sort of make-up on. And the ear-rings were new, and added to the change in her appearance.

" Out to kill," he commented inwardly, and was struck dumb by the aptness of the phrase.

Miss Freke purchased her ticket, and crossed the

diminutive platform to the other side. Crook waited till the train came in and saw her board it. It was a fast train, the only fast train of the day. Most of them stopped at every station. This ran through to Yarborough and thence to Bath, and at Bath, as Crook had ascertained, she could catch her connection to Bournehaven.

To his surprise, as he left his hidey-hole he found Peter Finnemore standing beside the Scourge. " It's all right," said the young man swiftly. " Uncle Corny's sent me out on some footling inventory job. It's about all he thinks I'm fit for. Fact is, he's in treaty with some fellow from Yarborough about a partnership, though he doesn't know I've twigged it, and this chap's coming out this morning to cross the t's and dot the i's, so the longer I'm away the more popular I shall be. What's cooking here ? "

" Just seeing Frostyface off on her fruitless journey, no doubt patting herself on the back (if she can reach as far) all the way. Quite sure, y'see, she's chucked enough dust in Arthur Crook's eyes to blind him for the duration."

" I saw the pink rose," Peter grinned, and Crook surprised him by saying, " That's no laughing matter. That's one of the things that's put me on the trail. Come on, if you're coming."

He jumped into the Scourge. " What's the hurry ? " asked Peter, following his example. " You've got the whole day. She can't be back before evening. I know the trains."

" I'm not worrying about her," said Crook, sounding grimmer than usual, grinding up the lane. " But I don't want blood on my hands, see ? "

" Not yet. Where do we go from here ? "

" The Cottage, of course. And don't tell me what we're goin' to do is illegal, because I know it. But there's a higher law than the law of man, whatever the courts may say."

They took a corner on two wheels, and Peter hung on to the side of the car. He hadn't brought his own this morning having hitch-hiked from Bath, which proved he had some sense, in Crook's estimation. The Mousetrap might be all right in its own way, but it didn't stand a chance against the Scourge. And nobody wanted a procession of noticeable cars wending their way towards The Cottage.

"Who—or what—do you expect to find at The Cottage?" Peter asked, reminding himself that he had no dependants and his lawyer had insisted on his making a will, though heaven knew no one was likely to benefit much from it, so what was he worrying about?

"Could be Miss Woodman."

"What's that?" Peter was so startled he nearly fell over the side. "But she's gone."

"Has she? Who saw her go? So far as I can find out no one saw her leave the house."

"Do you mean"—Peter sounded as dazed as he felt—"Miss F. murdered the pair of 'em?"

"Not much point gettin' rid of Miss Hunter so long as Bertha Woodman was above ground."

"And you know where she is?"

"I could make a good guess," said Crook, "though, mind you, I could be wrong. It was that rose that gave me the notion. And the make-up. I mean why, to go and see the old Mowbrays who probably think any woman with a bit of colour in her cheeks is one of Piccadilly's cast-offs? Yes, I'm expectin' to see Miss Woodman quite soon. Let's hope they give Frosty-face a royal welcome at The Ocean. It's the last good day she's likely to have for a long time to come."

"Well," confessed Peter frankly, "I'm all at sea.

I hadn't bargained for two corpses. Besides, they're not as easy as all that to get rid of. I know the woods come up near the house, but dragging a body by hand is a tough assignment, even for a man, and for an old maid like Miss Freke——"

"I wondered about that," Crook acknowledged handsomely. "Fact, I don't mind telling you I toyed with the notion that the old girl had packed the two of them into one coffin. But then I remembered the coffin never came to The Cottage, and Benson's got a reputation to keep up. It isn't likely she could buy him in. Besides, it 'ud entail buying in his chaps as well, so that's out."

"Perhaps she's keeping her drugged at The Cottage," suggested Peter, wanting to be helpful. "Like that chap in the film, who lured his wife's lover underground and kept him chained up for weeks while the hue and cry was on, so that if anything should slip up they wouldn't be able to take him for murder."

"She's still got to get rid of the body." Crook drove the Scourge at a reckless pace. "It's a funny thing about that note Miss Woodman was supposed to leave. Miss F. said she destroyed it. Maybe she did. Maybe it said a bit more than she cares to pass on. Or maybe there never was a note at all. Hope to be able to answer both points by the end of the day."

He stopped the Scourge outside The Cottage and both men alighted. The little house looked like something even Nature had forgotten. During the months of Miss Freke's tenancy the weeds had been suffered to grow, and no one had cut back the bushes or lopped the trees overhanging the gate. That long grass and unkempt border gave the place a great air of desolation. "From battle, murder, and sudden death, good Lord deliver us," said Crook in Peter's ear. Though he must have known it was a waste of time, he sent his companion on to pull the bell, while he himself kept an eye on the windows. But not a curtain fluttered, not a step sounded from within, as the echoes of the bell died forlornly away.

"No one at home?" said Crook. "Let's come round to the back."

Here the door was locked and the windows were shuttered.

"Does this mean she isn't coming back either?" Peter asked.

"All the luggage is there. By gum, I wonder if the old girl really has pulled a fast one." But he calmed down a moment later. Miss Freke hadn't gone to all this trouble and risk without hope of permanent gain and a disappearing woman can't claim dividends. He prowled round the house. "She certainly wanted to make sure no one would get inside," he said. Turning his back he stared out over the endless woods. As far as the skyline the trees were massed: it didn't need a lot of imagination to picture someone, dazed with terror, wandering and running and stopping again and going in another direction and finally turning a mad face to the unpitying sky before the darkness closed down for good. "If I don't take care," Crook told himself angrily, "I shall end up as a flicking poet, and a lot of good that'll do my clients."

"Best try the front door," he observed more calmly. "Most likely to be the one she left by, which means there's only the lock to tackle." He came back and stood thoughtfully staring up at the exterior. "No need to worry about bein' seen," he continued on a note of grim satisfaction, "because no one comes this way." Then he stiffened, then he moved forward, then he stooped and lifted something from the overgrown grass verge. It was a plated teaspoon and he stood staring at it till Peter joined him.

" Where did you find that, Crook ? "

Crook told him.

" Queer place to keep a spoon."

" You're telling me. What sort of game do you play with teaspoons ? Or wouldn't you know ? Anyhow, I thought housekeepers counted the silver every night. Mine would, if I had one, and there was any silver."

" Hasn't been there long from the look of it," Peter murmured. " No rust. Maybe there wasn't time for Miss Woodman to notice it was missing."

" You could be right at that. Though it don't seem quite in the picture to me for Miss Freke to be havin' a picnic on her lonesome with one woman vanished and the other a corpse. And if she wanted to scare a cat a teaspoon ain't quite the missile I'd choose."

" It's a bit large for a teaspoon," murmured Peter, turning it over. " And if it had been missing any length of time someone would have noticed it."

" And if you did think of having tea in the garden why choose the front ? " He shrugged and turned back to the house. " Come on. I'm going to get in some way if I have to go down the chimney," he said. " I have a hunch that spoon may mean something."

" Better leave this to me," Peter offered. " They taught us quite a lot about housebreaking in the Commandos."

" So that was your lay, was it ? Well, go ahead, young Oliver. Let your Uncle Bill Sikes in."

It didn't strike him as odd that the young man should unhesitatingly pick a lock ; Bill Parsons would have done it if he'd been there. And, seeing Miss Freke hadn't got wings as yet and therefore couldn't have flown out of a window, one of the doors must be unbolted, and it's the bolts that break a burglar's heart. They had all day and he wasn't in any particular hurry, not then, and in any case it wasn't long before

Peter had got a door open and they both went in. There was a charnel atmosphere about the interior that you find in houses where windows are habitually shut and blinds drawn. And during the latter weeks of her life in that house poor Alice Hunter hadn't been allowed to see much of the sun. Everything was in apple-pie order, all the dishes neatly washed and stacked, food in the larder covered with butter-muslin, raincoats hanging on hooks by the back door. Here Crook stopped. " Three fishers went sailing, three coats were hanging. That's funny. I thought Miss Woodman was never seen without a raincoat in any weather. And it was raining the day she left."

There was no doubt that one of the coats was hers. There was a handkerchief in the pocket marked B.W. But that wasn't all. There were abundant signs that if Miss Woodman had left The Cottage it had certainly been in very odd circumstances. For upstairs they found a respectable black leather handbag containing her identity card, ration book and various other personal possessions.

Crook pushed on to the dining-room where the silver was kept under green baize in a sideboard drawer. Here again everything was perfection, all the spoons and forks neatly graded, twelve of everything, with a monogram GHM on the back of the handles. The egg-spoons were in a case of a dozen, the teaspoons likewise. There was no empty groove ; and there were no other odd spoons.

" Perhaps that wasn't theirs," Peter suggested.

Crook took the spoon out of his pocket and looked at it. It bore no monogram and it patently was not silver. " Why only one ? " he said aloud, and then Peter supplied the clue.

" I've got it, sir. That's the sort of spoon you get in picnic baskets. If they've got one of those."

They found the basket in a cupboard under the stairs. It was a basket for four, but there were only three spoons.

" So that's where it came from. Who on earth has been going for a picnic in this weather? Surely the Snapping Turtle and Miss Woodman wouldn't go out gallivanting in the garden before their victim was cold in her grave? "

" No, that won't wash. Because Miss Woodman disappeared before the funeral. Well, then, the picnic took place before the Monday night. And this is Thursday. What sort of weather did we have on Monday? "

" Dampish in the morning, with a hint of fog, but it cleared during the day."

" You ought to be on the B.B.C.," said Crook admiringly. " Tuesday? "

" Rained all day."

" Then they couldn't have gone a picnic on Tuesday. Besides, that was the morning Miss Woodman disappeared. So—Monday was the last day she and Miss Hunter, the real one, could have gone into the garden for a nice cup of tea."

" And that wouldn't work, either," said Peter. " Because she was here on Tuesday, Miss Hunter, I mean. Dr. Mack saw her. I know she was dead, but she was here. It's Miss Woodman who was missing."

" Hold everything! " said Crook. " The wheels are starting to go round. Eureka! That's a neat trick she played. Don't you see, she meant to cash in on the dividends, and she didn't mean to go on sharing 'em with Bertha Woodman. So——" He brooded. " You do see, don't you? " he urged. " Suppose Bertha was missing *before* Miss Freke went down to call on Dr. Mack? After all, who was the last person who saw her alive? Beyond the shadow of a doubt, that is? "

"Well, obviously Miss Freke—or Miss Hunter?"

"According to Miss Freke, it was Miss Freke, Miss Hunter having departed to a better world. She must have seen her when she left the house, always assuming Miss Woodman was in the house, and Frostyface was telling the truth. But suppose she wasn't? Come to that, truth don't seem to be her strong suit. Now, suppose it was Bertha and Miss Freke went for a picnic in the woods, and one of them didn't come back? Who's to say? Miss Hunter's the only witness and she can't talk. Frostyface has seen to that. And nobody can swear to seeing Miss Woodman on the Tuesday."

"There was the stranger who bought the ticket to Bournehaven."

"Who can't be positively identified, not by the booking-clerk anyway. If they asked me I might give 'em a shock."

"You mean, you think——"

"It's perfectly obvious what I think. Come on, let's take a peek at her room and see if anythin' else is missing."

As he had anticipated, nothing was. The disappearing housekeeper had left her brush on the dressing-table, her toothbrush in its flowered vase; her night clothes were folded on the bed, her austere slippers were beneath it. But of the woman herself there was no trace. Crook almost literally didn't leave a stone unturned, but there were few hiding-places in The Cottage and, short of climbing up the chimney, a feat none of the three ladies could have achieved, and where none of them could in any case have been snugly accommodated, there wasn't an inch of the premises the two men did not examine. But of trapdoors, secret cellars, hollow walls, pits under the floor, cisterns of a convenient size for the concealment of a body or concealed cupboards, they found no trace. Only the handbag and its contents stood in mute refutation of Miss Freke's story.

"So there was never a farewell letter," ejaculated Peter at last.

"Not one written by Bertha Woodman in any case."

"You'd have expected Miss Freke to produce the forgery," Peter hazarded.

"May not have cared to take the risk and probably she was right at that. You have to remember she was only an amateur forger, and whereas nobody but your Uncle Corny had seen Miss Hunter's signature—and signatures and handwriting often don't agree—I dare say there were plenty of people who could recognise Miss Woodman's. Anyhow, even if she had left a genuine note, it couldn't be admitted as evidence until it's produced, just as you ain't supposed to find a chap guilty of murder without a corpse to back you up. Of course, as you and me know, that last isn't absolutely watertight. There have been two cases since the war in which men have been found guilty of murder where no body was forthcoming—in one case it won't be recovered until the sea gives up its dead—but the general rule holds good." He fell silent and remained in that state for so long that the young man beside him began to fidget.

"Where do we go from here?" he asked. "We can't so far even prove one murder, let alone two."

Crook turned his head. "Ever hunted a flea?" he asked. "But of course you have. You know how the game begins, sort of uneasy feelin' there's something wrong, general itch, makes you suspicious, but not localised as yet. Then you start scratchin' in an exploratory way, tickling the chap up, as it were." He was suiting his actions to the words. "Then ping! the brute's got home. First blood to him. Now you can start the hunt in real earnest. Slap! Squash! Got him? By gum, no, that one got away. Got to possess your soul in patience and wait for him to make another attack. Mostly you don't have to wait long. Now you're keyed up, ready for him, you're on his track, he jumps, you're after him, this time the beggar shan't get away. Hullo, nearly had him. No, that's a bit of fluff. Confound the brute, but you won't be beat. Ding-dong all the way till scrunch, there he lies never to bite again."

"Very pretty," said Peter. "You ought to do that on television."

"See my point. That's how it is with us. We're past the uneasy stage, we're pretty sure there's something wrong, only we ain't quite there yet. We've got the teaspoon and the bag and the ration book, and—— Wait a minute. We've got to go back a bit. All these amateurs make mistakes. All we need to do is start at the top of the road and work our way along. Now take this bag." He slapped it heartily as he spoke. "If Miss Woodman was O.K. she'd have it with her. Ergo, she ain't O.K. All the same, hiding a corpse ain't so simple. If you dig a grave you leave traces. You can bury 'em fair and square like they buried poor Miss Hunter. But—any lakes in the wood so far's you know?"

"I've never penetrated far. Why do you ask?"

"A lake's a nice convenient place for a body, specially if it's situated in the middle of a wood. And maybe the picnic wasn't in the garden after all." Suddenly his expression changed. He looked as if someone had tickled him up with a red-hot poker.

"Leave everything and come on!" Turning on the words he bolted out of The Cottage with Peter Finnemore hotfoot on his heels.

CHAPTER SIXTEEN

HE HAD LEFT the Scourge at the gate and now he leapt in and drove ahead, paying no attention to Peter, who had to take a flying leap to get aboard at all. " This lane's a blind alley, you know," he gasped, and Crook said of course he knew and there was a proverb about young chaps teaching their grandmothers. " Leads to the woods, don't it ? " he demanded. " Leastways I saw a path come snaking out first time I was up this way, and where a snake comes out it must have gone in first, or some other snake anyhow." Peter gave it up. They said genius was always mad, and if Crook really thought he was going to locate a body in this jungle he couldn't be far removed from genius.

" If that old woman got in and got home again she must have left some sort of trail," Crook amplified. " All we've got to do is to follow it."

" Trail ? " repeated the young man politely.

" Yes, Watson. I suppose you were born too late to be brought up on fairy tales. There was one I remember about a princess that dropped hairpins all the way through the haunted castle (or it may have been a maze) to be sure she could find her way back. I don't see Miss Freke, who, let me remind you, has shown a lot of enterprise, whether you admire her objective or not, letting herself be picked clean by the vultures who probably regard this wood as their happy hunting-ground."

He stopped the car and alighted nimbly. " Here's the entrance," he said. " You're right about it being a jungle. There's half a dozen paths she could have taken. Let's choose the widest, seeing there was two of them and neither of them sylphs." He began to crash through the undergrowth like a small brown elephant. A very few steps and he paused and began to look all round him. "The sea is so wide and my boat is so small," he said irritably. "Which way did that damn' woman go? She must have left some indications, clues, if you like, or the odds are she'd have got lost herself." He dropped down, hands on bent knees, and began to stare round him at the brambles and hillocks of sand that obscured the path.

"What are you hoping to find?" exclaimed Peter.

"Never heard of Sherlock Holmes?" asked Crook in an injured voice. "Well, here you perceive him in another guise. Well, hang it all, that old deerstalker couldn't last for ever."

Peter was wondering if Crook was expecting to find the body under the brambles, mysteriously shrunk like Alice after drinking from the bottle in Wonderland, when Crook whistled with satisfaction and straightened himself.

"This is the way she went and left the meadows rosy," said he, and held out a scrap of brown woollen material. "Sailed through regardless, or it could be was pushed through, and left a trace." Peter looked down at it thoughtfully. In that enormous palm it reminded him of the Silly Symphony Mouse in the mouth of the lion.

"Miss Hunter's suit was green," he murmured. "At least, the one I saw was."

"That's what you think. Most dames have more than one. Anyway, it don't have to be hers. Come on. They shut the road through the woods seventy years ago. Now keep your eyes skinned and sing out if you notice a quarry or a lake or any convenient place where a body could be hidden. Or a paper bag or anything to show folks have been picnicking hereabouts."

The next clue was a handful of fronds of bracken loosely put together and bound with grass and laid fanwise on a bramble bush.

"Nature never did that," said Crook. "First on the right and straight on, I take it. Funny thing about women, how they like discomfort. Men go to the trouble of inventing tables and chairs and roofs and plates and knives, and then dames think it's much nicer to lie about among thorns and thistles and eat their food out of pieces of paper, with all the wasps and flies to lend a hand."

"There's something," exclaimed Peter. "On that tree there. Something white."

"Attaboy!" Crook pushed forward unconcernedly through the bramble thicket as though he was a new version of St. Sebastian. "Well, that's proof the old girl came this way. This is a handkerchief, this is. See the initials? A.H. Alice Hunter. So it was Miss Freke who brought the other one here, not Miss Woodman as usual. Because Miss Freke 'ud be using Miss Hunter's handkerchiefs. Well!" He looked extraordinarily pleased, Peter couldn't think why. "That's the most cheerful thing we've found to date."

Peter shook his head, admitting himself to be a dumb cluck.

"You don't see what that means? Why, *that she's coming back*. She wouldn't leave anything as incriminating as a handkerchief there even for the crows to find. And if she's coming back it means the job ain't complete, so it could be we'll be in time to save the old dame after all. Though," he added in more sober tones, "that's what they call wish fulfilment in Harley Street. Still, miracles do happen, and why not to Arthur Crook?"

On they went, keeping a sharp lookout, which necessarily slowed their pace. But, as Crook said, he didn't want to be meat for the crows, and how the heck would it help anyone if he was?

"What else do dames wear that they can shed easily?" he inquired. "Hair ribbons? Or am I thinking of Bacchus?" While he rattled on he was moving steadily ahead, until his attention was caught by a newly-broken branch swinging in the light wind. "Who did that?" he asked sharply. "That's new, and we've had no storm lately; a little rain, I know, but nothing to account for a broken bough. No dear destructive little children hereabouts to have done it, no pumas leaping majestically from bough to bough, smashing one or two on route. No, you take your Uncle Arthur's word for it—that's arrow No. 4." Each clue marked a turn in the path—though track would have been a better word. Progress was necessarily slow, and Peter began to fret, but Crook soothed him saying the only way he liked a hare was in a pot, and give him the tortoise every time. Arrow No. 5 was an artificial flower, the stem wound round a twig, No. 6 was a checked scarf for which someone had once paid a coupon and eight and elevenpence.

"Must be gettin' near," suggested Crook. "Dame's runnin' out of clues."

That she was near the end of her tether was proved by the sight of a black felt hat swinging rakishly from a bush, though rakish was hardly the adjective to describe so sober an article. The next clue they found was the last and, to Crook at all events, the most illuminating. It was a daily newspaper weighed down with a large stone, and it bore the date the 14th September.

Crook took it in his hands and stood looking at it as though he were turned to stone. Peter, who had intended to ask some questions, sensibly held his tongue. He didn't know what thoughts were running through Crook's head, but he realised that in some manner this paper represented the crux of the situation.

"The fourteenth September," said Crook at last. "That was the day of the funeral. But Miss Woodman had disappeared the previous morning."

"According to Miss Freke. I take it we've no actual proof."

"And the doctor didn't see her. Miss Freke opened the door."

"Then could Miss Freke have had a solitary picnic?"

Crook shook his head. "I can believe a lot of that dame, but that she'd come out into the long grass because she's a poet *manqué* (if that's the right expression), who likes to wander like a cloud, sounds barmy to me. And if you had any such idea you'd better give up the law and go into one of these Government Departments."

He was so quiet after this that a bird whom neither of them could identify mistook him for a bird-watcher and just perched on a branch and stared back. Suddenly it nearly fell off its stance as Crook smote his thigh a blow that would have fractured anybody else's, exclaiming, "I'm losing my grip. Enough to make these police split their new nice blue shirts to hear this. Come on!"

"Got your flea?" asked Peter, who hadn't the smallest notion what this was all about.

Crook nodded. "Dead as mutton," he said. "And so will someone be if we ain't quicker than lightning."

"So you do think there's still a chance?" Peter put the question to Crook's back as it bustled along ahead.

"Always put my bob on an outsider. If she was only dumped there yesterday. Here we are."

Round the last bend he found what he had been seeking, a small secluded spot enclosed by trees, where the bracken was flattened as by the pressure of bodies.

"So this is where they had the last cup together," he murmured. "And a better spot Miss F. could scarcely hope for."

"You mean because of that ramshackle little hut in the background?" Peter sounded sceptical. "That wouldn't keep off much wind."

"Ah, but it has four walls and that's the important thing. What'll you bet that that's locked, too?"

At a first glance you'd say it was months at least since anyone had paid any attention to it. But one glance wasn't enough for Crook. Bracken had been heaped up against the door and soil scraped up from the path.

"And that's been done during the last twenty-four hours or I lose my guess," said Crook. He stooped and began vigorously clearing all the impedimenta away.

"Ahoy there!" he shouted, as he worked as busily as a terrier excavating a rabbit hole. "Hold the fort, we're coming."

But answer came there none.

Peter swept up an armful of bracken and then they made the discovery that the door was locked.

"And you don't need three guesses to know who's got the key," grunted Crook. "Come on. Young Lochinvar, do your stuff or we may be too late after all. Earth hath one weary soul the less, heaven one spinster more."

While Peter went to work Crook mooched off to see what lay beyond the hut. There wasn't a pond, but there was something very nearly as good—a steep slope running down to a great depth, the bottom of which was a dry overgrown ditch where a body could lie for months, years perhaps, without detection, except by chance. He hadn't a doubt in his mind as to Miss Freke's intentions. She'd be coming here on her return from Bournehaven—and *that* visit was all part of her careful game of bluff—to remove the body and shove it out of sight. Why, with any luck she herself might well lie in the churchyard along of her first victim before anyone found the mouldering bones.

When he came back Peter was so much absorbed in his task he had no thought to spare for the grisly discovery they would most probably find on the other side of the door.

" How's she coming ? " asked Crook.

" They must have made a practice of keeping either dead bodies or contraband here," was Peter's grim reply. " But she'll come all right. In time."

Time was of the essence of the situation, but Crook had too much sense to fuss the young man. He was doing his best and an angel could do no more. So he possessed his soul in patience until Peter, twisting his implement this way and that, at last made contact with the lock and the heavy door swung wide.

Crook was inside like a tiger leaping on its prey. For the hut wasn't empty as he'd known all along it wouldn't be. Someone lay there, hands secured at the wrist with a handkerchief, a scarf stuffed gagwise into the open mouth. The feet were fastened together, too, and the unhappy creature lay on its face half-smothered on the dirt floor.

" Who on earth——? "

" I told you," said Crook, impatiently, turning the figure over and tearing at the knots with his big capable hands. He removed the gag without much difficulty—it hadn't been very firmly affixed, since this wasn't to figure as a murder case—and knelt a moment with the unconscious woman in his arms. He dropped his big head and set his ear to the chest.

"Might make it yet," he said. "Chock-a-bloc with drugs if I get my guess. Bit peaky looking, too, ain't she? Not getting all her rations."

Peter came nearer. "But that's—that's——" He stopped dead.

"Cat got your tongue?" asked Crook irritably. "Who did you think it was going to be? The Man in the Moon?"

Peter's face was almost as white as that of the woman on the floor. "Look here," he said, in a curiously shaken voice. "Somebody's mad. Perhaps it's me. But I recognise that woman—and she's dead, Crook, I tell you, she's dead—and buried."

"Not she," said Crook, undaunted, "she's alive. She was buried but you and me have dug her up again. She's breathing nicely now, and before you know where you are we'll have her tucked up warm and cosy, spilling enough beans to keep the whole Cabinet going for a week."

"But she *is* dead," insisted Peter in the same incredulous voice. "You went to her funeral only yesterday. Miss Alice Hunter, buried as Laura Freke. So how on earth can she be here in this hut? Unless of course that was an empty coffin they put in the churchyard," he added dazedly.

"Not it," said Crook, who had pulled a flask of spirits out of his pocket and was skilfully pouring some of the contents down the unconscious woman's throat. "Benson's got a reputation to lose if Miss Freke ain't. There was a body all right, but it was the body of Bertha Woodman, the Disappearing Housekeeper. And if I'd had the brains of a louse," he added candidly, "I'd have seen that's the way it had to be before I picked up that newspaper a while ago."

While he waited for Alice to display sufficient signs of life for it to be safe to move her on he set down the case in black and white for his companion's benefit.

" See here," he offered kindly, " I'll fill in some of the gaps for you while we're waitin'. Mind you, the lady here'll have to cross the t's and dot the i's for us later on, but in the meantime we'll have a go. Reel One introduces Miss Freke, a female desperado if ever there was one, sick as mud of bein' kicked around most of her life and suddenly faced with the chance of cashin' in on a dead woman's inheritance. Right on her toes after it, too, and good luck to her. All goes merry as a weddin' bell till—Reel Two—she finds the dead woman ain't dead after all. If you want to start blaming anyone for what's happened you pick on that doctor at Yarborough Station at the time of the accident, who sent this poor old girl off to the mortuary on a maiden trip. Well, havin' got so far our heroine can't go back, not without landin' herself either in an asylum or chokey, most likely the last, so she beetles up to Yarborough and takes control of the real Miss Hunter. Now she's got to find some place to put her, and, harder still, someone to help her bear the burden."

" Reel Three," improvised Peter, " enter Bertha Woodman, complete with axe for emergencies."

" You're gettin' the hang of it," Crook approved. " Only as it happens, it's a case of for whom does the axe fall ? It falls for thee. Only luckily for her peace of mind she don't know it."

" Do you suppose Miss Freke took Bertha into her confidence ? " Peter wanted to know.

" My answer 'ud be in the negative, and if you're going to say she was taking an almighty chance, well, you do that every time you cross the road these days. Have a heart, man, she couldn't look after the heiress and do the chores, and anyway, why bother to safeguard a life that's not much better than slavery? And in the heart of a jungle at that. Of course, she never meant it to last long, and I dare say practically from the start she was wondering how soon she could put out our old lady's light, and, of course, it had to be in some way that would not throw any suspicion on her. And that's none so easy for the amateur, believe me. Well then, in comes Bertha Woodman. And she's like one of those medals they tell you about that have two sides. She was useful helpin' to spread the tale about there being a zany, a dangerous one at that, up at The Cottage. Folks listen a lot more readily to someone they know than to a foreigner, as Bob Day called Miss Freke. But she had eyes and ears of her own, Bertha I mean, and I dare say it wasn't long before she began to think there was something precious queer about the whole set-up. And after that, naturally, she became a nuisance, and Miss Freke wasn't standing for any nuisance in her plan. There simply wasn't room for them. So sooner or later, Miss Woodman must go, too. Miss Freke was lucky in one particular; neither of her victims appears to have had any relations, nobody to care if they were living or dead, and that's always a great help if you're out to commit murder. Remember that chap Rouse burned up in his car? No one to this day knows who he was. And there was the chap in the pond and Bella of the wych-elm, missing dear knows how long before anyone thought to ask why she hadn't turned up to tea. Miss Freke's headache was the same as all murderers who plan their crimes and don't just lash out in a rage on the spur of the moment. Neither of these deaths had got to look like murder and if she could stop people guessin' at a second death for a while, so much the better." He stopped and paid a little more attention to Miss Hunter.

"Coming on nicely," he encouraged, "soon be able

to start moving. Well, there you have the situation in a nutshell. If she's goin' to know any security for the future Miss Freke's got to get rid of both her girl-friends. And that's where Dr. Mack comes in."

" Do you mean he was in the plot, too ? "

" Not likely. No, he was a victim of circumstances arranged by the lady who's still calling herself Miss Hunter."

But Peter shook his head. " That can't be right; she must have bought the old man. He saw the dead woman and gave a death certificate for Laura Freke."

" Sure he did. Why not ? "

" But he must have known it was Miss Woodman."

" Why should he ? We have his word for it he'd never met the woman, so if he's called in to The Cottage and introduced to a female and told This is Miss Freke, why shouldn't he believe it ? Yes, you're getting there now, ain't you ? It was Miss Woodman he saw both times, though he didn't know it. I'd say the precious pair had started gettin' anxious. If and when our client (he indicated the unconscious Alice) passed out there'd have to be a certificate of death, and if she hadn't seen a doctor recently then there might be an inquest, a post-mortem anyway. And that didn't suit their book. But suppose the doctor's seen her quite lately and then she passes out, well, it's easy as kiss your hand. Especially when the doctor's a drunken old rapscallion like Mack. It wouldn't surprise me," added Crook meditatively, " to know Miss Woodman suggested the plan." (And here Crook displayed his usual perspicacity. This was, in short, the plot the housekeeper had outlined to Laura Freke, the real one, at which she had exclaimed, ' It would be too dangerous.' But Bertha had known that it would be more dangerous still to let Alice make contact with the doctor or anyone else from the outside world.)

" It all fits," Crook went on, urgently. " Mind you, she couldn't know Mack was going to hand her the case on a platter. That weak heart stuff was genuine. It must have made things a whole lot easier for the lady calling herself Miss Hunter. If Bertha Woodman could be persuaded to die a natural death, with just a little help, you understand, that only leaves our friend here for the lady to deal with. It'll look fishy if two old girls die under the same roof in the same week—no private enterprise encouraged these days, you see—so our one must look as if she put out her own light. Oh, the lady got it all nicely worked out. Y'know, I wondered why she got an undertaker all the way up from Bath, but of course Stan Haslett would recognise Miss Woodman and all the fat 'ud be in the fire and it 'ud be All hail the gallows-tree for X (easier to call her that, since we ain't proved which is which), so havin' got Miss Woodman buried as Miss Freke, she's got to dispose of the other one in some way that'll make it look as though she was Miss Woodman. Goin' too fast for you ? " he asked solicitously.

" No, I follow you to date. That's why she spread the news that Miss Woodman had walked out on her. And I suppose the trip to Bournehaven was just to add a little local colour."

" Partly that and partly, of course, she wanted to get her word in first. I happened to say something about the Misses Mowbray bein' informed, and she jumped to the conclusion that I'd be going down myself, so off she went like a bird."

" Which is what you intended, of course."

" We-ell," said Crook, " if you're going to break into somebody's house it's always nice to know they're sixty miles away and not likely to walk in on you unexpected. End of Reel Four."

" And she left Miss Hunter imprisoned here, to die

of exposure and madness? What an incredibly cold-blooded thing to do," exploded Peter. "When did she put her into the shed?"

"Yesterday, obviously. The paper was put down as the last clue to blaze the trail, and that only came out yesterday. She didn't do it this morning, there wouldn't be time, so it must have been before the funeral or as soon as she got back, and my bet 'ud be before. I don't think she'd chance leaving the old giri alone while she went to the graveside. (I can testify to the fact that she wasn't one-half of the mourners.) And if she'd been doped *before* the funeral Miss Freke would never have got her as far as this. She couldn't have carried her, so, ergo, Miss Hunter got here on her own feet. I dare say Miss Freke suggested it 'ud be a treat to get away from the house of death and have a nice cup of tea out of doors, and once she'd get her here she only had to drop something into the cup—it wouldn't be the first time she'd put the old girl out——"

"And dragged her to the hut. There's no sign of her being dragged." Peter sounded dubious.

"No reason why she shouldn't have come under her own steam. Say she felt faint—dizzy, more like, but she mightn't guess she'd been doped. A dame who can get herself into this jam can't be too bright. Miss Freke says it's the sun, you want to find a shady place, look at that sweet little shed, why not come and rest there? Easy as kiss your hand. It ain't likely anyone's to come looking for dames alive or dead in this bit of the forest. You can see she had a bit of a job getting the door open at all; then when she'd tied the old girl up and locked the door she threw down the bracken and scraped up some of the soil, and you'd have to look two or three times to see anything had been disturbed. What you have to bear in mind is that people mostly see what they're looking for, and they ain't looking for a body. I'd say it was a precious long time since anyone used that shed and it 'ud be a long while more before anyone wanted it again. And by that time who's to guess the old lady lay out for twenty-four hours or a bit over, before she was rolled out, either dead or as near as makes no difference, and pushed over the edge into the ravine? One thing, there's enough undergrowth there to dispense with the dear little birdies laying leaves on the lonely corpse."

"When did Miss Freke intend to do that, do you suppose?"

Crook looked up at the sky. "To-night, I dare say, as soon as she gets back from Bournehaven. No one to stop her, since she's not likely to have any visitors. I only hope I'm near enough to see her face when she opens the door and finds the bird—well, not flown—but flapped out on its drooping pinions, with a little help from yours truly."

"You mean, you're planning to return here?"

"Well, if we don't catch the lady red-handed we're back at the start. Yes, I'm plannin' to be there, and you, and maybe we'll give the police a treat and let them come in on the last act."

"Of course," said Peter, "*she's* allowing the body's never found."

"Oh, I think she's looked after that all right. No reason why it should be found yet awhile (she won't chance leavin' it in the shed), and by the time all that bracken's gone brown and some Nosey Parker digs her out what's going to be left to identify? A bag of bones and some utility clothing. Might have been anyone."

"The police are pretty fly," Peter objected. "They won't leave it at that. They'll start asking questions and they'll want the answers."

"Bless your heart, they're all goin' to be provided. Why do you suppose Miss Freke has kept Miss Woodman's ration book and identity card, all the bundle, if she ain't going to toss them down the ravine alongside the corpse? The inference'll be that Miss Woodman ran out through the woods, lost her way, got panic-stricken maybe, as anyone might, and in the darkness tumbled over the edge."

"You don't think they'll plump for suicide?"

"If I wanted to commit suicide I wouldn't take all that trouble. No, if a dame loses her way in a jungle, where every damn' path looks like all the rest, the odds are she'll lose her head as well, especially if she ain't so young as she was, and she knows damn' well no one's goin' to put a candle in the window for her. Come back, come back, your mother loves you still. Well, the inference is she'll go crashin' round, getting wilder and wilder, flailing her arms and bawlin' like a bull of Bashan, though if she stopped to think she'd realise there was no one but the old brown owl to hear, supposing any owl is fool enough to live in these parts, and sooner or later she'll start runnin' and that's fatal. Before she knows where she's goin' she'll be over the edge, crash, bang, kerblinkety-blink."

"It might seem queer to the curious that an elderly spin. should be barging about in the middle of a great wild wood all by herself," objected Peter.

"Half a dozen answers to that one," returned Crook, undaunted. "Romantic spirit, sense of adventure, hiding from the police, notion there's a pot of gold at the rainbow's foot, or just plain lunacy. After all, these Rum Old Girls are unaccountable; anyone'll tell you that. You never know what they'll be up to next, and anyway, there's no next-of-kin to weep for them, and life like a dome of many-coloured glass stains the white radiance of eternity—I saw that on a tombstone once, and I hope the chap that wrote it knows what it means, because I don't. You know, all the poets have so often and so violently declared it's better to be dead than alive you sometimes wonder if you ain't a bit dotty to hang on to your life the way you do."

"Now you're talking rot," said Peter frankly. "I never saw anyone outside Paris enjoy life so much. In Paris——"

"Keep it clean," said Crook sharply. "I'm not one of your intellectuals. Oh, this 'ud have passed as an accident all right; here and there chaps might remember there was some queer talk at The Cottage about the time the housekeeper disappeared. Old lady, said to be dotty, passed out. Could be there was some funny business. But it won't even be a nine days' wonder. As I said she don't seem to have any relations and she'd put herself in Queer Street with the Mowbrays. No, it was a good plan, but there was one thing Miss Freke hadn't allowed for, and that was you and me getting all tangled up in it."

CHAPTER SEVENTEEN

WHILE HE was speaking he had been cradling the unconscious Alice's head on his knee. Now he rose and said briskly, " Lend a hand, will you? We've got to get the old girl back to the Scourge. My guess 'ud be she was doped, but not unto death. Well, clearly not unto death or she'd have passed out by now. No, she was to die of exposure and neglect and cold——"

" And starvation ? "

" In twenty-four hours ? Be your age. That's why the scarf wasn't tied too tight ; Miss Freke wasn't goin' to chance a verdict of suffocation. When the body's found there'll be no marks of violence on it, except what you might expect if you fell down a miniature precipice. No shots, no smashed skull, no knife wounds. And if we'd been twenty-four hours later I dare say she would have passed out."

" You think she will recover ? " Peter didn't sound very hopeful. The body in Crook's arms looked as near dead as made no difference.

" Damned ungrateful of her, if she don't. Besides, there's my fee as well as my reputation. Don't look that way. I know chaps don't live by bread alone, but they don't yet know how to live without it."

If Alice Hunter wasn't dead she gave a very good imitation of it. It took the two men all they knew to get her back to where the Scourge was waiting for them. As Crook said, here was something that certainly wasn't a picnic.

He spoke truly. Alice was a woman of solid build, and though she seemed a little wasted her inert body made her an uncommonly inconvenient parcel to drag through the undergrowth and brambles. Even Crook seemed as though he'd met his match at last.

"This is a magic forest all right," he groused. "If we've passed that artificial flower once we've passed it half a dozen times, and what's the odds we'll meet it again round the next corner but one?"

Still, if he hadn't the faith that moves mountains he had the obstinacy that works miracles, and foot by foot and yard by yard they made their uncouth astounding journey.

Peter said presently, "Do you think Mack's in this?" But Crook replied, "Not he. Miss Freke wasn't going to let in any more people than she must. Miss Wells wasn't Rockefeller and three people were beginnin' to crowd the legacy out of the picture. No," as Peter seemed about to speak once more, "don't ask any more questions, there's a good chap. We shall have to write it out in words of one syllable for the police in any case. Thank heavens, there's the handkerchief. The harbour lights at last."

He thought he had never seen anything so beautiful as the Scourge standing in the lane where he had left her. Between them they squeezed the unconscious woman, who had begun to moan a little, into the seat alongside the driver, and "there's a sight for men and angels," remarked he. "Arthur Crook and a dame on a pleasure trip in the wilds of Southshire."

"Poor old lady!" said Peter compassionately. "She hasn't had much luck, has she?"

Crook looked astounded. "I don't know what you mean by that," he exclaimed. "She's got you and me on her side, hasn't she, and it beats me what more any woman can ask for. Now this is where we part brass-rags for a while. You're to stay here and hold the bridge while I take our mutual friend down to Dr. Lee. If Miss Freke gets back before I do, the odds are she'll make a bee-line for the woods. Bein' a female she won't feel safe till she's put the body where it won't need any robin redbreasts to cover it with leaves. Now what we've got to do is to take her red-handed. You hang around here under cover of darkness, though, come to that, it ain't exactly dark yet, like one of those sleuths they love on the B.B.C., who couldn't conceivably exist anywhere else, and if she starts trekking for the woods, trek after her. Tie your hankie to this bush if you have to leave before me, and I'll know you're on your way. This is zero hour, remember. We can't afford to make a botch of things at this stage." He looked doubtfully at the bunchy figure of Alice wedged into the seat beside him. "Clarice Mayne and That, 1949 edition," he murmured. "She looks as if she might hand in her checks any minute. Let's hope this is a case where appearances are deceptive."

"She'll be all right," Peter promised him. "She's like me, she wouldn't dare die with you around. She'd never know an instant's peace, even in the grave."

As Crook came driving into Great Moreton with his mysterious passenger he discerned the lights of a car coming in the opposite direction; when they passed he saw that it was Miss Freke returning from Bournehaven a lot earlier than he had anticipated. Now he was certain she intended to finish her fell deed before nightfall, and only hoped she'd want that feminine stimulant, a cup of tea, before she started operations. That would give him time to deliver his unwieldy burden at the doctor's and get back in time to see the fun from the rise of the curtain. (Mr. Finnemore, Senior, would have been horrified at such a description, but Peter would have known very well what Crook meant.)

Dr. Lee proved to be a man after Crook's own heart. He evinced no surprise at sight of the patient. Lawyers from London might turn up on his doorstep every day of the week bearing unconscious ladies whom they had just rescued from a horrid (and illegal) death. He didn't make any trouble about surgery hours or his own dignity; he examined poor Alice without ado and reported briefly, "Drugged. Not fatally, though. Should be all right, if she doesn't collapse from shock. Heart seems sound, though. Hope for the best."

Alfred Jingle could scarcely have been more terse. "Be leaving you," said Crook. "Playing the good old game of Hunt the Villain and I'm first base. By the way, use your phone?"

"Extension in the hall," said the doctor. So out Crook capered and put through a call. Then he leapt back into the Scourge and departed, as fresh as a daisy and right as ninepence, for The Cottage.

As he had anticipated, there was no sign of Peter Finnemore, but a white handkerchief fluttered like a flag of truce from a flowerless lilac. Pinned to it was a scrap of paper which said, "Zero hour 5.5." He pulled out his great turnip of a watch. It said 5.15.

"Ten minutes' start. Wonder if he'll be able to hold the old girl." He made all the pace he could. Not many minutes later another car drew up by The Cottage and two men got out; these also plunged into the woods. So there they were, four sorties going out in Indian file into the woods. They might be going Indian file, but they certainly weren't trying to emulate Indians in any other way. Crook crashed about like a wild animal, not bothering to pick his steps, but jumping dried ditches, and swinging over on branches of trees and crawling among the brambles in a way that would have endeared him to Walt Disney's heart. Ahead Peter was going carefully, anxious not to rouse suspicions in his quarry's mind. And last of all came the police, not bothering to disguise their footsteps, not so long as Crook went on his racketing way.

All the signs that had led them to the hut were there until they reached the place where the hat had been. And the hat had gone; but in its place the thoughtful Peter had hung his wrist-watch. Crook pocketed the watch and put his own bowler on the branch. He did it with some regret, he never felt quite his own man without his hat, but he reflected that even the police, who can be wily enough when opportunity offers, would scarcely pinch that, and anyway they couldn't conceal it, and he'd told them to look for a hat and like the rabbit, who is a creature of habit, they probably wouldn't realise that hats and watches can on occasions be interchangeable. After this stage he proceeded with great care, so that instead of looking like an elephant enjoying itself on Bank Holiday he was a great ginger cat prowling after its unconscious prey. And when the crashing ahead of them ceased the policemen took the hint and began to go quietly, too. Soon after the incident of the hat Crook heard a whistle; if he hadn't been anticipating some sign he'd have thought it was just another bird; they all sounded alike to him. But he looked about and after an instant he saw something that quite clearly wasn't a bird crouched behind some bushes and went stealthily forward to join it. Peter Finnemore was feeling as pleased as Punch about the whole thing; he hadn't enjoyed anything so much since he left the Commandos. Being a lawyer had seemed to him pretty tame, just sitting in an office and waiting for things to drift your way, discovering, too, the things men thought worth fighting for, which were quite different from what he and his friends had fought for "over there." This was different again. This was the goods. He wondered if the age of miracles was over, or if there was any possibility Crook might want an assistant.

Meanwhile, surprisingly unaware of her pursuers, for as Crook knew, people in the main perceive only what they expect, Laura made her way to the ominous shed. She was carrying the hat in her hand and now she set this on the ground while from a pocket she produced a key which she inserted in the lock. Peter's machinations had done it no good from her point of view. The key stuck, jammed, was retrieved with difficulty and thrust in again. Again it stuck. The truth never dawned on Laura; it simply didn't go through her mind that someone might have been here and discovered her secret. She imagined that there was some obstruction that she must circumvent. These old locks were rusty; no doubt it was some particles that she had dislodged the previous day when she turned the key on her victim that were causing the trouble. It was a matter of patience, and she didn't suppose there was any particular hurry. No one was likely to come calling at The Cottage, and if they did they'd find it dark and empty and, naturally, assume she had not yet returned from Bournehaven. She had by this time become so completely accustomed to the thought of what she was going to do that she felt neither horror nor repugnance. As for pity, she had left that far behind. Indeed, she had already stopped thinking about Alice as a human being; she was an obstacle, and more remotely, an object of peril. She'd got to be got out of the way and pretty soon she'd have disappeared and Laura herself might be lying in the graveyard with a nice stone memorial over her before anyone found the handful of rags and bones that had once been Alice Hunter. She hoped, and expected, that the other woman would be dead already.

Indeed, it seemed improbable that she could still be breathing. But either way her doom was sealed, and really, when you reflected how little she'd given to life or demanded from it, it hardly seemed like murder to put her out for the count. And then—then—for Laura Freke the days of freedom would begin.

She was so much engrossed in her struggle with the key and with the reflections that came pouring through her mind that she didn't hear the two policemen coming softly up to take up a position between herself and the ravine.

At last she contrived to make the key turn, the rusty lock creaked a little, and then the door swung outwards. She stepped forward, and stopped, incredulous, petrified, staring at the bare floor. Her unbelieving gaze roamed from the trodden boards to the walls and thence to the roof, as though Alice might have contrived to free herself and climb up the side of the hut but naturally there was no sign of her. Peter's thoughtful action in managing to re-lock the door had deceived her completely. Crook mentally gave him full marks; so many chaps he could think of would have been satisfied to leave it swinging.

Slowly Miss Freke moved back towards the fading light outside the shed. She took a couple of steps and found herself staring into the fox-coloured eyes of the common little upstart, the boor, the snooper who'd already had the insolence to come to The Cottage and make inquiries about Alice Hunter.

And if her eyes were devoid of pity, so, equally, were his. But his voice was cool enough.

"Evenin', Miss Freke," he observed. "Lost something? Maybe my friends and me can help you."

She knew then, being quick-witted by nature and experience, that all was lost—the money, the future, hope, life itself. But at least she could play her last card. Crook, however, was too quick for her. As she turned towards the ravine his great hand shot out and caught her wrist.

"Just a minute," he said.

"Drop your hand this instant," she flamed. "How dare you touch me!"

There was such a touch of the old Lyceum about her that Crook was taken off his guard. She wrenched her hand away, diving blindly past him. But it was no good; she was hopelessly outnumbered. Between her and the edge of the bank stood the two policemen and a young man whom she recognised as some connection of Cornelius Finnemore. Like that black hare that is a witch in disguise she doubled back, but now Crook was ready for her. Poor wretch, she never had a chance.

The two policemen closed in and told her she was under arrest. She denied furiously that she was Laura Freke but they paid no heed.

"What is the charge?" she demanded, throwing back her head, defiant to the last. You couldn't help admiring her spirit, thought Crook. She was the mare for his money, far more than virtuous insignificant Alice Hunter, at that very moment being restored to consciousness and life by the laconic Dr. Lee.

"Giving false information regarding Miss Woodman's death," they told her.

"Miss Woodman? You must be crazy if you imagine that I——"

But here Crook, who had his weaknesses like other men, though cowardice wasn't one of them, stepped forward to say, "Take the old dog's advice and hold your horses till you've seen a solicitor. I know you think they're mud but even mud has its uses. Face packs," he added hurriedly, not for the life of him being able to think of any other use for mud on the spur of the moment, except, of course, as an invaluable agency for registering the footprints of criminals.

Laura glared at him. Then her glance passed to Peter Finnemore. " I think I see my solicitor's representative here," she observed. But Peter, with commendable *savoir-fairè*, said their client's name was Hunter. Crook was grateful to her for not going into raving hysterics or suddenly justifying the psychological johnnies who'd have found some deep scientific reason for her behaviour, due, of course, to her spinster status, by raging and writhing and bawling obscenities. He suspected what was perfectly true, that she probably didn't know as much bad language as the average eight-year-old. She was simply a furious stony woman who'd played for high stakes and seen the throw go against her. She wasn't remorseful or weak or pitiable even now. If she could have called down thunder from heaven and slain them all she wouldn't have hesitated for an instant. He knew it, but he'd shot his last bolt. There was nothing more he could do. Then they were all on the move again, Laura walking between the two policemen for all the world like Eugene Aram, except that there were as yet no gyves upon her wrists.

CHAPTER EIGHTEEN

By next morning Alice was, as they say, sitting up and taking notice. Crook's diagnosis had proved true. She had been filled up with drugs, but the dose had been insufficient to cause death. Miss Freke had laid her plans well and carefully.

" You have to hand it to her that she followed out the copy-book maxim," urged Crook, who had a sneaking admiration for all thorough-going workers, whatever their objective. " Whatsoever thy hand findest to do, that do with all thy might. Now, sugar, you're not to over-exert yourself, so I'll start tellin' the story and you put me back on the right path when I go astray. I'm taking it for granted you never saw Dr. Mack ? "

" Never. I didn't even know he was coming. It was one of my bad days. I had a splitting headache ; I hardly ever had headaches before I came to The Cottage. Miss Freke brought me the bottle of aspirins, only, I suppose," she added naïvely, " they weren't aspirins really."

" Reinforced aspirin," agreed Crook. " Not dangerous, you know. Just powerful enough to make you feel hazy and ready for a nice long sleep."

" She told me after the doctor had gone that Miss Woodman's heart was in a very bad condition and we must be careful not to give her a shock, as that might prove fatal. I dare say she wouldn't have told me about his visit at all, only the doctored aspirins weren't quite as strong as she hoped, or else the doctor came much later than she expected. Anyhow, I heard his car drive away and I asked who it was and she told me."

"Believe her?" asked Crook.

"No."

"That's the worst of callin' Wolf!' from morning to night. When the wolf really does push his snout in you think it's another practical joke. Still, that time the joke was on Miss Woodman. She really had got high blood pressure and a dickey heart, and that's what killed her."

"I don't believe it," said Alice. "I believe Miss Freke murdered her."

"Don't you forget you've got the police here," Crook reminded her, indicating the two strangers who had followed him through the woods on the dramatic occasion of Miss Freke's arrest. "You can't make charges like that without proof."

"If they were to dig her up——"

"They have. Funny, you know, me saying that about knowing the truth when I set eyes on her. I must say at that time I didn't expect to find her in a coffin with your name on it. Mind you, I don't say Miss Freke didn't beat up some trouble, only it ain't murder accordin' to the letter of the law. What did she tell you about Miss Woodman's death? You did know that much I take it?"

"Of course I knew. She tried to make me believe it was my fault."

"How come?" asked Crook.

"She said she'd warned me that Miss Woodman's heart was in a very bad condition and whatever happened I mustn't make a scene, and that I'd been like a madwoman the night before, and it was enough to give anyone a stroke. And it wasn't true—that I'd been like a madwoman, I mean. But it so happened the night before I had a special dish for dinner that neither of the others had. They said they were feeling a little bilious and would just have bread and milk.

That was enough to make anyone suspicious, but I tasted the dish and it was bitter. There could be no question about that. So I said I'd be bilious, too, for one night, and Miss Freke was very angry. She said, Miss Woodman had taken a lot of trouble and now it was all for nothing. I said I wasn't going to eat food that was poisoned, even to please them."

"And that touched off the bomb?"

"Miss Woodman went a sort of peony colour, all blotchy, and said that was actionable, and I said 'Well, all right, why don't you tell the police and bring a case? You've got a witness. It's not me that's keeping them away from the house,' I reminded them both. Miss Woodman shouted, 'This is an intolerable situation,' and I said, 'You're not the only one who thinks that.' Then Miss Freke chipped in and said it was more than flesh and blood could bear, and I said that went for me, too. Miss Freke tried to shut me up, and she and Miss Woodman both got more and more agitated. Presently I went up to my room, and I could hear voices but I couldn't hear what they said. Later on Miss Freke came into my room with some hot milk. I said 'I'm not going to drink that,' and she said it was for Miss Woodman. She'd had a bad attack thanks to me, and if she wasn't better in the morning she'd have to send for the doctor. I didn't really believe her, but next morning she came in to say that she was going down to the village at once. It was maddening there being no telephone. I asked how Miss Woodman was, and she said, 'You're not to go in to her. I don't like the look of her at all, I believe she's had a stroke and if she has you can't be absolved from responsibility. I may bring a nurse back. Or, if the doctor thinks she can be moved, I shall try and get her into a hospital.' I said, 'I know something about nursing, I looked after Mother,' but she just looked through me. She was wonderful in her own way, you know ; even in a crisis like that, and I didn't know then what a crisis it was, she didn't forget that we'd changed places, so to speak. Whenever I mentioned my mother she put on that queer look that said, ' Poor thing, I believe you really do think you remember her, but of course you can't, because she died when you were just a baby.' She came across the room and took me by the shoulders and said, ' You understand, you are not to go into Miss Woodman's room. It's bad enough as it is, but if she were to see you after your mad accusation last night the results might be fatal. It's going to be awkward enough in any case, explaining things to Dr. Mack.' I said, ' If she was really as bad as he made out he won't be surprised,' and she looked at me like a gallows bird, you know that long thin neck and pointed face of hers, and said slowly, ' He may be an old toper, but even he is going to ask what happened last night to bring on the attack.' Then she went away. I thought for a minute she was going to lock me into my room, but I told her if she did I'd rattle the handle and scream the house down and that would be Miss Woodman's death sentence, and she could explain the situation to the coroner any way she pleased. She said harshly, ' You've done enough harm for the time being, haven't you,' and she went off. I saw her go. When she was out of sight I had the most extraordinary sensation, as though I were alone with death. Not just the fear of death, but death itself. If I'd turned my head and seen a figure standing in the doorway it wouldn't have surprised me at all. But when I looked round of course there was no one there. A long time went by and nothing happened, except that I began to think and it seemed to me queer that if Miss Woodman was really so ill

Miss Freke should have left her at all. And then I began to imagine that it was all a bluff. I was being kept in my room by a yarn, and she had really gone down to get the doctor to certify me. I went out on to the landing, and that awful hush as thick as fog hung over the staircase and the hall. It was like a physical thing. I can't explain it. When I looked out of the landing window it seemed amazing that the garden and the woods beyond should be full of light. I went along to Miss Woodman's room and knocked at the door, but nothing happened. I knocked again, then I thought perhaps she'd had another attack. My mother died of heart failure, so I knew something about it, and I thought I'd better go in. When I was inside I understood why she hadn't answered. She was dead; there was no doubt about it, and she must have been dead before Miss Freke went out, because she was quite cold. I wondered why Miss Freke hadn't told me, then I supposed she thought I'd be frightened—a lot of people are afraid of dead people—and she didn't want to take me with her. I didn't realise then how absolutely fatal that would have been, seeing that Dr. Mack thought the dead woman was me. Oh dear, that sounds very involved."

"We get you," said Crook. He supposed it was a long time since she'd had an opportunity of talking like a free being to anyone and it would be unkind to hurry her.

"Well—I may as well admit I was a bit frightened then, because I didn't for a minute believe this was a natural death. I'd been sure for a long time that Miss Woodman really believed my story, but of course it paid her better to keep in with Miss Freke, and naturally that wouldn't suit her—Miss Freke, I mean. So she'd got Miss Woodman out of the way, very cleverly getting a doctor to back her up, and I realised it would be my turn next, probably quite soon, unless I managed to get in first. So I went back to my room and began to make plans, but none of them was fool-proof. They all depended on Miss Freke doing what *I* suggested, and I couldn't see any reason why she should of her own free will, and, of course, I couldn't make her. I knew she would go to the funeral, and I thought I'd say I couldn't bear them, and then if she left me alone in the house I might try and get away. But I didn't really think she would give me such an opportunity, which meant, you see, that I had hardly any time left at all.

" I was still thinking about it when Miss Freke came back with the doctor. I stayed where I was. I didn't want to give her a chance of saying in front of a witness that I'd more or less murdered Miss Woodman. I didn't know then that he thought Miss Woodman was me.

" Well, after the doctor had gone I went on to the landing and I said I really must have some fresh air. Miss Freke began to laugh ; it seemed so heartless with that woman lying dead on the other side of the door.

" ' Don't be silly,' she said, ' of course you can't go out. It's begun to rain.' I suppose it does sound silly, but the fact is I hadn't even noticed it was raining, though actually it didn't come to much. Then she said, ' If it's better to-morrow we'll go out for a little, but I must arrange about the funeral. The sooner the better.' Well, the day dragged on. The undertaker came and they took Miss Woodman away. I asked if that meant an inquest, but Miss Freke said of course not, only it wasn't a good thing having dead people in private houses, it sometimes had an upsetting effect. The next day she asked if I'd like to come to the funeral, and I was so surprised I said, ' Yes, if she liked.' Then she told me, ' I think it would be a mark of respect, as her old employers certainly won't be able to get up here.'

"I said it was so nice after the rain and the house was so stuffy couldn't we go out before the funeral, and she said she'd been thinking that very thing. 'I know Miss Woodman is no longer here,' she went on, 'but somehow the shadow seems to hang over the house. We might take a thermos of tea, some of that cake Bertha made,' she went on, 'and have it in the wood. We needn't go far but we shan't have time for more than a snack, with the funeral this afternoon.'

"Of course I jumped at the idea. She told me I could make the tea then I shouldn't have any suspicions about it. I thought she was giving me a treat because I'd promised to come to the funeral."

"You'd have created a sensation if you had, seeing it was your official name on the box, I mean. But, of course, she never intended you to go."

"Of course not. But after she'd gone and I was in the kitchen while the kettle boiled I concocted what seemed to me a wonderful plot, almost as good as one of hers. Both Miss Freke and myself have a very sweet tooth, and both of us take saccharine in our tea and coffee. We each carried a little box of it—a bottle really—about with us. Sometimes she'd offer me hers, but I used to say I had plenty of my own, and she used to laugh in such a horrible way. When I'd cut the slices of cake I went upstairs and I saw the door of Miss Freke's room was ajar, and on the cupboard by the bed was the bottle of sleeping tablets Dr. Mack had prescribed for her. He said a person in her condition needed her sleep. Nobody was about, so I stole in and took the bottle, and the pellets were remarkably like saccharine. I should have called it dangerous really, asking for people to be murdered. Miss Freke's bag was in the dining-room, and she was talking to someone at the back door, the baker I think it was. So——"

"Don't tell me," pleaded Crook. "You substituted the sleeping tablets for the saccharine."

"There weren't many left but I knew she wouldn't know exactly how many so I put some of the tablets into her bottle and some of the saccharine into the phial of sleeping tablets. I didn't suppose anyone would ever examine that and find out the substitution. I just had time to slip out of the room when the back door shut. I said, 'Lunch is ready when you are,' and went upstairs. I was trembling so I could hardly put on my hat. I could scarcely believe that I was really going to regain my freedom. I was like someone shut up in a tomb; I could breathe and eat but I couldn't live. People talk about a living death but they don't know what that means, not at first-hand, or they wouldn't use the expression so lightly. And now, now at last I thought I was going to come back to life."

Crook had a vision of her feverishly watching Miss Freke shake the fatal pellets into her beaker, saw her grinning like the biggest croc ever as the woman put the drink to her lips, and the smile die out as gradually her enemy was overcome.

He said with more feeling, "Too bad! What happened? Did she rumble you?"

"I suppose she must have suspected something, though I still don't know how she did it."

"How she found it, you mean? It's pretty clear what she did. Just waited till your back was turned and changed over the saccharine bottles."

"Yes, I suppose so. I hadn't really thought. Did she tell you?" she added as an afterthought.

Crook shook his great head.

"She ain't telling me nuffin, though, mind you, if a word of hers could send me to perdition she wouldn't be able to say that word fast enough. No, I'm just goin' on the evidence of my own eyes. I mean, there were you, doped to the wide, and there was she as fresh as a flea. I dare say after your cup that cheers you don't remember very much."

"I remember pouring her out a second cup and having one myself. 'Such delicious tea,' I said, 'I can't resist another cup.' You see, I wasn't sure how many tablets were needed to send anyone off. And at first I thought I'd succeeded. She leaned back among the bracken and said, 'Dear me, what a pity we have to hurry back. A little nap here would be so pleasant. But we ought to start in about five minutes.'" Miss Hunter suddenly giggled. "I remember someone who came to a house where I was staying once—he only stayed a week, he said it was too constricted. He explained at the top of his voice that for the last ten years he'd slept under the stars in Patagonia where men are men and there ain't no dames."

"First good thing I've ever heard about Patagonia," said Crook unchivalrously. "Well, let's hope he sleeps in peace wherever he is now. Your move, partner."

"What? Oh yes. You know, I could hardly believe my luck when I saw her dozing off. I realised, of course, that I must get hold of my own ration book and identity card, which she carried about in her bag. I waited what seemed a long time till at last her head fell sideways and though I said her name twice she didn't answer. As a matter of fact, by that time I was feeling so drugged myself I was wondering how I'd ever get back to The Cottage. I put out my hand and felt for her bag, and as I did her fingers closed round my wrist like—like the teeth of a tiger. And then I heard a dreadful sound. I felt like someone standing in a high wind hearing a roaring some way off, as though a pride of lions were rushing from the horizon towards the place where I stood. It took me about half a minute to realise that it was her laughing. She laughed and laughed, till I began to think she was out of her mind, and at the same time I knew she thought the same about me, at least that was what she was telling everyone, so I began to laugh, too. I really was feeling rather queer by now, and it didn't seem so important to get back to The Cottage. I suddenly felt here we were, two of us in the same boat, so why not stick together ? "

" And that's about the last you remember, I dare say ? "

" No, not quite, though it all becomes rather hazy after that. I remember Miss Freke staggering up to her feet and saying ' The sun's too hot, let's find some shade,' and we saw a shed of sorts, and made for that, and then suddenly she was laughing again, not with me now, but at me, but it's rather vague and inconsecutive. Everything seemed to be going round, I just wanted to go to sleep. I must have said I wanted to sleep because she seemed to be saying ' Yes, so you shall, for ever and ever. Think of it, never wake up any more.' But perhaps I imagined some of that," she added. " By that time it didn't seem as if it was happening to me. Why, I wasn't even afraid."

" How many of the tablets did you take ? " asked Crook.

" I think—four."

" Darned lucky you didn't pass out, all things considered," Crook told her.

" Will they hang her ? " asked Miss Hunter abruptly.

" Hang her ? " Crook stared. " Why should they ? She hasn't killed anyone."

" If she hasn't it's not from want of trying. First of all Miss Woodman——"

" No proof she had anything to do with that death,"

said Crook firmly. "The lady had got a dicky heart and she died of a stroke. Mack says he's not in the least surprised, it was bound to happen some time. They dug her up, of course, to make sure there hadn't been any funny business, but if there was nobody found any traces of it. There's going to be no end of a hoo-ha about the false entry in the register though. Officially, you see, till that's changed you're dead and under the churchyard sod."

"Surely"—Alice looked alarmed again—"no one doubts now who I am?"

"Well, no one doubts that Miss Freke is Miss Freke. We've got evidence as to that that can't be upset, and since no one can be two people at once, though you have to hand it to her she made a damn' good try, you must be Miss Hunter. Seeing that the body in the coffin has been identified as Bertha Woodman. It's like that kids' charade where A loves B who loves C who loves B who loves A, and so on to Kingdom Come."

Peter Finnemore spoke for the first time. "Chaos and Old Night with a vengeance," said he.

"Knight?" repeated Crook perversely. "Where does he come in? Now be a good chap and don't start dragging Debrett into this. You know," he beamed affectionately at his latest client, "you must have been born under a gold star. Here are you hidden away in a cottage right out in the long grass and here's me snug as a bug in a rug in London, and yet by a miracle I come to hear about you—you'd have been a goner without this chap here, you know." He laid his huge hand on Peter's knee. "And then if Miss Freke had been a bit more thorough it 'ud have been too late after all, though it might have given you a certain satisfaction, wherever you found yourself, to know you weren't unavenged. Still, I always like it better this way." He came back to the point under discussion. "No," he decided, "they won't take her for the murder of Bertha Woodman. In fact, if ever a woman committed suicide, she did. If she hadn't pushed her claim so hard that she became a positive danger she might be alive still, though I dare say not for long. But at least she'd have been buried decently in her own name."

"It doesn't seem right," said Alice, "that she should get off scot-free."

"Not much scot-free about it," Crook told her grimly. "She's got plenty on her plate, choke as like as not before she's through. Fraudulent conversion, impersonation, making a false declaration of death, causin' a false entry to be made in the register—they'll take a very serious view of that. Trouble for the Civil Service, see? And then when she's digested that bunch maybe you'll like to bring an action against her for defraudin' you—if you've got the cash to chuck away, that is. Because she's only got what's marked up in her Post Office Savings Book, and that ain't goin' to frank you. And it's not one of those cases where the newspapers are going to compete for the privilege of payin' for the defence. No glamour, no secret love-life, just plain bread-and-scrape. Cake, that's what the public likes, and that's what the press has to give 'em. No, you don't have to be afraid she'll get off too light."

But to Bill Parsons he said afterwards, "There's something to be said for these whole-hoggers, you know. Most people are like the chaps in the hymn who start and shrink beside the narrow sea and linger shivering on the brink and fear to launch awee. If I had to spend my eternity with either dame, which heaven forbid, I'd put my money on that one, and leave virtuous Miss Hunter to the pretty angels."

EPILOGUE

SOME MONTHS after the trial and Miss Freke's subsequent disappearance from society for a period of years, unusual business took Crook down to the seaside. The man he had come to seek lived in apparent tranquillity with a wife who looked like a Victorian pin-cushion and was nearly as full of pins, at one of the hotels on the parade. On the whole, the place catered for residents, all of whom had settled there to await their last call in as much comfort as was possible in post-war Britain five years after the peace. On the whole, Crook reflected generously, they'd made a pretty good job of it. Not that it would ever have been his cup of tea. Sitting about on the cliffs till, like them, they crumbled away. But, also like the cliffs, they looked as if they had quite a future in front of them before the final dissolution.

Crook arrived at about four o'clock in the afternoon. His client, whose name very suitably was Hyde, was sitting in the main lounge watching a rough wind toss the spray on to the promenade.

To look at him, Crook reflected with admiration, you'd think he carried the bag round in church every Sunday and hooked his wife up the back every morning of his life.

He stood in the hall peering through the glass panes. He'd as soon have walked into a den of lions as into the hotel lounge. Everyone was looking rather lively as the hands of the clock approached four. Something obviously was going to happen, something of considerable importance. Presently a door at the back opened and waitresses appeared, carrying trays.

Immediately the occupants of the lounge began to push knitting into bags and books under cushions. A plump, prosperous-looking lady in a dark purple dress, wearing stud ear-rings and with her hair smartly waved, put down an article on miracles, in which she had been engrossed.

" No one has to convince me of their reality," she said to her companion, a neat little body looking like a small tidy fly in the grip of a large, comfortable spider. " If it weren't for a miracle I shouldn't be alive now."

The voice smote on Crook's ears. He looked at her in amazement through the protective glass.

As though aware of his regard the woman in the purple dress glanced up for a moment, and her face changed.

" What is it, dear ? " asked the bird-like companion, who was known in the Beach Hotel as the Shadow, since Miss Hunter was clearly a person with a complex of some sort and never went out alone.

" I suppose I'm suffering from hallucinations," acknowledged Alice Hunter with a weak laugh. " For a moment I thought I saw someone I knew—someone I used to know, that is—looking through the glass. But, of course, it must have been a mistake."

Resolutely she expunged the thought from her mind. " All that," she told herself, " is *over*. No sense dwelling on the past. You had a Narrow Shave, but you Got Through. You don't want to start imagining things."

All the same, the vision had been very solid—that was the only word that came into her mind. It brought back memories she had buried deep in her heart, memories of a time when she had been afraid to look over her shoulder, when doors had opened in the dark, and bodiless voices whispered. But that, she reminded herself courageously, was a long time ago. It couldn't happen twice. Miss Freke was in prison and everybody knew *she* was Miss Hunter, though, oddly enough, not many people seemed to recall her amazing story. A nine-days' wonder, Crook had said. It hadn't even been that. And now it was just as though it had never happened, except, of course, for the money that enabled her to live at the Beach Hotel and engage a companion.

" Tea, madam ? " said a sharp voice, and she looked up to see the waitress hesitating at her side. Bravely she thrust the past back into the shadows.

" That will be delicious," she announced in a firm voice. " I'm sure I'm always ready for a nice cup of tea."

THE END

››› If you've enjoyed this book and would like to discover more great vintage crime and thriller titles, as well as the most exciting crime and thriller authors writing today, visit: ›››

The Murder Room
Where Criminal Minds Meet

themurderroom.com

www.ingramcontent.com/pod-product-compliance
Ingram Content Group UK Ltd.
Pitfield, Milton Keynes, MK11 3LW, UK
UKHW010006031026
15589UKWH00008B/1483

9 781471 909948